This book is dedicated to Jim,
who emails me from another room
in the house when he knows he's not
supposed to distract me when I'm writing.
Love you, Mr. O.

HER DELTA FORCE PROTECTOR

Chapter One

"I need help."

Kade Church's heart skipped a beat at the voice he never expected to hear again, mainly because she was dead. "Harper?" The only reason he'd answered the call from a number he didn't recognize was because it could be from Talon Security, the Charlotte-based company he had an interview with in the morning.

"It's me. They found me, Kade."

"Harper, I…" Kade shook his head. This couldn't be Harper. "This isn't funny. Who is this?" He was all for practical jokes when they were good ones. This one was not good. Whoever this was had her voice down pat, and he felt the loss of his best friend all over again.

"I swear, it's me."

"Whose Celebration of Life did I attend?" Had it been only five weeks since he'd sat in the back of the base chapel and listened to her father and her friends give their eulogies for a daughter, a friend, and a woman he felt honored to know? It seemed like yesterday and at the same time, a lifetime of missing her. He stared out the kitchen window as he tried to wrap his head around hearing her very much alive voice.

"Mine."

"So this is a call from the beyond?" He'd grieved for this woman, still did. And all this time she'd been alive.

"Don't be ridiculous."

Ridiculous was getting a call from the dead. "You want to tell me what's going on?"

"I can't, not over the phone. Please, Kade. I need help. I don't know who else to call."

"Where are you?"

"Myrtle Beach."

That was why he was hearing motorcycles in the background. It was the Myrtle Beach Fall Rally Bike Week. "What kind of help?"

"Help staying alive. I have to go. I've been on this phone too long."

"Okay. Hole up in a motel and don't leave the room. Can you pay cash?"

"Yes, but I doubt there are any vacancies with all these bikers here."

"If not, lose yourself in the crowd or find a hole-in-the-wall bar that has dark corners. Can I reach you at this number?"

"I'm keeping my phone off, but if I know what time you'll call, I'll turn it on."

He glanced at his watch and did some calculations. Marsville, North Carolina, was about five hours from Myrtle Beach. "Turn your phone on at eight." He could be there tonight and get her back to his house, where she'd be safe. Although just barely, there would still be time to make it to his interview. That was one thing he didn't want to mess up. Talon Security had a stellar reputation, and he wanted that job.

"Okay. Kade?"

"Yeah?"

"Thank you."

"See ya tonight." He stared at the screen after disconnecting as his mind tried to wrap around the fact that Harper was alive. She sounded like she was fighting tears, but he wasn't ready to forgive her. Even if she had to fake her death, she could have come to him. No matter how grave the situation was, he would have been there for her. She knew that.

Duke, the dog Harper had conned him into fostering while she was in the Peace Corps, sat at his feet, wearing his goofy smile. Kade had brought the dog home for his brothers to take care of until he was back for good. The golden retriever believed humans were put on this earth for his personal pleasure. When Kade headed for his baby brother's art studio, Duke tripped over his feet in his excitement that they were going somewhere.

"You're a goofball."

Duke barked his agreement.

Parker's studio was a separate building from the house the three brothers shared, and at the door, he told Duke to sit. Duke rolled over. "Were you dropped on your head as a puppy?" He opened the door just enough to slip in and quickly closed it, keeping Duke out.

The dog had gotten into the studio once and had ended up with a coat of many colors. It had taken days to get all the paint out of his fur. Parker hadn't been happy with the mess Duke had left behind or the canvas Duke had destroyed.

Parker, a famous artist known as Park C, was standing in front of a canvas, giving it the stink eye.

"What's wrong with it?" The painting—an oil of Parker's young daughter and her cat staring out a window as it rained—looked great to him.

"The colors are all wrong."

"If you say so. Listen, I have to head over to Myrtle Beach."

Parker glanced at him. "You going to bike week?"

"Only for the day." He didn't bother explaining his reason for the trip. When Parker was painting, he tended not to retain anything said to him. Parker's attention returned to the canvas, Kade's presence already forgotten.

As he headed to his rooms to exchange his running shoes for biker boots, he called his older brother. Tristan was the Marsville police chief, while Parker, along with being a famous artist, was the town's fire chief.

As a Delta Force operator for ten years, Kade's life had been one of high-stress, life-and-death situations, and never knowing where he'd be tomorrow, or if he'd even live to see tomorrow. He was using his thirty days of leave time due him while he waited for his separation from the Army to become official.

His plan all along on getting out had been to chill for a month. Well, he'd had two weeks of chilling, and he was bored. Not that he'd choose for Harper to be afraid for her life, but he couldn't deny that he was amped to be on a mission.

"Hey, I've got to go to Myrtle Beach," he said when Tristan answered. "Wanted to give you a heads-up that Parker's closed up in his studio, so Duke's all yours until I get back."

"Oh, joy. Why the sudden trip?"

Poor Duke. Everyone liked him, but no one wanted to deal with his craziness. Kade told his brother about Harper's phone call.

"Do you know what has her afraid enough to fake her death?"

"Not yet. I'm going to bring her back here. Figure this is the safest place for her while I get to the bottom of it."

"You taking your bike or the Ram?"

"The bike. With bike week going on, I'll blend in better."

"Okay. Be safe. And call if you need help with anything. I'll head over now to get the goofball."

"Great. Thanks. He'll be in his crate."

After changing his shoes, Kade slipped on his leather jacket and put his gun in one of the pockets. His wallet went in his back pocket, then he grabbed his motorcycle key. Duke wasn't happy about being left in his crate, but he'd forget that as soon as Tristan showed up to get him.

Kade headed for the garage. Now that he was opting out of the Army, he'd treated himself to two things: a Harley-Davidson Road King and a Ram 1500 TRX pickup, both black and badass. He had his brothers to thank for being able to do that. They had refused to take money from him for household expenses while he was in the military. They said it was enough that he was risking his life for his country.

Because of his art, Parker was a wealthy boy, and he paid most of the bills. He'd also covered the cost of remodeling their house after their aunt had died. Now that Kade was getting out of the military, it was time to contribute his fair share.

He emptied his saddlebags, making room for whatever Harper might have with her. What wouldn't fit in them would have to be left behind. It still hadn't sunk in that she was alive. He took a few minutes to muddy the bike, including the license plate, obscuring all but two of the plate numbers. It killed him to dirty his bike up, but the less attention it got, the better.

As he rode toward Myrtle Beach, his thoughts drifted to

the first time he'd seen Harper. She'd been running down the street, chasing a dog. The dog would run, then stop and let the woman almost catch up, then he'd run again. The dog was having a blast, the woman not so much.

Kade and a teammate were doing a ten-mile run, and the dog veered their way, coming to a stop at their feet and giving them his goofy grin. He wore a collar, so Kade grabbed it and held the dog until the woman reached them.

"Lose something?" he said.

She stopped next to the dog. "Yeah. Thanks."

"No problem." He tapped the dog's nose. "And who are you?"

"This is Duke, better known as the military dog school flunky. He thinks everything's a game, even bombs."

"My kind of guy."

She laughed as she stood. "Figures."

Kade's teammate jogged backward. "I'm going to keep going."

"Catch you later, man." Kade took the leash dangling over the woman's shoulder and hooked it to the dog's collar, then held out his hand. "Kade Church."

"Lieutenant Harper Jansen."

"Nice to meet you, LT."

He walked with her back to her house, one she shared with another woman, a civilian. After that, they'd crossed paths several times, and one day he'd invited her to a party he and his roommate were throwing.

Over time, he and the lieutenant became friends. When he learned that she loved horror and action movies, they'd started a movie night. For the next year after meeting her, they'd been best friends. Nothing more.

They were both planning to leave the Army around the

same time, her a few months before him. She'd promised to come get her dog as soon as she returned home from her Peace Corps stint.

Then she'd died.

Since her promise to come get the dog ended with her death, Duke had become his. When he'd learned Harper had died, he'd wrapped his arms around her dog and cried against his fur. But she wasn't dead, as it turned out.

He wanted answers, and he was going to get them.

Chapter Two

Two months earlier

"Why don't we go out? Dinner and maybe a club after?" Harper had no desire to go out, but she was grasping at straws. Anything to get her roommate not to go meet her mysterious new boyfriend. "Please, Lisa. We haven't done anything fun for a while."

"Can't."

Harper leaned against the bathroom door while Lisa put on makeup. "Are you meeting…?" She waited for her friend to tell her this new guy's name. Lisa had been seeing him for a month now, and all she had ever called him was her boyfriend. He never picked her up for their dates, never came around, and the way Lisa had changed set off alarm bells.

"What's his name, anyway?" she said when Lisa ignored her question.

Lisa slammed the mascara tube down on the counter. "What's with all the questions?"

"I'm worried about you. You don't laugh anymore, and you've gotten really secretive. Tell me he isn't married." That was her biggest worry, along with the bruise on Lisa's cheek she'd come home with last night. She claimed she'd run into a door, but Harper didn't buy it.

"He's not married, okay?"

"Then why doesn't he ever come by or pick you up for your dates?"

"Stop it. Just stop with the questions."

"I care about you, and you're not happy anymore."

Lisa had grown up in foster care and never landed in a home where she was wanted or loved. Because of that, she looked for love and approval in every man she dated. With her long blond hair, blue eyes, and pretty face, she had no trouble getting dates. She just rarely got asked out a second time. One date and she was ready to have the man's babies. You'd think by now she would have figured out that was the best way to scare a man off.

"He's the one, Harper. Why can't you be happy for me?"

Because the alarm bells were clanging like mad. Something wasn't right with her friend, and she couldn't stand by and do nothing. Which was why she planned to follow Lisa tonight. "I'll be happy when you bring whatshisname over and introduce him."

"Why? So you can steal him away? You're just jealous because I have a boyfriend and you don't."

"That right there is why I'm worried about you. You know me better than that. The old you would never have thought that."

More worried than before their conversation, Harper went to her room. She checked her phone for a message from Kade. Still nothing. Yesterday, she'd asked him if he'd do something with her tonight but hadn't told him she planned to follow Lisa. He'd agreed, but today, he hadn't responded to any of her texts. That could only mean one thing. He'd been called out.

Even as close as they were, all he'd ever told her was that he was Special Forces. Being in the military herself—and hearing the whispers about Delta Force operators—how badass they were, how secretive, how they were a law unto themselves, all the way down to how many of the Army's regulations didn't apply to them—she'd always suspected he was Delta Force. Something none of those guys would admit to.

As a housing specialist, she helped relocated service members and their families find housing on and off the base she was assigned to. Her satisfaction and reward came from seeing a family's eyes light up when she took them on a tour of a home she thought would be perfect for them. What she was not was a combat soldier like Kade.

Kade was her best friend, and if she had a little bit of a crush on him, that was her secret. She valued his friendship too much to ever act on it. Nor had he given her any indication he thought of her as anything but a friend.

A very dangerous friend, one she wished was here to go spying with her. She briefly considered waiting for him to return, but that could be two or three weeks from now, and Harper was only here for another week since she was moving back to Florida. Tomorrow was her last day in the Army, then she planned to spend a little time wrapping her life up here. Then a few weeks in Apalachicola with her dad before her scheduled pre-training for the Peace Corps.

Another concern... Lisa was changing right in front of her eyes, and how could she leave if Lisa was in trouble?

All she planned to do was follow Lisa, see where she went, see if she could get a glimpse of the boyfriend. Hopefully see something that would ease her mind. She changed into black jeans and a black T-shirt, and not sure how close she could get, she grabbed her binoculars.

Lisa's bedroom door was closed, and Harper panicked, thinking she'd already left. She knocked on the door.

"What?" Lisa yelled, annoyance in her voice.

Good, she was still here. "Sure you won't change your mind?"

"I'm sure."

"Okay. I'm going out. See you tomorrow."

Lisa didn't answer, and Harper went to her car. Not wanting to live on base, she'd found a rental in Fayetteville, a city on the east coast of North Carolina. It was a convenient twenty-minute drive to Fort Bragg and the rent in the area was reasonable, so this part of town was popular with soldiers living off base.

Harper drove down the residential street, parked in the driveway of a house that was for sale and empty, and waited. "Here we go a snooping," she muttered when Lisa passed by.

Fifteen minutes later, Lisa turned into the parking lot of a warehouse. Harper stopped before reaching the warehouse and cut her lights. When Lisa went inside, Harper parked next to a semi in the lot across the street. Another car was already at the warehouse, and she took a picture of it with her phone, and then zoomed in on the license plate, and snapped another photo.

Why were they at a warehouse? She waited a while, but when no one came out, she decided to leave. She had a plate number and could look the person up, so it wasn't a wasted trip. Before she could leave, another car arrived. A man got out and walked to the passenger door. He opened it, and a woman got out.

Harper took more pictures, then put the binoculars to her eyes. The woman appeared drunk or stoned, and the man was supporting her as they entered the building. Harper picked up her phone again and snapped some more pictures, including the plate number of that car. "Time to go."

The next morning, Lisa was in the kitchen when Harper came out. "Morning."

"Can't talk. I'm running late."

Harper narrowed her eyes at what she saw on Lisa's arm. "Another bruise?"

"What is with you?" Lisa snatched her arm away. "It's nothing. I bruise easy. Big deal."

"You didn't used to."

"I have to go to work."

Lisa was a receptionist at a doctor's office. When Harper had advertised for a roommate to share the house she was renting, only Lisa had responded. They'd hit it off and over time had become friends. Until she'd hooked up with this new boyfriend, they'd talked about everything. Now it felt like Lisa barely tolerated her. Yet her friend wasn't happy. If she was, Harper could accept that things had changed between them and move on with the next phase of her life.

After Lisa left for work, Harper dressed. She spent a few extra minutes staring at her reflection in the mirror. This was the last time she'd wear an Army uniform, and she had mixed feelings. She'd matured during her eight years in the Army, had experienced living in Japan and South Korea, had rescued a dog that had flunked out of military dog school, and had met Kade and made him her best friend.

It had been a very good eight years, and today was bittersweet. She was leaving a life she loved for a new life. Joining the Peace Corps was what she thought of as her last chance to travel and to do her part for making the world a better place before she settled down and checked off the next items on her bucket list…falling in love and having babies. She'd been an only child, her mother dying when Harper was a baby. She'd always wished for brothers and sisters, and that was probably why she wanted a household full of kids.

Harper loved her father, a man who had wanted to be surrounded by children but hadn't found a woman he could love enough to replace his wife. For herself and for him, she would have those children and make him the happiest grandfather ever.

She was minutes from home, headed for the base, when she turned left instead of right. She'd just do a little drive-by of the warehouse, see if either of the two cars from last night were there. The lot was empty, and if she didn't know better, she'd think it was an abandoned building. She circled around and drove past the back. What was going on inside there? Whatever Lisa was involved in, Harper knew in her gut that it wasn't good. Before she could talk herself out of it, she parked down the street, then carrying only her car keys and phone, she walked back.

There was a window, but it was boarded over. Next to the window was a door, and Harper twisted the knob, expecting it to be locked. It was not. She opened it and leaned in. The first floor was wide open, and she didn't sense anyone in the building. In the middle of the room was a bed covered by a red velvet bedspread. Two cameras on tripods were aimed at the bed.

What in the world? Harper stepped inside. A table was against a wall, and she walked over to it. Photographs of women in various stages of dress were spread out over the top. She shuffled through them, sick at heart when she found ones of Lisa naked and tied to the bedposts. There were also some of the woman she recognized from last night. She put that one, the ones of Lisa, and a few of some other women in her back pocket.

The place creeped her out, and she needed to leave before someone showed up. But first she took pictures of the room, the bed, and the cameras with her phone. It was time to have another talk with Lisa.

Harper was waiting when her roommate arrived home from work. "We need to talk."

"Don't have time." Lisa blew past, heading for her room.

"Make time." Harper stepped in front of her, stopping her. "Are you making porno films?"

Fear flashed in her friend's eyes. "What? Why... Why would you say that?"

Harper handed her one of the photos. It was of Lisa wearing only black lace panties. "This is why. What have you gotten yourself involved in? Talk to me, Lisa."

Tears pooled in Lisa's eyes as she stared at the picture. "You don't understand."

"Explain it to me then."

When Lisa's lips trembled and the tears fell down her cheeks, Harper led her to the sofa. "Talk to me," she said after they were seated. "Are you making porno movies?"

"Yes," Lisa wailed. "But I don't want to." The story came out between sobs. "I was in love with him, Harper. In the beginning, he told me that he was filming us for only us. I didn't see any harm in it. It was kind of sexy. A few weeks later, another man was there, and..." She squeezed her eyes shut.

"You had sex with him, too?"

Lisa nodded. "I didn't want to, but then they gave me a glass of wine to drink. I think they put something in it because I felt really weird, and I don't remember much of that night."

Dear God. "You have to stop, not go there anymore."

"You don't understand. They won't let me stop. If I don't show up, they said they'd put the videos all over social media." She frowned at the picture. "How'd you get this?"

"I went to the warehouse. There were photos of other girls, too. You have to go to the police." She was furious that men would drug a woman to have sex, much less film it for others to see, and that just couldn't stand. She was also beyond disappointed in Lisa for letting herself be used like that.

Lisa vehemently shook her head. "No, they'll kill me if I do that."

"That's a bit drastic, don't you think? You can't let them do this to you. What's this guy's name?"

"I'm serious, Harper. They're not men you want to mess with. You're better off not knowing his name."

"Well, you can't go back there." Since she had the men's license plate numbers, she didn't need their names.

"If I don't show up, they'll come for me. I have to leave. Go somewhere far away."

That was a good idea. "What about your friend in Alaska? Can you go there?" Lisa and Stephanie were foster sisters, the only person Lisa had kept in touch with from her foster care days.

"Yeah, she told me I should come see her sometime. I'll call her."

"First, you need to call that man, tell him you're sick, that you have the flu and you're vomiting. He won't want to be anywhere near you. You can't go back there tonight."

Relief was in Lisa's eyes as she hugged Harper. "Thank you, thank you, thank you."

"Everything's going to be okay. Just promise not to let another man use you like this."

"I think I need to take a break from men for a while."

"That wouldn't be a bad idea." She hoped Lisa learned a lesson from all this.

After the phone calls were made, Lisa packed, managing to get almost all her clothes into two suitcases and a carry-on. Early the next morning, Harper followed Lisa to a used car dealer where she sold her nine-year-old hybrid for next to nothing. Then after a stop at an ATM, Harper took her friend to the airport. They'd agreed that Harper would call the doctor's office when she returned home and tell them Lisa had a family emergency and probably wouldn't be back.

"Take care of yourself," she said as she hugged her friend. "And don't call anyone here, even me. If there's anything you need to know, I'll email you."

"Okay. Thank you for everything. I'm going to miss you so much."

"Same. Just go and be happy."

What she didn't tell Lisa was that she was going to tell the police what was going on in that warehouse.

Harper read over the email she planned to anonymously send the police. After taking Lisa to the airport yesterday, she'd returned home and packed. She hadn't planned to leave until next week, mostly because she'd hoped Kade would be back by then, but she didn't want to be around if one of those men came looking for Lisa. The plan had changed, and she'd get on the road first thing in the morning. She'd call Kade after she got home.

The house was furnished, so all she had to pack were her personal things. She loaded her car, then cleaned the house. She called the owner, who promised to mail her deposit as soon as she inspected the house and confirmed there wasn't any damage.

She was taking the trash to the curb when a black SUV stopped in front of her driveway. A tall man wearing a knit cap got out, and as he strode toward her, his intense gaze narrowed on her, one word came to mind…*menacing*. Her gun was packed in its case and in the car. Why hadn't she kept it on her?

He stopped a few feet from her. "Where's Lisa?"

"At work."

"No, she isn't. Where is she, Harper?"

He knew her name? She told herself to stay calm, which was hard when her heart was pounding like a jackhammer on crack. "She left this morning for work. Who are you, anyway?" And how did he know Lisa wasn't at work?

"Someone you don't want to mess with, little girl."

A part of her wanted to roll her eyes at the scary movie dialog, but the smarter part wanted to run. She also sensed that the worst thing she could do with this man was show fear, even though internally she was shaking like a leaf. She was Army. She was badass. All she had to do was act like it. He wouldn't do anything—like kill her or beat her up—standing in her driveway in broad daylight…right?

"If Lisa's not at work, then she's probably with her boyfriend. Who did you say you were again?" Was this the *boyfriend*? He wasn't the man who'd arrived at the warehouse after Lisa.

"You better hope I don't find out you know where she is."

"Well, you better not threaten me again if you don't want me to call the police." *Pushing your luck here, Harper. Need to shut up.* Yeah, but this guy was pissing her off. She didn't get angry often, but when she did, she had no filter.

Pale blue eyes so cold they made her want to shiver roamed over her, pausing on her chest. "You'll make a good stand-in if I don't find your friend. And, Harper, make no mistake. I will come for you if Lisa isn't where she's supposed to be tonight."

Frozen to where she stood, the garbage can the only barrier between her and a man who made her want to take a hot shower and scrub her skin raw, she blew out a relieved breath when he returned to his car and left.

Her plan to leave in the morning had just changed. It was time to go. Like right now. She'd send her anonymous email to the police when she was at her dad's house. Leaving the garbage can on the curb, she went back inside and locked the door behind her. She raced around and put her toiletry bag, the clothes she'd left out to put on in the morning, and the few other things still to pack in her Army duffel bag.

After loading her car, she drove down her street for the last time.

"So, that's the full story," Harper told her father over dinner the next night. She'd driven straight home. With stops for gas, coffee, and a quick dinner, it had taken eleven hours, and finally feeling safe, she'd fallen face-first in her bed and slept most of the day.

Her dad swallowed hard, his Adam's apple rising and falling. "Sweetheart, you have to remove yourself from whatever's going on with Lisa and those men."

"I know, and I am. Promise." And she would, right after she sent the anonymous email to the police.

Which she did later that night.

Her first two days home she vegetated. Her third day, she broke her promise to her dad and went online, searching for news stories of a police raid on the warehouse. There was nothing. Maybe they were still investigating.

What she did find, though, was a story on the increase of drug deaths, especially from fentanyl, in the area around Fort Bragg. The article included a photo and the name—Abby Warton—of the latest victim, and Harper gasped. Abby Warton was the woman she'd seen go in the warehouse with the other man.

The one person she wanted to talk to was Kade. She trusted him, and he'd know the best thing to do. She called, got his voice mail, and left a message. When he hadn't returned her call by the next day, she knew he was still gone on whatever mission the Army had sent him on.

Unable to stand by and do nothing, she sent the police another email, attaching the photo she'd taken of who she now knew was Abby Warton and the man with her. Harper didn't know if the men were connected to Abby's death in any way, but her gut said they were. She also included the license plate numbers of the two cars. After a short debate with herself, she also sent this one from the anonymous email she'd created.

The biggest reason was Lisa. If these men, the one she'd seen with the dead girl and the one who'd threatened her, had killed Abby, then Lisa was in danger. If Harper gave the police her name, she'd have to explain why she was at the warehouse and that would mean giving them Lisa's name. As soon as an arrest was announced, making it safe for Lisa to talk to the police, Harper would convince her friend that she had to report what she knew. If she refused, then Harper would come forward.

The next reason was her father. She'd promised him she

wouldn't get involved. He was worried about her, and she got that. She was the only family he had, and keeping her safe trumped all else in his mind. Before she identified herself to the police, she owed it to him to tell him she was going to give the police her name. He'd worry less if the men in question were behind bars when she did it.

Also, she didn't know for a fact the men were guilty. She had no proof other than seeing Abby go into the warehouse and Lisa's fear of her so-called boyfriend. Even without proof, Harper believed with every fiber of her being that something happened to Abby in that warehouse.

The following day, there was a response to her anonymous email from a Detective Johnson demanding that she call the phone number he gave. She almost did, but the tone of his email rubbed her wrong. Why hadn't he asked any questions, even assured her that her identity would be kept secret? Plus, she wasn't ready yet to out herself. Would they want her to return, to talk to them in person? Would any meeting with them be kept confidential until the men were arrested? She wanted to think about it before giving him her name, so she replied with the truth, that she was afraid to come forward at this time.

If he responded with a promise that the police would keep her safe, she'd give him her name. Another day passed before he answered, and there was nothing about her coming forward. He only asked her to click on a link and tell him if she recognized any men in the attached photos. She studied the five pictures, but none were the two men she'd seen, and she replied no, she'd never seen those men before.

Detective Johnson never replied, so she'd wait for the arrests, which would surely happen soon since she'd given the detective the license plate numbers.

* * *

"Come in," Harper said, lowering her Kindle and glancing at the clock. If her father was knocking on her door at eleven at night, that meant he'd been called to the hospital for one of his patients.

He poked his head around the doorjamb. "I've got to head out."

"Okay. See you in the morning." She read for another hour, and when her eyes grew heavy, she set the Kindle on her bedside table and went to sleep.

The nightmare felt so real. Her scalp actually hurt when the monster dragged her out of bed by her hair. Wait. Why was she on the floor?

"Get up, bitch." The monster kicked her ribs.

Not a nightmare. Pain shot up her side, and she groaned. She scooted across the floor until she was backed against the wall. The man grabbed her arm and jerked her up. It was too dark to see his face, but she knew that voice. It was the man in the knit cap who'd threatened her on her driveway.

"I should have checked the security cameras sooner," he said, his fingers digging into her arm. "You're a nosy one, aren't you? Where are the pictures you stole? Where's Lisa?"

"You're hurting me." She tried to pull her arm away, but he tightened his grip. How had he found her? And they had security cameras inside the warehouse? That had never occurred to her. She'd make a lousy spy if she couldn't consider and plan for things like that.

"That's what happens to little girls who stick their noses in things that are none of their business." He slapped her. "Where. Is. Lisa?"

"I don't know. I swear." She cried out when he punched her in the same place he'd kicked her. Oh God, that hurt.

"Bitch." He wrapped his hands around her neck and squeezed. "Where is she?"

"Cho...choking me."

"Tell me, or I'll kill you and then wait for your father to come back and kill him, too."

Did she have a choice? He was going to kill her and her dad if she didn't tell him. *I'm sorry, Lisa.* "Ala..."

He squeezed harder and her world turned black.

Chapter Three

Present day

There wasn't one vacancy in Myrtle Beach, so Harper took Kade's advice and found a dive bar and settled in a dark corner. They didn't offer food, so she'd alternated between buying club sodas and cheap beers for the past four hours to keep from getting booted out. The three beers she pretended to nurse for a while before carrying each one to the bathroom when the waitress wasn't looking and pouring them out.

She checked her watch. One more hour and she could turn her phone on. So far, she hadn't noticed anyone paying attention to her, hadn't sensed she was being watched. The worst of her injuries, her two broken ribs, had finally healed, but she hated how the beating had changed her.

The confident, outgoing woman was gone, replaced by one who jumped at shadows. If her father had his way, she'd stay dead, because dead was safe. When he'd gone so far as telling her she should change her name after a man had knocked on his door, asking for her, that had been her wake-up call. She had to take her life back, and there was one person who could help her do that. Kade wouldn't turn his back on her, but would he help her once she told him her story?

"Another beer, hon?" the waitress asked.

Harper held up her forth and hopefully last bottle. "I'm good, thanks."

The woman glanced around. "Listen, if you're going to bring trouble in here, you need to leave."

"Why would you think that?" Although if one of those men found her, trouble would be an understatement.

"Well, you're hiding here in this corner with that ball cap pulled down, no one hangs in this place nursing beers for four hours, you keep watching the door, and you pay for your beers each time I bring you one so you're paid up if you have to run."

Harper blinked. "You're very observant." Too observant.

"I've had to run a time or two, so I know the signs." She glanced toward the bar where the bartender was staring at them. "That's Mako, my old man. You're making him nervous. We own this place, it's just the two of us working here, and we don't need cops storming the place. We barely get by as it is."

"I'm just waiting for a friend." She checked her watch. "He'll be here pretty soon now."

"You got a fifty on you?"

"If I do?"

"Give it to me. That'll buy you one more hour, then you won't have to keep buying beers that you sneak into the bathroom and pour out."

Harper choked down a laugh. And she thought she was being covert. She fished a fifty and a twenty from her wallet. "Here, plus a tip."

Like magic, the twenty disappeared into the waitress's

bra. "One hour, hon, then you leave." The woman headed back to the bar and handed the fifty to her old man.

It wasn't surprising that the couple was scraping by. Even with it being bike week, during the time Harper had been here, only a few men had come in, stayed for a beer or two, then left. At the moment, there were three customers besides her. Harper didn't think any of them were tailing her, but that was an assumption, so she stayed alert for anyone paying too much attention to her.

Everyone but her father believed she was dead. Her friends from Fort Bragg had held a Celebration of Life for her, which her father had attended. When they'd called her dad and asked if he could come up for it, he had agreed, telling Harper it would be suspicious if he didn't. That hadn't sat well, letting them believe she was dead.

Her biggest regret was that she'd given up her place with the Peace Corps. That dream was never going to happen now. How could someone who jumped at shadows traipse off to some foreign country and not see danger behind every corner? She just couldn't do it.

Eight o'clock finally arrived, and she turned on her phone. Seconds later, it vibrated, Kade's name coming up on the screen. "Kade."

"Where are you?"

"At a dive bar like you said. It's Bottoms Up." She gave him the address.

"On the way." He disconnected.

"A man of few words," she muttered. Did *on the way* mean ten minutes or another hour?

Since he should be here soon and she was thirsty, she drank a little bit of the warm beer. "Yuck." She hadn't stopped for food since getting off the bus in Myrtle Beach this morning, and that bit of beer didn't feel so great in her stomach.

She thought about asking for a glass of water, but the waitress was studiously ignoring her now, and she didn't want to be ordered out before Kade arrived. She wanted to call her father, but she didn't dare. Had he gone to her cousin's beach condo like he'd said he would? No one should be able to find him there. That was her hope, anyway.

A trio of men wearing biker leathers came in, loudly laughing and pushing each other. This was obviously not their first bar stop. Two of them headed to the bar, but one glanced around, then his gaze fixed on her, and he grinned.

"Crap," she muttered when he headed for her.

"Hello, there," he slurred as he swayed on his feet. "You want some company, babe?"

"No."

He sat anyway. "Aw, don't be like that. What's your name, babe?"

"Get lost."

"Well, now, that's a funny name. I think I'll just call you babe. Whatcha drinking, babe? I'll get us another round."

"I said get lost." Her gaze was caught by the man slipping up behind the biker on silent feet. Kade had shaved his beard since she'd last seen him, but his hair was still that messy, wind-blown look that she liked on him. Good gracious, he was hot.

"The lady said get lost, so do it."

"I'm busy here. You get lost," the creep said.

She wasn't sure exactly what Kade did, but he put his hand on the back of the man's neck and lifted him out of the seat. It made her think of a puppet controlled by a puppeteer.

"Walk away now," Kade said, menace dripping from his voice.

The man didn't just walk away, he ran.

Well, wow! She wanted to know how Kade did that.

He picked up her duffel bag. "Let's go."

"Okay." She slipped her purse over her shoulder, and for the first time since she'd "died," she felt safe. As he followed her out, the waitress fanned her face. Harper gave her a yes-he-sure-is-hot grin.

Parked on the sidewalk outside was a black motorcycle. When Kade stopped by it, she frowned. "That's yours?"

"Yes, ma'am."

"It's dirty." The Kade she knew wouldn't allow anything of his to look like that. He was one of the neatest people she knew, almost obsessive about it. Sometimes, when she was at his house to watch a movie, she'd purposely move something around or drop a jacket or sweater on the floor just to mess with him. It was funny how he'd try to subtly move the object back in its place or pick up whatever she'd dropped and fold it or hang it up. No way would he tolerate a mud-covered bike.

"The less attention we get, the better." He set her duffel on the seat, then opened one of the saddlebags. "Put what you can in here, then the rest in the other one."

She put her laptop, chargers, mouse, toiletry case, and purse in the first saddlebag. All that was left was two changes of clothes, running shoes, flip-flops, and the duffel bag with her gun in it, all of which fit in the second saddlebag.

"I was expecting to tell you that you'd have to leave some stuff behind."

"Well, I've learned to travel light lately." She noticed

that he constantly scanned their surroundings while she got her things put away, and the relief that other eyes besides hers were watching for danger was profound, especially when they belonged to a highly trained warrior.

He handed her a helmet. "Put this on so we can beat feet." As soon as they had their helmets on, he swung a leg over the bike. "You ever ride on a motorcycle before?"

"Yeah, a boyfriend had one."

"Good. Hop on."

There wasn't a backrest, so she put her hands on the sides of his waist. He shook his head, then pulled her hands around his stomach, which resulted in her pressed against his back. All righty then.

As they rode through the night, her arms wrapped around a man with a rock-hard stomach, she wondered what it would be like to have a boyfriend like Kade Church.

Chapter Four

Kade had never let himself think of Harper as anything other than a friend, but damn, he liked having her pressed against him. She'd let her hair grow longer since the last time he'd seen her. He'd have to see it in the daytime, but when she'd removed the ball cap to put on the helmet, the brown looked lighter than he remembered. Hazel eyes that lit up when she laughed, full lips that he'd never let himself think about kissing, and a body that rocked all made for a very fine woman.

Yeah, he was noticing now, but he shut that kind of thinking down. It had been too long since he'd had a woman's soft body wrapped around him, the reason for these stray thoughts. His best friend was hands-off.

They'd been riding for three hours now, and her helmet was bopping against his, and her hands had dropped to his lap. She was falling asleep, not a good thing to do on a motorcycle. He'd hoped to ride straight home. Stopping for a few hours of sleep would mean he'd never make it to Charlotte in time for his interview. Not the way to make a good impression, but he couldn't risk her falling off.

A motel was listed on the sign for the next exit, and he headed for it. When he shut down the engine, Harper mumbled something. He held on to her arm to keep her from falling off and twisted in his seat to see her. Her face fell to his shoulder. She was military, used to drills, sometimes long into the night. Normally she wouldn't have a problem staying awake. When had she last slept? He removed his helmet and set it over the mirror.

"Hey." He shook her. She mumbled something unintelligible again. "Ten-hut, Lieutenant!"

She jerked straight up.

"At ease." He chuckled when she sagged against him again.

"Where are we?"

He glanced at the sign. "The Blue Bird Motel, where sweet dreams are promised."

"You're making that up."

"Nope. Says so right there on the sign. Stay here while I get us a room."

"Why?"

"Because you're exhausted, and the last thing I want to see is your sweet ass hitting the pavement when you fall off." He tapped her helmet. "You can take that off if you want."

There were only a few cars in the lot, and the place looked pretty run-down, but it would do. They had a room with twin beds on the back side available, which was great. He doubted whoever was after her had tracked them here, but his motorcycle wouldn't be visible from the street.

After paying for the room with cash, and with an actual key in hand, he returned to the bike. He came to a dead stop at the view in front of him. The woman he'd never let himself think about sexually was bent over, her palms flat on the pavement, her butt in the air.

Killing me, LT.

"Ah…" He cleared his throat. "Looking for something?"

She slowly rose, lifted her arms over her head, and twisted her torso one way, and then the other. "Just getting the kinks out."

And now she had to go and put the word *kink* in his head. Eff him. Kink and Harper was a vision he didn't need. He cleared his throat. Again. "I have to ride to the room. You want back on or walk around?"

"I'll walk."

He handed her the key. "Room one eleven. Meet you there." He stuck his helmet back on his head, didn't bother to buckle it, and rode to the back of the motel.

She reached the room just as he did, and he came to a stop. She smiled when their eyes connected, and his gaze fell to her mouth. Something fluttery happened in his chest as she smiled at him. He gave a mental head shake. After some eight hours on the bike, he was tired and not thinking straight. That was the reason for these new thoughts about her. A little rest, and things would be back the way they were supposed to be.

"What do you need to take in tonight?" He opened the saddlebags.

She unlocked the door, pushed it open, then returned to the bike and collected some of her things. He followed her into the room. It was about what he expected. At least it was clean. He'd slept in much worse places over the years.

"I guess they didn't have two rooms available?"

He sat on the end of the bed closest to the door. "I'm sure they did, but I can't protect you from another room. Not that I'm expecting trouble tonight. Better safe than sorry, right?"

"I guess." She sucked her bottom lip into her mouth. "What?"

"Do they have a vending machine? I haven't eaten since

last night. I think my stomach is eating itself." She went to the other bed and dropped her things on it.

"There's a convenience store across the street. Why don't you get settled in, take a shower if you want, while I go get some snacks?"

"Thank you." Her gaze lowered to the floor. "I'm sorry if I've disrupted your life. I don't even know if you have a girlfriend now, and if you do, she's probably not happy."

"Hey." He stood and walked to her. "No girlfriend, and you're not disrupting my life. Truthfully, I was getting a little bored, so think of it as saving me from driving my brothers bonkers." He winked.

Her eyes lit up in that way they did when she was amused. "So, I'm doing you a favor?"

"More like doing my brothers a favor. Any special request from the store?"

"No, I just need to get something in my stomach. Oh, and if they have a bottle of green tea, that would be great. If not, just some water."

"On it. I'm taking the key, so you won't have to let me back in the room. Don't leave, and don't answer the door for anyone."

"I won't."

He stepped outside, stopped, and both listened and scanned the area. All was quiet, and he didn't sense anything that didn't belong. An awareness of danger, of being watched, was something he'd honed over the years of sneaking in and out of places under the noses of his enemies.

The convenience store was directly across the street, and he was able to keep an eye on the motel while he piled up an assortment of snacks on the counter. He added four bottles of green tea to the pile, along with a couple bottles of water.

Harper liked ice cream sandwiches, so he got her one. A few packages of beef jerky for him, and he was done.

"Dude, that's some serious munchies," the young clerk said, admiration in his voice as he bagged the snacks.

"I'm a growing boy." Again, not wanting to leave a trail, he paid cash.

Back at the motel, he stopped at the door and let his senses reach out. Nothing was out of the ordinary. He didn't know who Harper was running from, how well she'd covered her tracks, if she had at all, or what the danger was. As soon as she had something in her stomach, he'd find out what was going on so he could make plans.

He unlocked the door and went in. She was slipping into bed, wearing nothing but a T-shirt and panties.

"Um, I was in a hurry and didn't pack any pajamas," she said when she caught him looking at her. She scrambled under the covers.

"S'kay." It wasn't. It was a sight he wished he could unsee because now the vision was imprinted in his mind.

"Wow," she said, when he dropped three bags of snacks on her bed. "Did you buy the store out?"

"The clerk thinks I'm a pothead with a serious case of munchies." Thankfully, she'd pulled the covers up to her waist.

She leaned forward and rummaged through one of the bags. "Oh, good, they had the tea."

"There's an ice cream sandwich in there you might want to eat before it melts."

"You remembered."

There was so much pleasure in her voice that it made him feel like some kind of hero for remembering she liked them. He couldn't think like that where she was concerned.

He was no one's hero, just a man trained by the United States government to be one of its elite assets.

"I'm going to take a shower, get the road dirt off, then we'll talk," he said when they finished eating.

"'Kay."

When he came out of the bathroom, she was asleep, and although he didn't like not knowing what he was facing, she was exhausted and needed to sleep. He wanted to be back on the road as soon as possible, so they'd talk when he got her home. He'd keep her safe, solve her problems, and then send her on her way.

Chapter Five

Harper was exhausted down to her bones. Kade had woken her at sunrise with a cup of coffee and a Danish, and then had stood at the door, anxious to leave. Any other time, she'd enjoy the ride on a motorcycle, but today, she just wanted off the bike.

They came around a curve, and she got her first sight of the Blue Ridge Mountains in the distance. A blue haze hung over the peaks, and she wondered if that was how they got their name.

She'd grown up in Apalachicola, a small town in the Florida Panhandle. Their claim to fame were their oysters. The mountains seemed mysterious to a girl who was raised in a beach town in one of the flattest states in the country.

She wanted to keep going, up to those blue-crested mountains rising to the sky. Would it be easy to get lost in them, to find a mountain cabin, maybe with a creek running through the land, a place where she couldn't be found?

As the motorcycle cruised along, people in the cars they passed looked over at them, and she imagined they were envious, wishing they were enjoying a ride on a bike on a warm fall day. They would think she and Kade were a couple, and she liked the idea of that a little too much. A girl couldn't help but appreciate the hard body she was wrapped around.

For a while, until they reached their destination, she let herself pretend they really were a couple out for the day on her boyfriend's bike. It was a nice dream, but that was all it was. Kade was nothing more than a friend who might or might not help her after he heard her story.

They left the highway for a two-lane country road, and she watched the passing scenery with interest. Kade had told her stories, some hilarious, of his hometown. Located in the foothills of the Blue Ridge Mountains, Marsville was infamous because of a supposed alien abduction years ago. They even had a UFO museum of all things. She hoped she'd get a chance to see it.

Not long after leaving the highway she saw signs welcoming her to Marsville. The town was just ahead, but Kade leaned to turn onto a cross street. The town looked charming from the brief glimpse she got of the main street. What really stood out were the colorful awnings on the buildings.

A few minutes later, Kade turned the bike onto a private drive that led to a beautiful three-story Victorian-style house. He stopped in front of a four-car unattached garage. Who had that many garages?

Before they could get off, a little girl came running out a side door of the house. "Uncle Kade! Where'd you go? You didn't tell me! Uncle Tris took Duke to work with him 'cause you weren't here. He's not a police dog, Uncle Kade! Only Fuzz is. Can we go get him?"

The girl came to a sudden halt, her eyes widening at seeing Harper. "Who are you?"

"That's Miss Harper. Harper, this is my niece, Everly, who has lost the volume control on her voice. We're hoping she finds it again and soon." Kade stood, his long legs straddling the bike as he held it upright. "You can hop off."

She swung her leg over, then stepped to the ground. "Hello, Everly. It's nice to meet you."

"Are you my uncle's girlfriend? Are you coming to live with us? My uncle Tris has a girlfriend, but she doesn't live here. Sometimes she stays here. Do you know her? When my uncle Tris marries—"

"Ev! Give Miss Harper a chance to answer a question before you ask another one."

The girl sighed. "But I have so many, Uncle Kade. I don't want to forget one."

Harper shared an amused glance with Kade. His niece was adorable. Harper guessed her to be around five or six, and she shared Kade's dark chocolate eyes and dark brown hair.

"I'm not your uncle's girlfriend, but I am his friend. Is it okay if I stay here for a few days?"

"Do you like pickles?"

Harper managed not to laugh. Was that a condition of staying? This girl was a charmer, all right. "I do like pickles."

Everly took her hand. "Let's go have some."

"You're now her new best friend," Kade said. "Go on in with her. I'll bring your things."

Harper let her new best friend lead her into a kitchen that was to die for. Kade had told her that he shared a house with his two brothers, each of them having a separate floor. He hadn't told her that their house could be on the cover of *Architectural Digest*.

"I can have five pickles, Miss Harper," Everly said. "How many do you want?"

Five? Harper had her doubts about that. She was pretty sure she was in the presence of a miniature con artist. A precious one, definitely, but for sure a talented one.

"You can have one, Ev," a man said, walking into the kitchen.

"But, Daddy! Miss Harper wants five, and I—"

"Save it, kiddo." Her father tapped her on the nose. "One. End of discussion."

The man turned his attention to her. "Hello. I'm Parker and this pickle freak's father." He glanced around, then back at her as if wondering what a stranger was doing in his kitchen. "And you are?"

"Harper Jansen, a friend of Kade's. I hope I'm not imposing." So this was the artist slash fire chief brother. Kade's family had always fascinated her, especially his stories about the three brothers raising a baby. He'd have her in stitches talking about changing diapers.

He shrugged. "Can't see why you would. A friend of my brother is always welcome." He took the jar away from Everly. "You need to leave for school in fifteen minutes, so if you want a pickle, you better eat it now." After opening the jar and putting one on a saucer for his daughter, he glanced at Harper. "You know you don't have to eat a pickle if you don't want one."

Everly appeared shocked that someone might not want a pickle, and Harper didn't want to scandalize her little friend. "I'd love one." She slid onto a bar stool next to the girl. "This granite is gorgeous." She'd never seen anything like it. The shades of blue, gray, and purple swirling through it made her think of storm clouds.

"Thanks," Parker said as he stabbed a pickle with a fork, then held it out to her.

Kade came in, carrying her duffel and purse. He set everything down on the end of the kitchen island. He grinned at seeing her eating a pickle. "If you're not careful, that will be your breakfast every morning."

Harper studied the two brothers. They had similar characteristics except for their hair. Parker wore his pulled back in a low ponytail, while Kade sported his new short cut.

"Uncle Kade, can we go get Duke now? Jellybean misses him."

"You, my little pickle monster, are going to school," Parker said. "Go get your backpack."

"But Jellybean wants Duke."

Kade picked her up and set her on the floor. "Duke will be here when you get home."

"Oh, goody." Everly clapped her hands as she skipped out of the room.

"Jellybean does not miss Duke, believe me," Parker said.

"Um, who's Jellybean?"

Kade slid onto the stool Everly had vacated. "He's Everly's cat. Duke loves him, but Jellybean doesn't return the affection."

"Duke loves everyone and everything. I've missed him." There were a lot of things she'd missed, but Kade and Duke were at the top of the list. The freedom to go and come as she pleased was up there, too.

"I still don't know how you conned me into taking that goofball." He shifted on the stool to face her.

"Because you can't say no to me?"

Something flashed in his eyes, then he grinned. "That must be it."

What had she seen? If she didn't know better, that had been heat in his eyes.

Chapter Six

"My brother and his fiancée are on the way over. Skylar's the sheriff." Kade had called Tristan before coming in. He wanted the two of them here when Harper told her story.

"He's the police chief brother?"

Kade nodded. "Yeah. They both need to know who to be on the lookout for if someone figures out where you are and shows up in Marsville. You good with that?"

"Yes, it's a smart thing to do. I hope that doesn't happen, and I've been as careful as I know how not to leave a trail, but they found me once already."

Kade wanted to know who *they* were. She'd called him one morning and asked him to go with her somewhere that evening. Something about being worried for her roommate. She'd said she'd fill him in when they met up. He'd agreed, but two hours later, his team was summoned. She knew the drill—no phone calls, no communication to the outside world when an operation was in progress. When he didn't show up, she'd know why and understand.

On returning, he'd learned that she'd died, the victim of a mugging gone wrong on a visit home to see her father. Her absence had left a hole in his heart, and not a day had passed that he hadn't thought about her, hadn't missed this girl who'd become his best friend. Now, seeing her alive and breathing, the relief that she wasn't dead was profound, but there was anger, too. She'd let him grieve for her when she could have come to him for help.

"I need to make a phone call. There's a bathroom around the corner to your left if you need one."

"Oh, thanks. I would like to freshen up a little." She opened her duffel and took out a toiletry bag.

"You want coffee?"

"That would be great, thanks. Be right back."

Coffee started, he called Chase Talon. Nothing like canceling an interview twenty minutes before it was supposed to happen. When Chase answered his phone, Kade walked outside, not wanting Harper to hear the conversation and realize he was missing an interview because of her.

"Chase, it's Kade Church."

"Hey, man. You're in town already? Come on over. I'll grab Nick, and we'll go talk over breakfast."

"I'm not in Charlotte. That's why I'm calling." Damn, he hated having to make this call. "Something's come up. I'm going to have to reschedule." Hopefully the brothers wouldn't write him off as unreliable.

"You want to tell me what's more important than your future?"

Yeah, the man's friendly voice had icicles in it now. "A friend's in trouble, the life-or-death kind. The kind I can't turn my back on. Look, I want this job, but—"

"You're hired."

"Just like that?"

"Yep. You risked losing a job you wanted because a friend needs you, and if you're telling the truth about it being a life-or-death situation—"

"I am."

"That's loyalty, and the kind of man we want on our team. But there's one condition. How long do you think it will take to deal with the situation?"

"Not really sure." He hoped only a few days. "What's the condition?"

"I need you on board no later than two weeks from today. If you can't make that happen, I'll have to bring someone else in."

"Thanks for understanding. I'll keep in touch."

"You do that, and if Talon Security can be of any help, all you need to do is ask."

"Thanks. I might just do that." As soon as he learned exactly what the situation was. He was glad Chase hadn't asked since Kade wouldn't have had an answer for him.

He'd been on a joint operation with Chase's team a few years past, and they'd hit it off. When Chase learned that Kade was returning to civilian life, he'd called and asked if Kade might be interested in coming on board. He was, and with Chase's reaction to the missed interview, he was more certain than ever that it was going to be a good fit.

He hadn't met Chase's brother yet, but Nick had called him after he'd scheduled an interview, and they'd had a good conversation. Chase was the CEO, and Nick, former military intelligence, was the operations vice president. According to Nick, Talon Security had their fingers in a variety of things from providing bodyguards for the rich and famous to government jobs that he couldn't talk about until Kade was officially on the team.

The item that most appealed to Kade, though, was Talon Security's involvement in rescuing people who found themselves in danger, especially abducted children. That might not have interested him as much as it did before Parker returned from France with his baby girl. Kade would hunt down anyone who dared to hurt his niece, and the results wouldn't be pretty. The thought of any parent having their child taken from them, the fear and heartache that he would feel if it was Everly…yeah, he wanted in on those missions.

It was a weight off his mind that he hadn't ruined the opportunity to work for Talon Security. It was an ideal situation in that not only did the company appeal to him, but Charlotte was only about an hour from Marsville. He wouldn't have to move. The job wasn't nine-to-five, and he didn't need to be there every day, so the commute wasn't a problem.

What he needed to do now was find out what kind of danger Harper was in, take care of it, then she could get back to her life, and he could get on with his. The little tug of regret in the back of his mind at the thought of not having Harper in his life was annoying, so he ignored it.

Tristan and Skylar walked in a few minutes after he finished his phone call, both holding cups from Sweet Tooth Bakery. Duke bounded in behind them, and when he saw Kade, he gave an excited yelp and tripped over his feet trying to get to him. He got his feet back under him, then skidded across the floor to Kade.

"You're a doofus." He kneeled, letting the silly dog jump around him, barking his happiness. "I was only gone overnight."

"To a dog, that's eternity," Tristan said.

Suddenly, Duke stilled and lifted his nose in the air. He looked at Kade and gave an excited bark, then he raced in circles with his nose to the floor. Kade stood. "I think he just picked up Harper's scent."

After Duke ran out of the kitchen Tristan whistled, and

his police dog, Fuzz, peeked around the open door. "You can come in now."

"What's with Fuzz?"

"Duke wore him out," Skylar said. "I think if we hadn't brought him back, Fuzz would have driven the car himself to deliver Duke to you."

"Poor Fuzz. Duke's a handful." He didn't mean to be, he just loved people and other dogs and cats and...well, everything. He loved life. Would that everyone loved the way Duke did. The world would be a better place.

Harper returned with Duke jumping around her. When she reached the kitchen, she sat on the floor. Duke landed on her and knocked her onto her back. "I've missed you so much, sweet boy." She laughed as Duke tried to lick the skin off her face.

Kade smiled at seeing her loving those Duke kisses. During the time they'd been friends, they'd laughed at a lot of things. This felt different, this weird feeling in his chest at seeing her happy.

He grabbed Duke's collar and pulled him off Harper so she could get up. "I didn't get a chance before Duke attacked you to introduce my brother and his fiancée. Tristan, Skylar, this is Harper Jansen."

"It's great to finally meet you, Tristan." Harper smiled at Skylar. "It's a pleasure to meet you, too. I'm just sorry I'm bringing trouble with me."

Kade shook a finger at her. "Stop that right now, okay? Your coffee's on the counter. Why don't you grab it, and we'll go sit on the deck? That'll get Duke outside where he can run some of that energy off." When everyone was settled around the patio table with Harper between him and Skylar, he nodded at her. "Time to talk. Start from the beginning."

She stared at Duke for a moment as he ran around the backyard, snapping at things in the air only he could see. Then her gaze scanned the three of them. "The beginning. That seems a lifetime ago." She blew out a breath, then her gaze fell on him. "I'm afraid you're going to be angry when you hear what I did."

That might well be true since whatever it was had ended with her playing dead. "If I am, it will only be because you're now in danger."

"I don't regret what I did, I just wish…" She shook her head.

"Take your time," Skylar said, placing her hand over Harper's.

Harper gave her a grateful smile. "Okay. I had a roommate, Lisa. When she started acting weird, I got worried."

"Did you know her?" Tristan asked him.

"I met her a few times, but when Harper and I hung out, it was always at my place." He shrugged. "I had the bigger TV. Lisa was…how do I say this without sounding like a douche?"

"Flirty? Too forward? Handsy?" Harper said.

"All of the above."

"Yeah, you told me once not to leave you alone with her. She thought you were hot and was always bugging me to set her up with you. I finally told her you had a girlfriend back home."

"How come you never told me that?"

"Because you would have been even more uncomfortable around her, and I had no intention of trying to get the two of you together, which you never would have agreed to, anyway. Lisa was desperate for a boyfriend, but a guy would ask her out, and she'd fall in love with him on the first date and be all clingy."

"Fastest way to run a guy off," Kade said.

She nodded, then continued with her story. As he listened, he grew angrier by the minute. When she told them about the man finding her at her father's house and what he'd done to her, Kade couldn't take any more.

"Let's take a break." He stood and then walked away.

Chapter Seven

Harper recognized the expression on Kade's face as she told her story. Anger, pure and simple. But was it directed at her—because yes, she could admit that she'd brought this mess on herself—or was it for the men who were threatening her? Probably both.

When he walked away, she pushed up, intending to follow him. Kade had never lied to her, and if he wanted her to leave, he'd tell her.

"He just needs a minute," Tristan said. "Do you know who the men are?"

She eased back onto the chair. Kade's oldest brother wasn't as intense as Kade, but intelligence shone in his dark chocolate eyes so much like Kade's and Parker's. The biggest difference between the brothers was their hair. Parker had long brown hair that he kept pulled back in a ponytail, and Tristan's short hair was a caramel color. Kade's was almost black and scraggly, a style he seemed to favor, and more than once she'd wondered how it would feel to comb her fingers through it.

Her eyes strayed to Kade as he strode across the yard, his fists clenched at his sides. Tristan had asked her a question, and instead of going to Kade like she wanted, she turned to him. "No. After that one hurt me, I was afraid to do a search on the plate numbers. I didn't know if they could somehow find out if I did, so I decided to wait and give the numbers to the police, which I did."

Her quiet time as a dead woman had ended three days ago when she had gone on the run, afraid for her father, afraid for herself, after a man showed up at her dad's, claiming to be a friend from Fort Bragg. Any friend of hers from the base would have believed she was dead, her dad reasoned, so he was suspicious. And rightly so.

She told them about the man. "He was the same one who hurt me. I'm the only family my dad has, and he's afraid of losing me. He wanted me to change my name, and I did think about it. But I don't want to be dead. I want my life back."

Out of desperation she'd called Kade, although she hadn't been sure he would answer. He could have been out of the country, or he might have blown off an unknown number. Her father had told her that Kade had attended her Celebration of Life, and she'd cried at hearing that. She'd almost called him then, her friend who was hurting for no reason. She had wanted him to know she wasn't dead. But they were just friends, a guy and a girl who sometimes hung out, sometimes watched movies together, and her problems weren't his to take on.

In the end, she'd called him anyway. She shouldn't have, but she couldn't bring herself to regret it. He was the only person she trusted who had the skills to help her. She hadn't missed that after his surprise at finding she was alive, that he was angry at her for letting him believe she was dead. She got that and didn't blame him. Even not happy with her, he hadn't hesitated to come for her. That was Kade, a man who was loyal to those he called friends.

He returned to the table, the anger she'd seen on his

face when he'd walked away replaced by…nothing. It was a warrior's face, the one he wore into battle. She didn't know how she knew that, but she did.

In the year she'd known him, Harper had never seen him lose his temper until now. There was a wild side to him, and she'd learned to never dare him to do something. He was always up for a challenge, especially in the name of fun. She'd seen him serious and intense, particularly when he was training or leaving for an operation.

They'd lived on the same street, and although he couldn't tell her whenever he was heading out, she'd been walking Duke a few times when he was leaving his house, his go bag slung over his shoulder. The first time it had happened, she'd stopped to talk to him. It was as if something had taken possession of her friend. A robot maybe. A mindset that left no room for anything but the operation he was setting out on.

There was something so desolate about that blank look on his face now, that she wanted to wrap her arms around him and make the world go away. She wanted to be the one to put light back in his eyes, the one to make him smile.

Where were these thoughts coming from? It had to be from the sexual tension left over from having a powerful motorcycle's rumbling vibrations between her legs while she was wrapped around a man's hard body. She willed the hands that wanted to touch him to stay on her lap. He wanted nothing more from her than to be his friend, so that was what she would stay.

"Give me the plate numbers, and I'll run them," Skylar said.

"They're in my computer. I'll go get it." Her first impression of the sheriff had been wrong. When Kade had introduced her to the tall blonde with ice-blue eyes and a gun on her hip, Harper had been a bit intimidated by the confidence and authority pouring off the woman. But Skylar proved to be warm and friendly with a great sense of humor. Harper really liked her.

"Just email me the numbers," Skylar said. "Kade can give you my addy."

"Okay. I'll also send you the pictures that I took of the things I told you about seeing at the warehouse. They're on my laptop, too." When she'd called Kade, begging for help, she hadn't expected to have a sheriff and a police chief also ready to help her. For the first time since that man had shown up in her bedroom, she thought this was a battle she might win.

Tristan stood, smiled at his fiancée as he pulled her up with him. "We have a meeting with the mayor and Miss Mabel in twenty minutes, so we need to head out." He turned that smile on Harper, and she could see why the sheriff was besotted with the police chief. "You have friends watching out for you now, Harper, who know a thing or two about bad guys. The only person we fear is Miss Mabel. Kade can tell you why you should run in the opposite direction should you see her coming at you."

Skylar laughed. "That's the gospel truth. You see her and her cane, run. Unfortunately, Tristan and I are at her beck and call. We'll come back tonight and bring dinner." Fuzz came out of hiding and raced to the car ahead of Tristan and Skylar.

"He really doesn't like Duke, does he?" Harper said.

"It's not so much that he doesn't like Duke, but that your dog wears him out. They do play together until Fuzz has had enough." Kade whistled when Duke, seeing that Fuzz was leaving, chased after him.

Duke put the brakes on, stumbled, got his feet under him again, then raced back to them. He took a flying leap, hit the middle of the table, skidded across it, and landed on Harper, taking her thankfully empty coffee cup with him.

"Oomph," Harper muttered when seventy pounds of dog fell on her. She laughed. "You big lug."

"Crazy dog," Kade said.

"Aw, he just wants some lovin'." If nothing else, Duke's antics had put a smile on Kade's face.

"What male doesn't?"

She wasn't sure what to make of the flash of heat in his eyes as he looked at her. Was that heat for her or for women in general…like it wouldn't matter to him who he got that lovin' from? The thought of him with another woman sent a streak of jealousy though her, and what was that about?

She'd never known him to have a girlfriend, but he wasn't a monk. He'd never hid his hookups from her. Not that he'd paraded women past her, but she had been out with him and his teammates sometimes, and on occasion one of them would leave with a woman they met at a bar, including Kade. It had never bothered her…okay, more like she'd refused to let it bother her.

Those men worked hard and played hard, and she understood. When you did what they did, and every day could be your last on earth, you'd live life to the fullest, and boy, did those guys ever. Only one of his teammates was married, and when Todd did come out with the team, he always brought his wife with him. Todd had earned Harper's respect for that.

Kade Church was the hottest man she knew and had a body to drool over. He was also funny and kind…as long as you weren't the enemy, of course. But he was her friend, the reason she'd locked down any stray feelings she might have for him. If she thought they could have some playtime and still come out the other side with their friendship intact, she'd sure be tempted, though.

"How did your playing dead come about?" He slid an arm under Duke's stomach and lifted him down to the deck.

Harper blinked as she dragged her mind back to the business at hand. Too bad, since thinking of her and Kade skin to skin beat the reality of her life now. "One of my friends from Fort Bragg called when I was still pretty out of it. Dad panicked and told her I'd been killed in a mugging. He wanted the people after me to think I was dead. I wasn't real happy to let everyone think that, but I wasn't in any condition to protest.

"We don't know if he meant to kill me and maybe something scared him away, thought he had killed me, or if he was just giving me a warning. I blacked out, so I don't know if he left right away or what. After the attack, my dad found an apartment on St. George Island for me to hide out and heal. The island is just across the bridge from Apalachicola, so I wasn't far from him." She told him about the man who'd come to her father's house a few days ago, saying he was a friend.

"Tell me he didn't fall for that."

The anger was back in his voice and the ice was back in his eyes, and she understood it was for her and not at her. "No, he didn't. Any friend of mine thought I was dead, so he was suspicious. The next day, he drove to the island to show me the video feed from his doorbell camera. The man on the video was my attacker."

"He's a dead man."

"Don't say that. I don't want you killing anyone for me. Let's just see that these men have to answer for what they've done."

"There you go, taking away all my fun."

"Not sorry." She didn't know what effect being in Special Forces had on these men, what demons they returned home with. They all held their feelings and those demons close. She was not about to let him add to whatever rested heavy in his mind because of her.

"What I don't understand is why you went back to that warehouse the next day, and especially why you went inside. What the hell were you thinking? What if one of those men had been there?"

"Well, they weren't, and I was worried about my friend, okay?" She'd done what she'd thought she had to. She'd saved her friend from...well, she hadn't known it at the time, but she'd saved Lisa from predators of the worst kind. She'd do it all over again, but smarter.

He pinched the bridge of his nose with his fingers. "I thought you had more sense than to do something like that, Harper."

Now he was making her mad. "You know what? You can take your surly attitude and stuff it up—"

"My *surly* attitude?" He stood, paced to the end of the patio, then returned, put his hands on the arms of her chair, and lowered his face to within inches of hers. "I thought you were fucking dead. I held your goofy-assed dog in my arms and cried into his fur. You could have come to me for help. Did you even consider that?"

"You cried for me?" Her anger at him melted away. After the attack, she'd wanted to call him, almost had.

"Like a bawling baby."

That this man, a man who'd faced death more times

than she could probably guess, would admit such a thing stole her breath. "I'm sorry. I wanted to call you."

He sank onto the chair next to her, making her think of a deflating balloon. "Why didn't you?"

"I wish I had." She impulsively reached over and put her hand on his. He turned his hand, palm up, and wrapped his long fingers around hers. She stared at their hands, joined together. The intimacy of her skin pressed against his was something she'd never experienced with him, had never dared to hope would happen.

It was unnerving how right it felt.

Chapter Eight

Kade reached for the control he'd honed over years of special operations. What he really needed was to go do a hundred laps around Marsville or five hundred push-ups before he exploded. He could have lost his best friend, and although he couldn't help being sent out on a mission, the guilt sat heavy that he hadn't been able to go with her when he'd said he would. If he had known what she was up to, he would have made her promise to wait for him to return.

"I'm sorry I wasn't here for you." He rubbed his thumb over the top of her hand. "But I'm here now, and I'll keep you safe. That's my promise to you."

Funny how her touch calmed him. But she'd always kind of had that effect on him. When he would return from a mission, his mind sometimes a bit screwed up, the first person he'd want to see was Harper. His best friend had a way of getting him out of his head.

Her eyes were focused on his thumb as he caressed her hand. Something was changing between them, but he wasn't sure exactly what. He was trained to pick up on clues that people put off, and by the puzzled expression on her face, she was as clueless as him on what those changes meant. He eased his hand away because he liked touching her too much.

Duke raced up with a stick and dropped it at Harper's feet. "Aww, someone's getting bored with all this talk." She picked it up and threw it into the yard. He looked at where the stick landed, then back to her and tilted his head as if to say, *Why'd you do that?*

"That dog has a few loose screws," Kade said.

"I think he was giving me the stick as a present and doesn't understand why I tossed it away."

"Watch." He pointed at Duke. "Roll over." Duke jumped in his lap.

She laughed when Duke tried to lick Kade as he put his hands over his face. "Don't tell me you don't love him."

"Not about to admit that," he said, while trying not to laugh with her. Her laughter, that was what he'd missed and thought he'd never hear again. The way she could make his worst day better with the joy that lived inside her.

He set Duke back on the deck. "Why don't we get you settled in, then go grab some lunch."

"Sounds great."

"Tristan's giving you his floor while you're here."

"Really, he has a whole floor?"

"We each do. Parker and Everly have the first floor, Tristan the second, and the third floor is mine. Although Tristan spends most of his nights at Skylar's downtown loft now." He slid the glass door open, and then followed her in. Duke raced past them, headed for his water bowl, and ran headfirst into the wall. He backed up and barked at the wall.

Kade shook his head. "That boy's elevator is stuck between floors."

"Aw, he just marches to the beat of his own drum. But you have to admit he's the sweetest dog you've ever met."

"Can't argue with that." He was supposed to have Duke for a year, until she returned from the Peace Corps. Was her joining the Corps off now? If so, did that mean she was going to want Duke back? He'd grown attached to the goofball.

At seeing a cat sitting on the kitchen island, she headed straight for it. "You must be Jellybean. Aren't you a pretty kitty?" The cat bumped his head against her arm.

"He's Duke's best friend, and he's not supposed to be on the counter."

At hearing his name, Duke came to the island. He lifted, put his front paws on the granite, and edged his face toward the cat. Jellybean boxed Duke's nose.

"For reasons only he knows, Duke loves getting his nose punched. Come on, let me show you your room." Leaving Duke to play with his cat friend, he picked up her duffel, slung it over his shoulder, and was halfway through the living room when he realized he'd also taken her hand. He'd done it without thinking, but her hand in his felt right.

"Wow, this room is gorgeous. So many books."

It was a combination living room and library, and the books had belonged to his aunt. He and his brothers hadn't been allowed to touch them. One of the first things he and Tristan had done after she'd died was make a pact to read every damn one of them, whether it interested them or not. But he wasn't going to drag out life with his aunt with Harper.

"You're going to love this room." He led her to the room he knew she was going to freak out over.

She came to a sudden stop after taking a step inside. "Holy cow!"

"Pretty cool, huh? Parker designed it." It looked like one of those old ornate movie theaters, except with rows of leather recliners instead of movie seats. There were even floor-to-ceiling red velvet drapes and crystal chandeliers.

His gaze was on her as she took everything in, and he smiled at the way her eyes lit up. One of their favorite things to do together had been to watch movies, and they'd do some of that while she was here.

"Well, he did an amazing job. Oh, look, a popcorn machine. Can we watch a movie and make popcorn one night?" She fluttered her eyelashes. "Pretty please?"

He laughed. "As often as you want. Let's go upstairs." When they reached the foyer, she gasped at seeing the matching curved staircases on each opposite wall and the massive crystal chandelier hanging between them.

"Your home is beautiful, Kade."

"Thanks to Parker's success as an artist, we were able to do a lot of work on it after Aunt Francine died." They wouldn't have touched a thing in the place while she was alive, not that she would have let them even if they wanted to make improvements.

"Parker and Everly have their rooms down that hall." He pointed to the hallway between the stairs. "The common rooms belong to all of us, but our bedrooms are off-limits to each other."

"That probably saves a few arguments."

"Exactly." As they were going up the stairs, Andrew

came down, carrying a hamper of Kade's dirty clothes. His eyes widened at seeing Harper, and he stopped a few steps above them.

"Andrew, this is Harper Jansen, a friend of mine. Harper, this is Andrew Shaughnessy. We would be lost without Andrew." Kade swallowed a smile when Andrew's cheeks turned pink at the compliment, but it was true.

"It's very nice to meet you, Andrew," Harper said. "I imagine it's a big job to keep three brothers, a little girl, a dog, and a cat organized."

Andrew's blush deepened. "I cook for them, too. I can cook for you if you want."

When Harper darted a glance at him, Kade answered for her. "She'll be eating dinners with us, so all you have to do is make a little extra."

Andrew beamed. "I can do that."

"You're the man." Kade hugged the wall to let Andrew pass.

"Thank you, Andrew," Harper said as she moved next to Kade.

Still blushing, Andrew smiled. "You're welcome, Miss Jansen."

"You can call me Harper."

"Okay."

He headed down, and when he was out of sight, Harper said, "He's a sweetheart. He has Down's, right?"

"Yeah. Word of warning. Don't try to help him do his job, which includes any housecleaning, cooking when it's his night in the kitchen, or cleaning up after dinner. He takes it to mean that you don't think he's doing a good job, and it upsets him."

"Gotcha."

He led her to Tristan's second-floor rooms. "This floor is all yours."

"What about your brother? I don't want to—"

"Not a problem. Like I said, he spends most of his time at Skylar's. I'm on the floor above you. I need a shower. We'll leave in about thirty minutes if that works for you."

"Oh, we're not eating here?"

"No, I thought you might want to check out our little town."

"Great. If there's a clothing store, I need to pick up a few things since I packed so light."

"There is. See you shortly."

"Wait, I need to send those license plate numbers and the photos to Skylar. She said you'd give me her email address."

"Right. Let's do that now."

"I'm ready," she said after turning her computer on and logging in.

He gave her Skylar's email address.

"I'm sending her the whole file. It's got everything in it plus a timeline of events I created."

"Skylar will let us know when she has something. I'll be back in a few." He headed for the stairs, stopped, and said, "I'm really glad you're alive, Harper."

"Me, too."

And he was going to keep her that way.

"We'll eat first, then you can go shopping." Kade clipped Duke's leash to the hook screwed into the outside wall of Katie's Corner Kitchen. Duke knew the drill and didn't fuss about being left outside.

"He'll be okay here?"

"Yep. Katie makes sure there's water for him and Fuzz, and half the people around here carry dog biscuits to give the two of them. He loves the attention." He opened the door of the diner. "The locals just call this the Kitchen. Katie serves up some damn good food, but her cheeseburgers are the best."

As usual, the diner was busy, and he should have considered that because every head in the place turned their way, wondering who the woman with him was. The phone lines would be burning up. He put his hand on Harper's back and guided her to the only empty booth. He nodded at people he knew as they passed, but he didn't stop and talk. Let them wonder who she was.

They'd barely gotten seated when Katie appeared with two glasses of water and a menu, which she placed in front of Harper. "Hi, Kade." She gave Harper a friendly smile. "Welcome to the Kitchen. Would you like something besides water?"

Harper smiled back. "Thanks. Water's fine, and Kade said your cheeseburgers are the best, so sign me up for one."

"Kade's right. Fries, a side salad, or a bowl of homemade wild rice and mushroom soup?"

"The soup sounds yummy, so I'll have that."

Katie turned to Kade. "The usual?"

"Always." He lifted a chin toward Harper. "Katie, this is my friend…" He grinned at Harper. "Petunia. Petunia, Katie Dawson, who will get a hundred questions as soon as we leave from all the nosy locals wondering who you are."

Katie laughed. "True story, but they should know by now they'll get nothing from me."

"If any strangers come in asking about her, you've never seen her before."

"Seen who?" She winked at Harper. "Your food will be up shortly." She chuckled as she walked away.

"What about everyone else in here?" Harper said after Katie left. "Maybe it was a mistake to come to town."

"You're with me," Kade said. "That makes you one of us, and not a person in here will take kindly to a stranger asking questions about you, Petunia."

She wrinkled her nose. "Petunia? Really?"

He swallowed a laugh. "You have a problem with petunias?"

"Not when they're not my name. I don't think Katie believed you."

"But she was amused." Because Katie knew he'd made the name up, she'd understand Harper wasn't to be talked about and would put a stop to any questions.

"She seems nice."

"That she is."

"And she's pretty."

"She is." He chuckled. "You're dying to ask if I ever dated her."

"No!"

Her gaze lowered to the table, and he outright laughed. "Yeah, you are. The answer is no." Was she a little jealous, and was that relief in her eyes? He'd examine how he felt about that later.

She glanced around. "Why is everyone staring at us?"

"Because they've never seen me with a woman before."

Her eyes snapped to his. "Never?"

"Yep." He knew everyone in Marsville, and most of the people in the diner were locals. The few out-of-towners would be gone before anyone came around asking about her. If the locals believed she belonged to him, they'd close ranks if any nosy strangers showed up. There was one way to do that.

"You want to really give them something to talk about?"

Chapter Nine

Mischief danced in Kade's eyes, a look Harper knew well. There was nothing he loved more than stirring up trouble. How many times had he goaded her into doing things she'd never consider doing, pushing her out of her comfort zone? Too many to count.

The thing was, she'd never been able to resist that fun side of him. And not once had she regretted going along with his shenanigans. His pranks were never harmful, but they were almost always sidesplittingly funny.

Like the time in Fayetteville when he'd called her in the middle of the night, asking her to come to his house, that it was an emergency. The emergency had been to help him hide the door of the bathroom with plywood that they painted to look like the wall, and to draw a fake door next to the real one. He'd actually screwed a doorknob into the fake door. Then they'd sat next to each other at the end of the hallway, drinking beers as they waited for his drunk roommate to go to the bathroom.

During the hour they'd sat there, they'd whispered stories from their childhoods to each other. Most of his stories had been of the pranks he'd played on his brothers, but there was one that had broken her heart. That was the night he'd told her how his mother had abandoned him and his brothers, how she'd left them at her sister's house, promising to come back in a few days. She never had, and their aunt had resented being stuck with three young boys. It was the one and only time he'd talked about his childhood.

Harper had somehow managed not to cry as she listened to him talk of a life where no one wanted him and his brothers. It had been hard to relate to that kind of rejection because all her father had ever wanted was for his daughter to be happy. She'd been too young to remember her mother, so she didn't really miss what she'd never known. But there had never been any doubt that her dad loved and wanted her, so to think of her father rejecting her…it just didn't compute. She hadn't cried that night listening to him talk of being unwanted, but she'd wanted to.

She didn't know why he'd told her any of that because that was not Kade. He didn't share, so it made her feel special that he had confessed something that was very private to him. Before she could tell him how amazing he was, considering the obstacles he'd had to overcome, his roommate staggered out of his bedroom.

Kade had elbowed her to hush her as they watched Reid zigzag his way to the fake door. She and Kade had fallen against each other, uproariously laughing as Reid tried to open the wall.

"Don't think about it." Kade leaned closer, interrupting her trip down memory lane. "Just say yes."

She grinned. "Sure, why not. Let's give them something to talk about."

He grinned back. "That's my girl." He left his seat across from her and came to her side of the booth. "Scoot over."

What was he up to? With Kade, you never knew. She made room for him. The only warning she had was that devilish gleam in his eyes before he kissed her. At first, she didn't respond, because… Kade. Was. Kissing. Her.

Then, oh, then, she forgot where they were, that people were watching, and her mouth softened against his. She slid her tongue across the seam of his lips, and when he hummed his approval, that low, growly sound sent hot need rushing through her.

She blinked when he pulled away and sat back. "What the hell was that?"

"What I said, just giving them something to talk about."

The kiss meant nothing to him, just another of his jokes, only this one hurt. She forced a smile. "Well, you got everyone looking at us." And whispering. She didn't care about that part, but she had been better off before she knew how much she liked kissing him. Katie was heading their way with their lunch, and Harper poked him. "Move back to the other side."

"Yes, ma'am."

As Katie set their plates in front of them, she shook her head at Kade. "Still doing your best to cause trouble, I see." Her lips twitched, belying the stern expression on her face.

"Who, me? Cause trouble? You must have me confused with one of my brothers."

Harper and Katie both snorted and exchanged eye rolls. Harper decided she liked the woman.

"Enjoy," Katie said before walking away.

Ordering herself to forget about a kiss that was a joke, Harper started with the soup. "This is delicious." And Kade was right about the cheeseburger. It was one of the best she'd ever had. If she lived in Marsville, she'd eat here every day. She really liked what she'd seen so far of Kade's hometown.

Kade pushed his plate to the side when they finished eating. "I still have a few questions. You good with answering them now, or do you want to wait until we get back to the house?"

"Go for it." Although her wish was that it was all a nightmare, and she would wake up any minute now.

"First one, how'd you get to Myrtle Beach, and why go there? And are you sure you weren't followed?"

Before she could answer, Katie came back to collect their plates. "Can I get you anything else?" She glanced at Kade. "I have apple pie today."

"You know I never refuse apple pie. A cup of coffee, too."

"With vanilla ice cream still?"

"Absolutely."

"What about you, Petunia?" Katie's lips twitched.

"I'm too full from that delicious cheeseburger and soup. Just coffee for me." When they were alone again, Harper said, "Why did you kiss me in front of everyone? Now they're going to really remember me." Okay, so forgetting about that kiss wasn't going to be so easy apparently.

"Because now they know you're mine."

"Excuse me?"

"Well, they think you are. That sound better?"

"No." What was wrong with him?

"If they believe you belong to me and someone shows up asking questions about you, they'll swear they've never seen you before. Also, they'll let me know a stranger is in town. We protect our own, Harper. If you doubt me, ask Skylar. She learned that, too."

It was hard to believe no one would breathe a word about her, but there wasn't anything she could do about it now. The damage was done.

"Tell me about your father. Do we need to worry about his safety?"

He was giving her whiplash. "Okay, my dad. After that man showed up again, I knew it was time to come out of hiding and do something about this situation before the worst happened. My dad's in a practice with four other doctors who could cover for him. I got him to promise to take a leave and go stay with a friend of his in Gulf Shores. The only way he would agree was because I was coming to you. Dad was a medic in the Navy, and he has a lot of faith in special operations people."

"So he's safe?"

"Yes."

"How did you get to Myrtle Beach?"

"Dad dropped me off at the bus station on his way out of town. Not that he was happy about that. The first bus leaving that would get me closest to you was to Myrtle Beach. Dad stuck around until the bus left to make sure I wasn't followed. Any more questions?"

"Not at the moment."

Katie returned with Kade's pie and their coffee. When she set the bill down, Harper said, "Two checks, please." Kade frowned at her but didn't argue.

He held his fork out. "Want a bite of the best apple pie you'll ever taste?"

"Sure." She leaned forward, and he fed her a bite. "That is really good." First he'd kissed her and now he was feeding her. It felt like something had changed between them, or it could just be her imagination because she wished there was something there, especially after that kiss.

"I'm going to run to the restroom while you're finishing your dessert." She needed to splash some cold water on her face and give herself a little talking-to.

He pointed his fork behind her. "Down the hall back there."

When she returned, their table had been cleared, and Kade was walking out the door. She followed him out. "You weren't supposed to buy my lunch."

He smirked. "You should know by now that I rarely do what I'm supposed to."

There was a truth. "Well, thank you, but don't do it again."

"Yes, ma'am." He unclipped Duke's leash. "Come on, I'll take you to Fanny's. She should have just about everything you need clothing-wise. If you need shampoo or something, we'll stop at the pharmacy."

"Yeah, I do need some of that kind of stuff. Marsville's a cute town. I love all the different-colored awnings. It looks so festive."

"That was Parker's idea back when Main Street was pretty drab. A few of the merchants thought it was ridiculous, but enough agreed and did it. Everyone loved the way it made downtown look, so the few that had refused came around."

They passed an ancient pickup truck, and she stopped. "Is that a goat?"

"Yep, that's Billy, Old Man Earl's goat. Go look in the window."

She did. Billy the Goat was busy eating the truck's headliner...or what was left of it. "There's no material left on the bench seat. It's just springs. He ate everything?"

"Just about everything but the metal. Don't say anything negative about his goat to Earl. He won't like you if you do."

"Wouldn't dream of it." She got her phone and took

some pictures of Billy and the inside of the truck to send to her dad. He'd get a kick out of this.

Duke put his paws on the door and barked. Billy stopped his chewing, then hopped to the window, which was open a little. The dog and goat rubbed noses.

"They know each other?"

He nodded. "Duke's friends with every person and animal he meets." He pulled Duke away from the window. "Come on. Fanny's just down the block."

The shop he took her to was adorable with its pink awning, rose-colored door, and whitewashed brick exterior wall. There was a hook next to the door like the one at the diner, and he secured Duke's leash to it. When they stepped inside, a silver-haired woman who couldn't be more than five feet tall rushed to them, her bangle bracelets jingling as she clapped her hands.

"Kade Church, I heard you were back. Took you long enough to come see me. I thought I was your favorite girl."

"You are my favorite girl, Fanny, and I have no excuse." He bent over and hugged the petite woman. "Forgive me?"

"I could never stay mad at any of you Church brothers." She turned an assessing eye on Harper. "And who is this?"

"This is Petunia, a friend of mine." He grinned and winked. "And no competition to you, Miss Fanny, love of my life."

Harper swallowed a smile when the older woman blushed.

"You're a silver-tongued devil, Kade Church," Fanny said.

He really was, and Harper was tempted to tell Fanny that the man was also the best kisser in the world...well, in her world of experience, anyway, but she decided that was information she wanted to keep to herself.

"Petunia needs some things, Fanny, but can you give us a minute?" Kade said.

"Of course."

When they were alone, he stepped in front of her. "It would be best to pay cash for whatever you buy. Do you need any money?"

"I'm good. Dad sent me off with a full purse so I wouldn't have to use a credit card."

"Okay, that's good. Take your time. I'll be outside when you're done."

"Kade," she said when he turned away from her.

He glanced over his shoulder. "Yeah?"

"I don't know how to thank you."

"My best friend staying safe is all the thanks I need."

He winked, then walked out, leaving her with tears stinging her eyes.

Chapter Ten

Why had he kissed her? Well, he knew why, he just hadn't thought it through. A part of it was because he wanted to put a claim on her in the minds of those in the diner. But he'd also done it because everyone in the diner who knew him had been staring at them, wondering who Harper was. He didn't play in his backyard, so they'd never seen him with a woman, and if they couldn't mind their own business, then he'd give them a show. That was him, the class clown.

He was the brother who disappointed. Tristan and Parker had been the favorites of their teachers as boys and still were for the people of Marsville. Those two could do no wrong because they never did anything wrong.

Kade, though, had been the one people pointed to and said, "Don't be like him." He'd finally matured enough to regret the headaches he'd given his oldest brother. Tristan had done his best to step into the role of father/mother/brother to him and Parker when they'd been abandoned by their mother to an aunt who hated them. What had Kade done to thank him? Rebelled at every turn.

He really needed to tell Tristan how much he appreciated the sacrifices he'd made for his two younger brothers, and that he wished he hadn't caused so much trouble.

What he should do was get with Parker and do something special for Tristan. Maybe send him and Skylar on a romantic weekend getaway. Man, he really was growing up if he was thinking stuff like that, but it was about time he thought beyond his own self.

Which he had not been doing when he'd kissed Harper because there was another reason he'd done it. He'd wanted to kiss her. And now he wanted more.

He unhooked Duke's leash from the wall. "I kissed a girl, and I liked it," he told Duke as they walked down the sidewalk. "Can't do it again, and that pretty much sucks."

Duke stopped, sat, and lifted his paw.

"You really are a goofball. I said *sucks*, not *shake*." Since Duke still had his leg in the air, Kade shook his paw. "You're a real clown. Have you considered joining the circus?"

Harper was going to want her dog back when it was safe for her to return home, and he was going to miss the silly boy. Unless she still planned to spend a year in the Peace Corps, and then he'd get to keep Duke a while longer. He needed to ask her what her plans were. Too bad she didn't live here so they could hang out like they used to. He missed that.

If the Peace Corps was now out, maybe he could talk her into moving to Marsville. She loved to read, and while she was in the Army, she'd had a part-time gig going as an assistant to a few authors, something she really enjoyed. For one thing, she got to read advance copies of their books, which she thought was super cool. She also did stuff for them, helping with their marketing and whatever. She'd talked about developing that into a full-time job after the Peace Corps. No reason she couldn't do that here. Something to think about.

"Sean!" a woman down the block screamed.

There was hysteria in her voice, and when she screamed again, Duke whined, then took off toward her, only getting as far as the end of the leash. Something was obviously wrong, so Kade headed for the woman with Duke pulling him along. He had a bad feeling on seeing the child's tennis shoe she held in her hand.

"Ma'am, can I help you with something?"

"Oh, please. My son is missing."

"How old is he?"

"Six. We were in the ice cream store, and he was standing next to me, then I took my eyes off him to pay. He must have wandered off… Oh, God, do you think someone took him?"

Kade hoped to hell not. "I'm sure he's around here somewhere. We just have to find him." If they couldn't turn him up in a few minutes, he'd call Tristan.

Duke took the shoe out of her hand.

"Your dog. Did he take the shoe so he could find my baby?"

No, he took the shoe because he liked it, but maybe Duke could give her a little hope while they searched. Kade took the shoe away, then held it to Duke's nose. "Find the boy, Duke."

Duke snatched the shoe back, then took off with his nose to the ground. Kade ran behind him, with the woman following them. Hell, the dog thought this was a game. About the time Kade decided to put a stop to this and call his brother, Duke raced around the hood of Earl's pickup, and damn if there wasn't a little boy—one shoe on, one off—standing on the running board and reaching his hand inside the truck to pet Billy.

His mother scooped him up. "Sean Luke Dawson, you never ever leave my side."

"Look, Mommy, there's a goat in that truck."

"I don't care if there's an elephant in there, you don't leave Mommy like that."

Duke dropped the shoe at her feet, and she kneeled in front of him. She glanced up at Kade. "What's his name?"

"Duke." Duke, the dog he'd yet to figure out. Had he known they were looking for the boy, or had it been a game and it was by chance that they came across him?

"Well, Duke," she said. "You're my hero. Thank you so much for finding my baby."

"I'm not a baby," Sean grumbled.

Duke offered her his paw, and after more gushing of her thanks to both him and Duke, the woman headed back to the ice cream shop. Kade wondered if one of Miss Mabel's space aliens had taken possession of the dog, one with brains.

Kade eyed him with suspicion. "Dude, was that pure luck, or have you only been masquerading as a goober?"

Duke answered with his goofy grin.

Chapter Eleven

"I think for reasons only known to him, Duke's hiding his smarts," Kade said after finishing the story of Duke's afternoon. The whole family was here along with Harper, and they were sitting on the deck, eating the pizzas Tristan and Skylar had brought.

Tristan watched Duke chase a bumblebee around the yard. "I'm not so sure about that. Smart dogs know to avoid bees."

"Duke finds me all the time when I hide from him," Everly said.

"We should experiment. Dogs can track from scent, but can Duke? Or was that a fluke?" Harper slid a second slice of pizza onto her plate. "After we finish eating, I'll hide. See if he can find me."

Everly jumped up. "Let's go, Miss Harper. I'll hide with you."

"Not until we finish our dinner," Parker said. "Sit, Ev, and eat the rest of your pizza."

"But Daaaddy, I need to show Uncle Kade that Duke knows how to find people."

"And you will, as soon as you finish your dinner."

Kade's niece was just too adorable. Harper leaned toward her. "I have to eat the rest of my pizza, too, before I can go play. Let's finish together."

"Okay, but don't eat faster than me."

"Wouldn't dream of it."

Twenty minutes later, after everyone was done eating, she stood on the lawn with Kade's family, preparing to test Duke. Fuzz sat on the deck, watching them, and Harper wondered if the police dog resented all the attention her dog was getting.

But was he her dog anymore? Romping around the Church brothers' yard, Duke seemed happier than he'd ever been when living with her. She wanted him back when she had a place of her own, but seeing him with the brothers and Everly, would she be doing the right thing to take him away from here? Even though it would break her heart to give him up, where he'd be happiest was something to think about.

"I'm going to take him inside so he can't see where you're hiding," Kade said.

Everly tapped his arm. "You mean where Miss Harper and me's hiding."

"Yes, Miss Everly, that is what I meant." He grinned at Harper over Everly's head. "She's a bossy one."

The amusement in that private look between them had Harper wishing she could wave her hand and make everyone but him disappear. Then she'd walk right up to him and…

"Harper, you with us here?"

Heat spiraled up her neck and across her cheeks. "Um, yeah." Had he been saying something?

"What did I say?" Her silence and glare must have gotten her point across because he laughed. "I actually haven't said anything yet."

"Asshole," she mouthed, but by the snickers coming from his family, she hadn't been covert.

Tristan grinned. "Don't even ask how many times I thought that very word over the years where my brother was concerned."

She glanced at Kade, wondering if he was mad, but there was only laughter in his eyes. "So, we doing this or not?"

"Doing it." He put his hands on Everly's shoulders. "After I take Duke inside, go with Miss Harper."

"You need to give him something to bring us," Everly said.

Kade turned Everly to face him. "What do you mean?"

"He finds me when he wants to give me something. Sometimes he brings me a toy, and sometimes a sweater, like if it's cold and he thinks I need to be warm."

"Okay, we'll try that," Kade said. "But let's really test him. You hide first, Ev, then if he can find you, Miss Harper will hide."

"He'll find me."

"Make sure you hide somewhere good. Wait until I take him inside so he can't see where you're going."

"I know that, Uncle Kade." Everly rolled her eyes. "And don't forget to give him something to bring me."

"Yes, ma'am." Kade glanced at Harper and winked. "Bossy."

What was it with a guy winking at you that had your stomach feeling funny? Harper turned away from him so she wouldn't be tempted to admire his backside as he took Duke into the house.

"Where are you going to hide?" Parker asked his daughter.

"I can't tell you, Daddy. You might tell Duke."

"Yeah, I can see how that would be a problem. Okay, go hide yourself."

"She's adorable," Harper said as Everly took off, zig-zagging across the yard. She disappeared around a separate building.

Harper had only been here a day, but she already saw how close the family was and how much they cared for each other. Someday she'd have a family, children who loved and took care of each other like the Church brothers did.

"Is she hiding?" Kade said, returning with Duke.

Parker nodded. "Yep. She wouldn't tell us where she planned to hide because she was afraid we'd tell Duke."

"Can't say I blame her. Y'all are a shifty bunch."

Skylar chuckled. "I can attest to that." She glanced at Harper. "Tristan once gave me a Danish filled with may-onnaise. You can't trust a one of them."

"Eww." Harper wrinkled her nose. "That's gross."

"She deserved it after making me think there were spiders crawling on my neck." Tristan grinned at his fiancée. "But I love you anyway."

Kade waved a stuffed frog in front of Duke's nose. "Duke, find Everly." Duke sat. "I think him finding the boy today was a fluke." He held the frog in front of Duke again. "Where's Everly?"

Duke yawned.

"Everly said he had to bring her something for it to work," Harper said. "Give him the frog and see what he does."

Kade dropped the frog in front of Duke. "Take Everly her frog."

Duke snatched up the frog, put his nose to the ground, and zigzagged across the yard in the same pattern as Everly had taken.

They all followed Duke, who led them around the building Everly had disappeared behind, then down a slope to a pond. The branches of a beautiful weeping willow touched the ground at the edge of the pond. Duke ran through the branches.

"Duke! You found me!" Everly yelled.

Harper parted the limbs and peeked in.

Everly held her frog in the air, showing off Duke's success. "He did it, Miss Harper."

"He sure did." She grinned at Kade. "Are you impressed with my dog now?"

"I'm halfway there. He still has to find you."

"So little faith."

The side of his body was pressed against hers, and she resisted the urge to lean into his touch, but she breathed in his citrusy scent. Did he have to smell so good?

Before she did something like lick his neck in front of his family, she dropped to her knees. "Who's a good boy? Duke is! Duke's a good boy." Duke took a flying leap, landed on the ground in front of her, and rolled over on his back for a tummy rub.

"Your turn, Miss Harper. Give something of yours to my uncle to give Duke!" Everly scooted over and tugged on Kade's leg. "You hold Duke, and I can help Miss Harper."

"The boss has spoken," Harper said, grinning up at Kade.

"Guess we better get on it then." He reached a hand down to help her up.

As she got to her feet, her hand still in Kade's, Duke pushed on the back of her knees, knocking her against Kade. With her breasts pressed to his chest, she lifted her gaze to his.

One side of his mouth quirked. "Hey."

How could one word sound like there was an entire message in those three letters? Was he also feeling this crackling in the air between them?

Chapter Twelve

"Hey, back," Harper said, her voice soft and her eyes dreamy.

Kade's gaze fell to her mouth. One kiss wasn't enough, he decided, but they had an audience. The woman was messing with his head, and he didn't understand why that was happening now. He'd gone out for beers with her, had movie nights with her, just the two of them, and he'd never thought of her as more than his best friend. She was his calm in the middle of a storm. He wasn't feeling so calm around her anymore.

Everly took Harper's hand. "We can have a pickle while we're in the house."

"Good idea," Harper said, glancing over her shoulder and giving Kade a smile.

Something fluttered in his chest, something he'd never felt in his entire life. Both his brothers caught him admiring her ass as she walked away with Everly and had smirks on their faces. He scowled at them. Even Skylar looked amused. "Don't you people have things to do?"

"Not really," Tristan said.

Parker shook his head. "Nope."

"Me either." Skylar laughed. "Isn't family wonderful?"

"I used to think so, but I'm revising my opinion." He snapped his fingers, getting Duke's attention. "Let's go, boy." He walked away to their laughter, glad his back was to them so they couldn't see his smile. Family actually was pretty wonderful.

He and Duke walked into the house as Harper and Everly came out, both eating a pickle. Harper handed him the T-shirt she'd been wearing when they'd left the hotel this morning. That brought him up short. She'd only been at his family's home for a day, yet it felt like she belonged here, with him and these people he'd die for. Every one of them liked her. How could they not? She was...he searched his brain for the right word. *Special.* As his best friend, she always had been, but this *special* was something new.

He had a lot to think about, but he had to see if Duke could find the woman who was growing ever more fascinating before it got dark. After giving her a few minutes to hide, he dropped Harper's shirt. "Harper needs this." Duke barked, grabbed the shirt up in his mouth, and took off. As he followed Harper's dog, he met up with his brothers, Skylar, and Everly.

Skylar paused as the others headed toward the garage. "You owe me," she said. "I'm taking them to town for ice cream. Well, you also owe Everly for jumping on that idea, and making it impossible for her father and uncle to deny her."

"Okay, thanks." He wasn't sure exactly what he owed her for, but at least his smirking brothers would be gone.

"I like her, Kade."

"Me, too." Maybe too much. Skylar squeezed his arm, then followed his brothers and Everly. He'd lost track of Duke while talking to Skylar, and he stopped and listened. There. Off to his left. That was her dog giving a yip of joy at finding her, the sound muted because they were inside the walls of the barn on the back end of their property. He headed for them. On silent feet, he slipped into the barn and paused. His gaze focused on the last stall, where Harper was quietly admonishing Duke to be quiet. This was supposed to be a game of Can Duke Find Harper, but she appeared to be turning it into a game of hide-and-seek.

He grinned. He loved games. Harper knew that, so was she wanting to play? So be it. Keeping to the shadows, he stealthily made his way to the stall. A rope was coiled up on the floor, and he picked it up. From Harper's whispers, she was near the stall door. He eased to the back of the stall and peeked over. Her back was to him, her attention on the gate.

Perfect. The hayloft was above the stall she was hiding in, and with the stealth of a covert mission, he climbed up the ladder. Now the trick was to walk on the beam above her without her noticing. She was so focused on watching for him to come through the gate that she wasn't giving any attention to what was going on above her. Duke was, though. He was on his back, getting a belly rub, and he barked and tried to turn over.

"Shhh," she whispered. "You're going to give us away." She wrapped her arms around him and pulled him onto her lap. "We have to be quiet, okay?"

Kade secured the rope around the beam, then tied it off. He'd done this once on a mission—eased down a rope behind his target, tackling the man and taking him out without a sound or a shot fired. The difference this time, he was going down headfirst. He grinned as he wrapped the rope around his leg, then lowered himself down. This was fun.

She screamed and fell over on her side when he came

down behind her and tugged on her ponytail. "Oh, God. Give me a heart attack, why don'tcha?"

Kade let go of the rope, falling next to her. She had her hands over her face, and her shoulders were shaking. "I'm sorry." Was she crying? He was an ass. "Harper?" He peeled her hands away from her face. Not crying. Laughing.

She beat her fists on his chest. "I think I peed in my pants."

Because she was still laughing as she punched him, he grabbed her wrists, and when he did, she managed to yank one hand away, and then tried to tickle him. They ended up in a wrestling match with Duke trying to get in on the action.

Somehow she ended up straddling him, and she threw her hands in the air. "I won!"

Ha! She thought she had him pinned? They'd just see about that. He flipped her over, and she peered up at him with surprise in her eyes. Then, as his legs pressed against her thighs, and his groin rested on her sex, their gazes caught and held.

Her eyes turned soft and liquid. "Kade," she whispered.

"I'm right here."

When she parted her lips, drawing his attention to them, he put his hands on her face, cupping her cheeks.

He brushed his thumb over her bottom lip. "I want to kiss you, but you should tell me no."

"I can't tell you that."

"Permission granted then," he murmured. Her lips were warm and soft, and when she touched the tip of her tongue to his mouth, he groaned. Electricity buzzed through his body as their tongues tangled. He slid a hand down to her neck and pressed his thumb on the pulse beating erratically under her skin. The beast inside him thrilled with how she was responding to him. His own heart had invited a jackhammer to take up residence.

He moved his hand from her neck to the curve of her breast, and when he flicked his thumb over the nipple, her breath hitched. He kissed his way from her mouth to the lobe of her ear, and…a long, wet tongue slurped across his face.

"Damn it, Duke." He rolled off Harper. He'd been so lost in her that he'd forgotten they were on the floor of a stall with a goofball dog wanting to join in. He'd forgotten that he'd declared Harper hands-off.

She giggled. "He was feeling left out." She turned on her side to face him. "We can put him outside the stall."

"I'm sorry. I shouldn't have—"

"Don't say it." Anger flashed in her eyes. "And don't be sorry." She pushed up, then glared down at him. "I'm a big girl, you know. If I didn't want you to kiss me, I wouldn't have let you, so don't go feeling all guilty and martyr-y." She snapped her fingers. "Come on, Duke. Let's go…" She threw her hands in the air. "I don't know, eat a pickle or something."

"I don't think *martyr-y* is a word."

She rolled her eyes. "Whatever." She opened the gate, then glanced over her shoulder at him. "And just so you know, we will kiss again. And maybe do other naughty stuff. If you're lucky." With that said, she walked away from him.

Whatever. He hated that word. He really shouldn't have kissed her. He wanted more. Much more. She was apparently his catnip, and that wasn't good. He didn't do relationships, and Harper was a relationship kind of girl.

How many times had she talked about her plans? The

Peace Corps because she wanted to give something back while having an adventure before falling in love with an amazing man, getting married, and having a houseful of children. Marriage and children were a firm no for him, and he wasn't amazing. Not amazing enough for what she deserved, anyway.

The last thing he ever wanted to do was hurt her, and he would. That was inevitable. He needed to explain that to her. It was the right thing to do.

A red hair tie caught his attention. It must have come off her hair when they were wrestling. He put it in his pocket to give her later…when she'd calmed down and wasn't tossing *whatever*s at him.

Chapter Thirteen

Theo Watson answered a call from his cousin Rex Sorenson.

"I got her," Rex said.

"I'm with Stockton." Theo glanced at their business partner Stockton Rawls. "Rex found her." He put his phone on speaker so Stockton could hear. "Where is she?"

"Not sure yet," Rex said. "She just used her computer for the first time since she clicked on my link. Give me a little time to trace her location."

"Call me as soon as you know where the hell she is." Theo disconnected from Rex without waiting for an answer.

"Explain to me again how Rex can find her?" Stockton asked.

Theo resisted the urge to roll his eyes. He'd explained it twice already, but Stockton barely knew how to turn on a computer. That was fine because as the owner of three successful strip clubs around Fort Bragg, Stockton was their money man. They were in Stockton's office in his original and biggest club, Venus, and Theo had to admit that Stockton had the best girls of any of the local clubs.

Theo kept his resentment over Stockton's wealth hidden. A detective barely made enough to exist, and he sure as hell couldn't afford to enjoy the finer things in life. He was fucking tired of living paycheck to paycheck, and this venture was going to change that.

From the time they'd discovered girls, he and Rex been each other's wingman. They shared the same taste—dark and bent. They often shared a girl or girls at the same time when they could talk the women into it. Sometimes that required a little help. Get them drunk or slip them drugs and you could get them to do almost anything.

They'd met Stockton here at Venus, and over time, the idea to make and sell porno movies had been born. Stockton provided the funds for the equipment, Theo the muscle and the ability to keep the cops out of their business, and Rex was their filmmaker. Rex had a full-time job in the IT department of a bank, but just for the thrill of it, he was also a black hat hacker, which was coming in handy in finding Harper Jansen.

Little did she know that when she'd clicked on the link from the nonexistent Detective Johnson that Rex had installed a Global Positioning System and Wi-Fi tracker in her computer. They'd just been waiting for her to log on. He knew he hadn't killed her, so the story that had circulated among her friends that she was dead was as phony as the tits on a stripper.

He should have killed Harper Jansen when he'd had the chance, would have if her father hadn't come home. He'd barely made it out of the house without getting caught.

Luck had been on their side when he'd been the one to intercept her email to his police department. He didn't even want to think how things would have gone down if someone else in the department had gotten it before him. She had to be stopped before she ruined everything.

"You better hope he can find her," Stockton said. "You sure the police can't tie Abby's death to us?"

"I told you, the case is closed. Accidental overdose."

Stockton had supplied the pills. The ones they'd given Abby were supposed to be ecstasy, like they had been for Lisa. Theo had almost taken out his gun and shot Stockton when the asshole admitted he'd given Abby fentanyl instead.

Because he had, and Abby had died in the warehouse, they'd had to close that site down. Well, they would have vacated it anyway because of Harper Jansen not minding her own business, but he was still pissed at Stockton and the headache he'd caused.

The man was damn lucky Theo knew how to hide evidence and set a scene that wouldn't raise questions. They'd moved Abby's body back to her efficiency apartment in the deep of the night, and Theo had made sure he was assigned the case. None of the other cops particularly wanted another overdose case, so that part had been easy. Abby in her bed, a small baggie with some fentanyl pills still in it on her nightstand, and there you go…drug overdose. Case closed. And it needed to stay closed, which meant Harper Jansen had to be eliminated.

"Anything comes back on me, you won't like the consequences," Stockton said.

Theo gritted his teeth. He didn't like Stockton. The man was a bore and a slob. Theo managed not to curl his lips in disgust as his gaze roamed over the red stains on his shirt. There was no excuse for not keeping in shape and looking your best. The guys at the station had nicknamed him Dapper, thinking they were insulting him. They weren't. Theo was proud of always looking his best.

Chicks loved a well-dressed man, and it didn't hurt

that he was good-looking. They told him so, but he didn't really need them to. He had a mirror. He knew he was what women considered hot with his black hair, blue eyes, and handsome face, and he worked hard at keeping a six-pack women licked their lips over.

All he had to do was give a woman the look he'd perfected…the hooded, smoldering eyes, and just enough of a smile to show off his dimples, and he could have them on their knees in no time flat, begging to pleasure him.

The first time he'd had Harper Jansen's roommate on her knees, Lisa had only known him an hour, not even a challenge. The girl was a talented thing, eager to please. Entirely too clingy, but useful. She'd balked at making a porno movie, but a little happy pill, some wine, and a bit of warming up, and voilà, they had the star of their first movie.

When he found Lisa—because Miss Jansen was going to damn well tell him where she was—he was going to have to punish her for disappearing. She had a movie to finish.

And as soon as Rex located Harper Jansen, Theo was going to make her sorry for interfering. But first, he'd have a little fun with her.

Chapter Fourteen

Early the next morning, no one seemed to be around when Harper got up and went for a run. Running was something she'd learned to enjoy in the Army. She liked the burn in her muscles, the runner's high, and the benefit of keeping in shape.

The street the brothers' house was on was residential, the homes spread out. The leaves of the trees lining the road were starting to turn their fall colors, the air was brisk, and she settled into the rhythm of her run, the only noise her trainers slapping the pavement.

Okay, that wasn't right. There was more than one pair of shoes sounding in her ears. Preparing to fight if necessary, she glanced over her shoulder and blew out a breath of relief at seeing Kade. When he reached her side, she smiled.

Uh-oh. Not only did he not smile back, but his lips were pressed together in a firm line and anger flashed in his eyes. She didn't want to start her day with tension between them, but it looked like that was what it was going to be.

"Good morning." She hoped his attitude was nothing more than he wasn't a morning person.

"Have you lost your mind, Jansen?"

Okay, she was the reason for that grouchy face. "I don't think so."

He grabbed her arm and pulled her to a stop. "Have you forgotten why you're here? You don't take off anywhere on your own. You want to run, you take one of us with you."

Jeez, overreacting much? "I'm safe here." Those men couldn't possibly know where she was.

"And you know that how?"

Fine, he might have a point. "I guess I don't."

"Exactly." He started running again. When she just stood there, he turned and jogged backward. "You coming?"

She wanted her life back, the one where if she wanted to go for a run, she didn't have to have a bodyguard. But if she had to have one, the man waiting for her to catch up with him would do. Letting go of her irritation, she sprinted to his side.

"First one to the stop sign has to give the loser a foot massage." Because, duh, who the winner would be was a no-brainer, and she wanted his hands on her.

He snorted as he glanced at her. "That's not how it works."

"My run, my rules."

"All right. Looking forward to my foot massage."

"Oh, no you don't," she said when he eased back, jogging behind her. "You can't purposely lose."

He smirked. "Watch me."

By the time they were only a few feet from the stop sign, they were both moving slower than a snail. She was not going to lose out on that foot massage. When they were inches from the finish line, she jumped behind him and pushed him past the stop sign. That was when she felt the gun strapped under his T-shirt, and reality reared its ugly head.

At Kade's house, surrounded by him and his law enforcement family, it had been easy to forget the danger lurking out there. She hadn't thought of the possible consequences of being caught alone because she didn't believe anyone outside the Church family and her father knew where she was. Kade was right, though, and she was embarrassed by her mistake.

"Ha! You won, and I get a foot message," she said, but the fun wasn't there anymore.

"So you're just going to pretend you didn't cheat?" He tossed his arm around her shoulders as they walked back to the house.

"Me cheat? Never." In all the times they'd spent together, he'd never put his arm around her. Well, he'd never kissed her until recently. She was beginning to think they'd wasted a whole year of possibilities. She wanted to rest her head on his shoulder, but after his rejection yesterday, she didn't want to give him a reason to push her away again.

Duke was in the yard, and at seeing their approach, he barked his excitement and launched himself at them.

"Incoming," Kade said. He stepped in front of her. "Duke, sit!"

Duke skidded to a stop and rolled onto his back.

Harper kneeled next to her dog and gave him a tummy rub. "Good morning, silly boy. What's that in your mouth?" She pried the scrap of blue material away and held it up. As soon as she realized what it was, she wadded it up in her hand.

Apparently, she wasn't fast enough because Kade made a laugh-snort sound.

"Shut up."

He laughed harder. "I'm gonna need Duke to teach me his panty-stealing talent."

"Stay out of my panties."

"Not a chance."

Because she couldn't resist, she said, "I was talking to Duke." As she stood, she peeked over at him. Yep, mischief was in his eyes, and she sucked in her bottom lip to keep from smiling as she waited to hear what was about to come out his mouth.

Then he blinked the mischief away. "Sorry, that was out of line."

She wanted to stomp her foot like a toddler having a tantrum. Why was he being so stubborn? This chemistry between them might be new, but it was there, and not just for her. Turning her back on him, she headed for the house.

Duke scrambled to his feet and trotted ahead of her. "Where does Duke sleep?" she asked Kade to get things back to normal.

"With Everly."

Again, she wondered if she'd lost her dog to the Church family.

"I'm hungry," Kade said. "Let's get some breakfast."

In the kitchen, Parker was churning up something green in the blender. Everly was sitting at the island with a plate of scrambled eggs and a pickle in front of her.

"Did Duke find you, Miss Harper?" Everly said…well, more like yelled. "I gave him something of yours so he'd go look for you."

Kade's lips twitched, and he whispered something to Parker. Harper caught the word *panties*.

"Everly Church, we do not take other people's things without asking," Parker said. His gaze slid to Harper, amusement in his eyes. "Tell Miss Harper that you're sorry and you'll not take her things without permission."

"What's permission?"

"It means what I just said, without asking."

"But Daddy, Duke needed to find her."

"Don't 'but Daddy' me. Tell her you're sorry."

"Sorry," Everly muttered.

The girl wasn't at all sorry, and although Harper wanted to laugh, Parker was right to reprimand her for doing it. She put her hand on Everly's shoulder. "I'll forgive you this time, but I might not next time, okay?"

"'Kay. But what am I supposed to do if Duke needs to find you again?"

"Tell you what. I'll give you a pair of my socks to keep just in case. That work for you?"

Everly clapped her hands. "Yes! Then my daddy won't get mad at me." She gave her father sad eyes and pouty lips. "I don't like when Daddy's mad at me." She put her hand on her chest. "It hurts in here."

Aaannd Parker Church just about melted right in front of his daughter.

Harper stepped next to him. "She's a future star of stage and screen."

"Don't I know it." He laughed as he shook his head. "I'm shaking in my boots at the thought of her teen years."

"You don't have boots on, Daddy."

"And you're not dressed for school. Hop, hop like a bunny."

Everly hopped out of the kitchen. Parker picked up his glass of green stuff and followed her out, muttering something about teenage daughters.

"She's a trip." Harper leaned back against the island.

Kade nodded. "That she is." He opened the refrigerator door. "How's an omelet sound?"

"Sounds perfect. You cooking or me?"

He glanced over his shoulder. "We're cooking together, panty girl."

"Stop it." Jeez, that smirk of his did something to her. He seemed to be back to her playful friend, which was good.

"Don't think I will. So—"

His brother and Skylar walked in, both with serious expressions on their faces.

Without thinking about it, Harper moved next to Kade, and when he slipped his arm around her waist and pulled her closer, she gratefully leaned into him. Bad news was coming.

"Good morning," Skylar said.

"Cut the niceties and just say whatever has you here so early." Kade squeezed her waist, reminding her he was there for her.

"The license plate numbers you gave us don't exist," Tristan said.

"Not possible. They're right there in the photos I took."

"And that's why I think something's fishy," Skylar said.

Chapter Fifteen

"Fishy how?" Kade wasn't liking this. People stole license plates to put on their car if they were up to no good, but plates with numbers that didn't exist? That didn't make sense.

Skylar shrugged. "I don't know. Neither Tristan nor I have ever heard of fake license plates. That would be a risky thing to do if you were stopped by the police and they ran the number."

"Nor have we ever heard of legitimate plate numbers just disappearing from the system," Tristan said. "Skye and I talked about possible reasons for that, and the only thing we could come up with was that someone who knew what they were doing managed to hack into the DMV's files and change the numbers. Sounds far-fetched, but anything is possible if someone knows what they're doing."

"So, two different people would have had to get new license plates, then one of them hacked into the DMV and changed the numbers to the new ones," Kade said, thinking out loud. "Or someone did it for them, which, if it's that, takes our bad guys from two to three."

"I'm not liking this at all," Harper said. "Their plates numbers were the only way to identify them."

Tristan nodded. "For us, yes." His gaze slid to Kade.

Kade caught on right away. "But not for someone else, say a black hat who might be able to dig deep and see if those plate numbers actually existed once?"

"You didn't hear that from me or Skye."

"Copy that."

"I wouldn't know a black hat if one walked by me wearing a black hat." Harper glanced at him. "Do you know one?"

"Maybe, although I'd say they were white hats." Talon Security had offered their help if needed. He didn't know if this was something they'd agree to, or even if they had someone on the payroll who could hack into the DMV, but he was sure going to ask.

"And this is where Skye and I stop listening," his brother said. "Oh, one other thing, Harper. We couldn't identify the one man you got a photo of. It was too dark to see his features. All we could tell was that he was heavy-set and medium height."

"So nothing I got helps? I don't even know if I can identify the man who showed up the day I was moving back home and then came to Florida and broke into my dad's house. I can tell you he had blue eyes so cold that he gave me chills. That's it. He wore a knit cap the first time, and I couldn't tell you what color his hair was. He scared me so much that I don't remember his face. The night he came into my bedroom, it was too dark to see him, but I recognized his voice."

All of that was said with fear in her voice, and when he found the man who'd hurt her and had her afraid now, it wasn't going to be pretty. He slid his hand into his pocket and hooked a finger around the hair tie she'd lost in the stable, intending to give it to her. But he didn't. Letting go of the tie, he left it where it was. He refused to examine why he was keeping it.

Skylar stepped in front of Harper and touched her arm. "You aren't alone. You have some pretty awesome people vowing to keep you safe." She glanced at Kade and smiled. "Tristan and I are the law watching your back, but the man at your side is a scary devil. Whoever decides to get his dander up is a fool. He'll protect you with his life."

Kade didn't think he'd ever loved his future sister-in-law more than he did right this minute.

"I don't want him risking his life for me," Harper whispered. "I shouldn't have come here."

Kade looked at his brother and lifted his chin toward the door. *Go away.*

Tristan gave him a slight nod. "Let's go, Skye. I'll treat you to breakfast."

Once they were gone, Kade put his hands on Harper's shoulders and turned her to face him. "Hey, none of that, okay? You're right where you need to be."

"Just promise you won't let anything happen to you."

"Who, me? Haven't you heard? I'm the baddest badass there is. Villains quiver when they see me coming."

The hint of a smile appeared. "Quiver, huh?"

"Fucking A." He pulled her to him and wrapped his arms around her. "Everything's gonna be fine. We'll figure this out. That's why you came to me, because you knew you could count on me. Right?"

"Yeah."

She rested her head on his chest, and he liked her in his arms. She smelled like coconuts, which made him think of the beach on a lazy summer day, and her in a bikini. *Don't go there, Ace.*

He'd planned for them to get down to business this

morning, but they could take today and have a little fun. Give her a day to relax and recharge after what she'd been through and her trip to get here.

"Tell you what. Why don't you get dressed and we'll have a play day? There's someplace I want to show you."

She leaned back and studied him. "Am I interrupting your plans? I mean, you didn't know I'd—"

He put a finger over her lips. "Hush. I was just hanging out, bugging my brothers until I have to go back and finalize my separation." His missed job interview wasn't something she needed to feel guilty over, so he didn't mention it.

"You're really going through with it? I guess I thought you'd stay in the Army until you couldn't pass the physicals anymore."

"Nope. It's time. Go. I'll meet you back down here when you're ready."

"Give me thirty minutes."

While she was changing, he walked outside and called Talon Security. When he got Chase on the phone, he gave a brief summary of Harper's problem and explained what Skylar had discovered with the license plates and their theory.

"That is disturbing," Chase said.

"I didn't know if you'd be willing to dig into it, or if you had someone who could."

"My brother. Send those numbers my way, and I'll see what he can find out."

"Appreciate it. We need names, and right now we're shooting in the dark. I'll text them to you in a few."

"It's to our benefit to get your woman's problem taken care of so you can get your ass to work."

"Copy that." After disconnecting, he went up to the second floor.

Harper came out of the bedroom before he could call out to her. "Oh, hey. I thought I was supposed to meet you downstairs."

He momentarily forgot why he'd come up. Her hair was down around her shoulders, and she had on a red sweater that looked thin and soft and hugged her curves, snug hip-hugging black jeans, and red Chuck Taylor high-tops. And damn if she didn't look both cute and sexy.

She glanced down at herself and frowned. "Is this not okay? Do I need to change?"

His brain had derailed, and he shook his head to get it back on track. "No, you look…" He searched for a word. "Adorable." Huh? He'd just used the word *adorable*? Who was he?

She tilted her head and peered at him. "Are you okay?"

No, he was not. He was not supposed to be seeing her as cute and adorable, and especially not as sexy. She was the girl he palled around with, his movie-watching buddy. He should have never kissed her, that was for damn sure. How was he supposed to put that genie back in the bottle now that it had escaped?

"Fine. I'm fine. Your sweater's pretty. You get that at Fanny's?"

"I got everything I have on at Fanny's."

He should have told Fanny to load her up with old lady clothes. "I need to send those photos with the license plate numbers to my contact at Talon Security. They're going to see if they can learn anything."

"That's great. Hang on a minute, and I'll get them." She disappeared into the bedroom and returned a minute later with her computer. "It'll take a few seconds to boot up. Do you think they can find out the deal on the plates?"

"Let's hope so."

"Who's Talon Security?"

"How about we shelve that question for now and we'll talk about everything later?"

"Okay."

After the photo files were sent to Talon, she shut her laptop down, and they headed downstairs. When they walked outside, Duke lifted his head from where he was taking a nap in the sun. He yawned as he got to his feet.

"Are we going somewhere that he can come with us?" she asked.

"Depends. Bike or truck?"

Her eyes lit up. "Bike!"

"Was hoping you'd say that, so no, obviously he can't."

She leaned over and kissed the top of Duke's head. "You can come with us next time." She glanced at him. "Do we need to put him inside?"

"No, he's got a doggie door, so he can come and go as he pleases. He won't leave the yard."

As they walked to the garage, she said, "Where are we going?"

"What's your opinion on UFOs?"

Chapter Sixteen

Harper knew exactly where they were going, and she was giddy with excitement. He'd told her some months ago about the Marsville UFO Museum, how it had been closed for years and was reopening, which he thought was nuts.

It was another beautiful fall day, and she was relaxed and safe, not to mention spending time with a man she really liked, and she planned to have fun…something that had been missing in her life recently.

"Put this on." He handed her his leather jacket.

"This is yours. I'll be fine."

"It's going to be chilly once we get going. We'll stop at Fanny's and get you a jacket, then you can give it back. Deal?"

"Okay." She slipped his jacket on, and of course, it was huge on her, but there was something intimate about wearing it. It was something couples would do. Then he stepped in front of her and zipped it up for her.

As he raised the zipper, she lifted her eyes to his, and that heated look in his…no, not *heated*. That wasn't a strong enough word. Hot. Scorching hot. Like there was a fire raging inside those orbs. He leaned toward her as if he was going to kiss her, then, inches from her mouth, he blinked and stepped back. Her breath swooshed out of her, and disappointment settled in her chest.

Why was he fighting this new attraction between them? She wasn't imagining that heat in his eyes or the almost kiss. Maybe he was afraid she was looking for a permanent place in his life? She'd known him for a year, knew he didn't do relationships, so she had no intention of trying to change him. Besides, she wouldn't be around after they resolved this mess she'd found herself in. She would probably end up back in Florida, so why shouldn't they have a fling while she was here?

She almost wished he'd never kissed her in the first place. Then she wouldn't know how good it felt to have his mouth on hers, and she wouldn't be dying to kiss him again. The operative word, though, was *almost*. She wasn't giving those kisses back.

"Let's roll." He threw a leg over the bike, then held it upright while she got on.

When she was settled behind him, she put her hands on the sides of his waist, and like he had the night he picked her up in Myrtle Beach, he pulled her hands around him. Once he was satisfied that she was holding on, he pushed the ignition button and the Harley roared to life.

Marsville was such a pretty place, a great place to have a bike. Since it was in the foothills of the Blue Ridge Mountains, the landscape was…well, hilly. Then, the blue-hazed mountains rising in the distance were breathtaking, and she could just sit and look at them all day. Even the air was different. It was fresh, crisp, and a little piney smelling versus the heavy salty scent of the air back home.

The fall leaves on the trees were spectacular, and for a girl born and raised in Florida, the red, gold, yellow, and orange leaves were a sight she'd never take for granted.

She wondered if people who grew up in places that had four seasons forgot to see the beauty surrounding them. Shame on them if so.

As they rode down a curvy two-lane country road toward town, Harper decided she wanted to live somewhere that didn't have basically the same temperature year-round, that she wanted seasons in her life, wanted to feel this breathtaking joy at seeing fall leaf colors. And snow. She wanted to live where it snowed. It rarely did at Fort Bragg, and even when it did, it was never more than an inch or two. Even that had thrilled her. A white Christmas was on her bucket list.

She thought she'd like living in Marsville, but that was out. She'd never make things awkward between her and Kade and moving here would be so awkward. He'd think she was stalking him, and on her part, she wouldn't want to see him around town with some other woman on his arm. So, something to look into—where to live when this was over.

The bike slowed, then stopped. She glanced around to see why they were at a standstill in the middle of the road. Kade squeezed her leg, then pointed up. "Oh," she breathed. A black bear and her cub were in a tree. The mama was sitting on a lower branch watching her baby climb to the top. The mama bear looked over at them, then dismissed them and went back to observing her cub.

It was one of the most awesome things she'd ever seen. How had Kade even seen them up there? She supposed it was proof of how honed his observations skills were from his years in Special Forces. The kind of talent those guys needed in order to return from their missions alive.

She leaned around his shoulder. "That's so cool. The baby won't fall?"

"No. Mama wouldn't let it go up there if she thought it would. This is probably the cub's first tree-climbing lesson."

There were no cars on the road, and they watched the bears for a few more minutes, then he throttled up, and they were on their way again. As they passed the tree, Harper waved to the mama bear, then laughed at herself for doing so.

Some minutes later, they were riding down Main Street, and she again smiled at all the different-colored awnings. Everything was so festive. She wondered if there was another small mountain town somewhere with colorful awnings. If so, she'd go live there.

A parking space was available in front of Fanny's shop, and Kade pulled into it, stopping next to an old turquoise Cadillac. She hopped off the bike and removed her helmet, which he set over one of the rearview mirrors and his helmet on the other. She slipped off his jacket and gave it to him.

"That's Miss Mabel's car, so she's around here somewhere," he said. "If we come across her, don't take anything she might say personal."

"Who is Miss Mabel anyway? Tristan said if I saw her coming to run in the opposite direction, and Skye said to stay out of reach of her cane."

"Mabel Mackle and her nephew own half the town. Luther's the mayor, and he's as scared of his aunt as we are."

Harper thought there probably wasn't a female around who didn't like the brothers. All three were that hot, although in her opinion Kade was the best looking of the three. Skylar would disagree with her, but Skylar would be wrong.

In Fanny's shop several women were looking through

the clothing racks. Fanny was at the register talking to an older woman, or more like just listening and nodding her head.

"Speak of the devil," Kade said.

As they approached, Harper noticed the older woman's cane. So that was Miss Mabel. She was a thin, tiny little thing.

Relief flashed in Fanny's eyes. "Good morning, Kade and Petunia," she said. "Petunia, dear, did you need some more clothes?" She came around the counter. "Come, I'll help you find whatever you're looking for."

She was going to kill Kade for "Petunia," and she was going to do it right here in front of witnesses if he didn't wipe that smirk off his face. "I'm looking for—"

Miss Mabel swung her cane up in front of Fanny, stopping her. She then turned curious eyes on Harper. "And who are you?"

"This is my friend Petunia. Petunia, this is the lovely Miss Mabel."

Harper smiled. "It's a pleasure to—"

"Since when do you have a girlfriend, Kade?"

Rude much? From the disapproval in Miss Mabel's voice, Harper decided to heed Skylar's advice and stay out of reach of the woman's cane. She stepped back.

"Aw, you know you're my best girl, Miss Mabel."

The woman actually fluffed her blue tinted hair, which Harper found amusing. She decided to remove herself from the conversation and the allegedly lethal cane, and as she wandered off to see if she could find a jacket Fanny slipped up next to her.

"Miss Mabel loves the Church brothers, so we'll leave Kade to her. Were you looking for anything in particular?"

"A jacket. Do you have any leather ones?"

Fanny leaned away and skimmed her gaze over Harper, then snapped her fingers. "I have a perfect one for you."

Harper followed her to a rack of coats. Before she could look through them, Fanny pulled one out.

"A medium, right?"

"Usually." The jacket was a zip-up red leather with two pockets that zipped. It was simple and classy, and Harper loved it.

"Try it on." Fanny slipped it off the hanger.

It was a perfect fit. She'd gotten a glimpse of the price tag as Fanny held it up, and it was more than she wanted to spend out of the cash her dad had given her. But she did need a coat, and she did love this one.

"This comes with the family and friends' discount. Twenty percent off," Fanny said.

Harper grinned. "I think you just made that up on the spot, but I'll take it." If she ran out of money, her father would send her more, so that really wasn't a big issue. Still, she didn't want to irresponsibly blow through the cash she had. She'd be more careful with how she spent what was left.

She kept it on but pulled off the tags and handed them to Fanny. "I love your store. I could spend a fortune in here."

"That works for me," Fanny said, smiling. "Let's get you checked out so you can get on with your day with that sexy man of yours."

"Oh, he's not my man. We're just friends." As much as she wished otherwise.

"The way he watches you, hon, could've fooled me."

Harper snuck a glance at Kade, and sure enough his eyes were on her. He winked, then turned his attention back to Miss Mabel. When he winked at her like that, it felt as if they were sharing an intimate moment. The man was sending her mixed signals, and it was confusing. She didn't know whether to ignore this attraction between them, or to go for what she wanted.

As she was taking her wallet out, Kade reached past her and handed Fanny a credit card. "That jacket looks awesome on you, P."

She'd forgotten how he shortened her name to letters. She'd been both H and LT to him during their year of being friends. Now she was P, and she'd take that over Petunia. She tried to bush his arm away. "Thank you, but you're not paying for it."

"Am, too. Happy Birthday." He turned mischievous eyes on Fanny. "You take her money, and I'll sneak Earl's goat in here. You know how much he loves to eat dresses."

"But it's not my birthday," Harper said.

"Don't care," Fanny said. "Earl's dress-eating goat tops all. Been there, not letting it happen again." She slid Kade's card through the machine, then handed it back to him. "You might want to go rescue your motorcycle. Miss Mabel's backing out."

He glanced out the window. "Oh, shit."

"What?" Harper said as Kade ran out of the store.

"The woman's a menace behind the wheel of that boat she drives."

"Whoa! She almost hit Kade." Was he out of his mind? He'd put himself between his bike and Miss Mabel's car, and her front bumper had come awfully close to his legs. He hadn't moved an inch. The man had nerves of steel.

Once Miss Mabel was backed out of the space, she gave a merry wave, then the car jerked, and then...good Lord, she floored it and the car shot forward.

"You should go make sure his heart's still beating," Fanny said.

"Good idea."

Outside, she expected to see him look irritated or mad or something. Nope, none of those. "Why are you grinning? I thought she was going to run over you."

"And hurt her favorite boy? Not a chance. Ready to go check out some space aliens?"

Men!

Chapter Seventeen

"This is the coolest hokey place ever," Harper said as she peeked in the window of a spaceship about the size of a dining room table. "Look, there are even little green men and women in here. Who knew space girls had boobs and wore lipstick?"

Kade grinned. "What? You didn't learn that in school?" He knew she'd get a kick out of the museum. She'd examined every supposed moon rock and photo of spacemen and UFOs in the place.

She glanced over her shoulder and grinned back at him. "That must have been the day I skipped class to make out with Jimmy Brickell behind the bleachers." She turned and leaned back against the fake spaceship. "I had a huge crush on him, and I was so excited he was going to be my first kiss."

"Something tells me this story isn't going to have a happy ending."

"Bingo! He stuck his tongue in my mouth, and it was gross." She wrinkled her nose, but there was laughter in her eyes.

There she is, the fun girl I know. He stepped closer. "How do you feel about tongue now?"

"Depends on who's doing the tonguing."

She winked, then walked away, and he laughed as he followed like a puppy wanting her attention. "Come on." He took her hand. "If you're done here, let's take a ride out to the lake for lunch."

"Oh, what's that?" She pulled him to the counter with a *Space Candy & Ice Cream* sign on the wall behind it. "Two space ice creams and a bag of moon rock candy, please," she told the woman behind the counter.

"You do know none of that is really from outer space, right?" he whispered into her ear.

She elbowed his stomach. "Hush. I know no such thing."

They walked outside to eat their ice cream, green mint, which he didn't care for, but pretended to for her. He was having fun, though, and more importantly, she was having a blast.

It was almost like they were on a date, something he did not do. Ever. Dating was risky. Take a woman out on dates and they started having feelings for you and talked about weddings and babies. That was not something he wanted, not being who and what he was…a man who left for days or weeks at a time with no notice, a man who might never return.

Could he see himself dating a woman like Harper and enjoying his time with her? Yeah, he could. Could he see himself with a wife and some kids? Not even. He was too solitary, needed to spend more time alone than would be fair to a family. He wasn't husband material, never would be. He didn't know how to be that kind of man. If he tried, he'd just fuck it up.

"You're deep in thought there, Ace."

"I'm wondering how Miss Mabel got this ice cream all the way from Mars without it melting."

She'd been around his teammates enough to know Ace

was his call name, yet his brothers hadn't known that until recently. Just went to prove how secretive he was, and he didn't know how to un-be a man who didn't let himself need anyone.

So, bottom line. Despite how much he wanted Harper, and how much those soft looks she gave him had him wanting to be a man he never could be, he had to keep his mouth off hers and his pants zipped up tight. Today wasn't a date. It was a day for her, an escape from the fear she'd been living with.

It was simply a friend day because a friend was all he could ever be for her. And if that hurt somewhere deep down in his chest, it was his hurt to bear. Quietly and alone.

"I had a great time today," Harper said.

Kade was sure he'd had an even better time. "Good." They were sitting on the back deck keeping an eye on Everly until Parker returned from the firehouse.

He'd purposely put an empty chair between him and Harper so he wouldn't be tempted to touch her. Swear to God, having her body wrapped around his most of the day, her arms circling his waist, her fingers pressed against his stomach…yeah, torture of the best kind.

The ride to the lake had been beautiful. As they'd cruised along the country road, no other traffic in sight, and as the fall leaves floated around them, she'd leaned against his back and put her mouth next to his ear, and said, "I feel like we're in a magical land."

It pleased him that she got it. He loved taking rides on his bike on the country roads, losing himself in the feeling of freedom and the wind on his face. Bikers loved to say that it was the journey, not the destination. A cliché, all that about journeys and freedom, but it was true. He truly felt at peace when he was off by himself on his bike.

Until today, he would have said that he could only achieve that peace and rightness with the world alone, no passenger on the back. He had been wrong. At least where Harper was concerned. He couldn't imagine enjoying it as much with another woman. And that was his problem.

He'd almost taken her to his lake cabin, his sanctuary from the world. That was how much he'd wanted to share something private that only his family knew about. Simply wanting to do that had surprised him, and not in a good way. He didn't need to be wanting to make her happy. He couldn't make her happy.

While Harper's attention was on Everly and Duke playing in the yard, his eyes were on her. He liked the longer hair and highlights that were new. While in the Army, she'd kept the length even with the bottom of her ears. She'd always been pretty, but the new look added a sexiness to her that hadn't been there before.

Was he seeing her in a new light? Yes. Did he want her? Hell yes! And because she'd made it clear that she was interested, he wouldn't hesitate to go for it if it was anyone but her. Harper was his best friend for one, and the last thing he wanted to do was mess that up. For another, she was a girl you put a ring on her finger and gave her babies. He wasn't pulling that out of the air. Over time, she'd talked about wanting a family. That future dream had included a dog, and Duke had been her first step in getting what she wanted.

Although he'd helped out with Everly, he'd only done so when he was on leave or had squeezed in a few days home here and there. He'd even learned to change her diapers, and he should have gotten a medal for that. But one of his own running around? He just couldn't see it.

He didn't plan on putting a ring on anyone's finger, so to mess around with her was out. It wasn't that he was against marriage. It was that he would make a shitty husband, and he wasn't going to make any woman's life miserable.

"It's really lovely here," she said.

You're lovely. "Yeah. It's a great place for Everly to grow up."

"You told me once that your mother dropped you and your brothers here and never came back. Do you know why she did that?"

He shrugged. He'd stopped caring about his parents a long time ago. "Our mother liked to party, and three boys were apparently too much of a burden for a party girl. I was nine when she brought us to her sister's house. Said she'd be back in a few days. That was the last anyone saw of her."

"What about your father?"

"He split before Parker was born." Were those tears in her eyes? "Don't pity me or my brothers. We've done just fine without them." Better probably. Did he wish they'd been lucky enough to have a mother who hadn't abandoned them and a father who hadn't walked away from his responsibilities without a thought to the consequences? Sure. What kid in those circumstances wouldn't wish for parents who'd loved them enough to stick around? Another thing he'd stopped doing a long time ago…wishing for things that would never be.

She gave him one of her soft smiles. "I don't pity you, but parents should put their child first. That yours didn't is wrong and sad. Have you ever tried to find either of them?"

"Hell no." He and his brothers had talked about it once, and they'd all agreed that they had no desire to find people who couldn't care less about them. Not to mention they'd just be looking for trouble.

"You never wonder—"

"No." At first he'd spent his boyhood wondering *when* she'd come back, then as the years passed it changed to wondering *if* she'd ever come back. For a long time, he'd believed she left because of him. Tristan had been the perfect son, Parker the adorable baby and her favorite, but Kade had been the one to try her patience.

He knew that because she'd said it often when he resisted going to bed early or taking a bath or any of the numerous things that got on her nerves. "You're giving me a headache, boy." Or "Why can't you be like your brother?" Meaning Tristan, the good son. Or her favorite, "You're getting on my nerves, boy." He was always *boy* to her, never *Kade*.

After some resentful and rebellious teenage years when he'd sorely tried Tristan's patience, he'd enlisted in the Army after getting caught stealing a car with a buddy, and the military had knocked some damn sense into his head. The Army had taught him to lock down his shit and just soldier on. And why was he thinking of all this now? The past was best left where it was, in the past.

He wanted to ask Harper about the Peace Corps, if that was something she still planned to do, but talking about his mother had him antsy. He checked his watch. "Ev," he called, "your dad's going to be home soon. Let's get your bath done so you'll be all sweet smelling for your daddy."

"I don't wanna, Uncle Kade." She wrapped her arms around Duke. "Duke wants me to play with him some more."

"Fine, but no pickle for you tonight."

She jumped up. "Duke, come on. We have to go in the house."

Harper chuckled. "Well, that did the trick."

"Always does," he said. Everly stopped next to him, and he leaned over and sniffed. "Yep, you're a stinky girl. Go on inside. I'll be right there."

"I'm not stinky, Uncle Kade." She ran to Harper and stuck her neck in front of Harper's face. "Do I stink, Miss Harper?"

Harper made a show of smelling her. "You smell like Duke, grass, and sunshine. In other words, you smell yummy." Harper pretended to nibble on her neck, making Everly giggle.

"Inside with you, pickle girl. I'll be in right behind you." His niece was the one female in his life that he'd give his heart to.

"She's about the cutest thing ever," Harper said after Everly and Duke went inside.

"No argument on that from me." He stood. "Why don't you stay out here and enjoy the rest of this beautiful day while I…" A flash of metal from the trees reflected in the sunlight, and Kade dived for Harper, taking her down to the deck with him a second before a bullet split the air above their heads, right where Harper had been sitting.

"The hell, Kade," Harper sputtered as she struggled to get out from underneath him.

"Quiet. Someone's shooting at us." At her specifically, but he didn't want to scare her more than necessary.

"Uncle Kade." The glass door slid open, and Everly stepped out. "Are you coming?"

Harper stopped fighting him. "Oh, God, don't let her come out here."

There had been times when he wasn't sure he was going to walk away from an operation unscathed. He'd walked into the middle of firefights, had been shot at, had almost stepped on an IED, and nothing—nothing!—he'd endured had ever scared him more than the sound of his niece's voice as she stepped onto the deck.

"Don't move," he ordered Harper. He pulled the wrought iron table onto its side so it was in front of her, hiding her from view to whoever the fuck was shooting at her.

"Uncle Kade, why are you and Miss Harper on the floor?"

A bullet pinged as it hit the table. He raced across the deck, grabbed Everly, brought her against him, shielded her with his body, then ran into the house. Duke, thinking this was a new game, bounced around them, barking and trying to lick him and Everly.

"Sit," he commanded the dog. Duke sat, but Kade didn't take the time to praise him for getting it right. Kade had to face the hardest choice he'd ever made. Stay inside with Everly, keeping her safe and leaving Harper outside alone with whoever was shooting at her, or leave Everly unprotected while he rescued Harper. He couldn't turn his back on either one.

"Hey, kiddo, want to play a game?"

"Yes!" she yelled.

"Your daddy's almost home, so you hide from him, and I'll tell him to find you." He had to get back to Harper. "He'll never think to look for you under my bed. Take Duke and go hide there." He set her down. "Go now, baby girl!"

She giggled with delight. "Come on, Duke."

The dog hesitated as he gave Kade a worried look.

Damn dog knew something wasn't right. Kade pushed Duke's butt. "Go with her. Keep her safe." As if Duke understood the seriousness of his job in this strange situation, he raced after Everly.

As Kade headed back to the deck, he pulled out his phone and called Tristan. He'd give anything to have his gun, but he'd locked it up in the safe in his closet when they'd gotten home, and he didn't have time to go get it. While the phone rang, he grabbed a knife from a kitchen drawer. He doubted the shooter would dare come to the house, but if he did, he'd have a weapon. He went to the open door and peered around the door frame.

Harper was still behind the overturned table, her body flattened to the deck. One advantage of her being military, she knew how to follow orders. She looked over at him and gave him a thumbs-up. *Good girl.*

When Tristan answered, Kade said, "Active shooter on the property. Come in hot." He disconnected without waiting for his brother to answer. Tristan would know what to do, and he'd bring reinforcements. If the shooter was still hanging around, the sirens would scare him off.

If it wasn't for Everly and Harper, and needing to protect them, Kade would go after the asshole who dared to try to hurt his people. But their safety came first, and he wasn't about to leave them unguarded.

First order of business was getting Harper inside, and the table was too heavy for her to drag to the door. He army-crawled—pulling himself along with his elbows—to her. "You okay?"

"Yeah. Is Everly safe?"

It warmed him that her first concern was Everly. "Affirmative. Now let's get you safe. I'm going to pull the table to the door while you stick to my side like your life depends on it." Because it did.

She nodded. "Ready when you are."

Sirens blared in the distance, and it sounded like Tristan's entire police force was barreling down on them. Good. "Go." He dragged the table along as they crawled to the door. With the noise the cops were making, Kade was positive their shooter had beat feet, but he wasn't taking any chances.

When they reached the doorway, he let go of the table. "Go." He followed her inside, and as soon as they were away from the sliding door, she jumped into his arms and wrapped her legs around his waist.

"Well, that was exciting...not." She smashed her face against his neck.

He wrapped his arms around her. "You did good, babe." And now that she was safe, his heart could stop trying to pound itself out of his chest. *Anytime would be good, heart.*

Tristan burst in with Parker right behind him. "Where's Everly?" Parker said.

"Upstairs hiding under my bed with Duke."

Parker rushed out of the kitchen, and Harper dropped her legs to the floor. Kade wanted to haul her back, keep her safe in his arms, but he let go of her. He'd rather face a dozen tangos alone than have someone shooting at her.

"I can't stay here," she said. "I won't risk Everly getting hurt. Or any of you."

He'd already decided they had to leave for that very reason. "We're not staying. Go pack your things."

"You're not coming with me. I'll never forgive myself if something happens to you."

Silly girl. "You're with me until we catch these bastards. Go pack. That's an order, LT."

Her eyes narrowed as she huffed an annoyed breath. "I don't like you."

"You'll get over it."

"Doubtful," she muttered as she stomped off.

"Talk to me," Tristan said after she left.

Kade told him what happened. "We need to go look around. Can you put two of your men on the front and back doors while we do that?"

"On it. I'll meet you out back in a few minutes."

"Tell them not to let Harper sneak out." She'd totally do it.

"I was planning on it."

After a detour to his closet to get his gun, he went hunting.

Chapter Eighteen

After Theo Watson had found a perch that allowed him a view of the yard, he'd expected to settle in for however long it took for Harper Jansen to appear. Luck was on his side because she and Kade Church came out to the deck thirty minutes later. Problem was that a little girl was with them.

He was tempted to shoot Kade Church first, before he put a bullet through Harper Jansen's heart. From his perch in the lower branch of a tree, he put his eye to the scope of his rifle and sighted it between the man's eyes.

So tempting. But Church's brother was a police chief, and the chief's fiancée a sheriff. That was trouble they didn't need. Kade Church was spoiling his fun, though, and that pissed him off.

Getting close enough to Jansen to grab her with a man like Church around wasn't worth the risk, even for the fun he would have with her before he killed her. After Rex had located her and learned who the people she was staying with were, he'd done a deep dive in the Church family. Bad enough that it was a family of cops, but Kade Church was the one who got their attention.

Rex had discovered that he was in the Army, but that was about all. "The dude's records are classified."

Theo had shrugged. "So, you're already in the Army's files. Just get into those records."

"Too risky. One wrong move that alerts someone I'm in classified files, and we'll have the Army and probably the FBI and Secret Service breathing down our necks. His records being classified means he's Special Forces of some kind, a man whose radar we don't want to be on."

"So we just walk away?"

"Might be the smart thing to do."

Theo considered putting his fist through his cousin's face. Rex needed to grow some balls. "And what if Jansen gets impatient with Detective Johnson stalling her and decides to go to some other police department?"

"So, let her. The only real evidence she has to connect us to the warehouse are your and Stockton's license plates, and I took care of that problem. Besides, she's probably already talking to other cops, Tristan Church and his girlfriend, and they got nothing on us."

"It's the fucking principle of the thing, Rex. Harper Jansen stuck her nose where it didn't belong. She hid Lisa from us." That last one burned. Lisa was his creation. He'd taken a girl looking for love in all the wrong places and was making a porn queen out of her. He never left a job unfinished. This one might not finish the way he'd planned, but sometimes plans changed and one had to adapt.

He peered through the scope again. Good, the little girl had gone inside. He wasn't a monster, and he hadn't wanted to risk her running into the line of fire. He aimed the rifle at Church. "Bang," he murmured, his finger itching to pull the trigger, but control was one of his strengths, so instead of taking the shot, he pointed the gun at Harper Jansen.

Church stood a second before Theo pulled the trigger. Theo stared in disbelief as Church tackled her, taking her down to the deck. How the fuck had the man known? Church toppled the table they'd been sitting at, hiding them from view. The little girl came to the door, and Church grabbed her and raced inside the house, leaving Jansen alone.

"Gotcha," he whispered. He lowered the barrel, aiming for the bottom of the table, and fired. He wished to hell that he could see her, know if he'd aimed true. For good measure, he shot again. Church came back out of the house and dived behind the table, then the table began to slide across the deck toward the door.

Was Jansen hurt, hopefully dead? Was he dragging her body to the house? When the table stopped moving, Theo peered through the scope. "Shit," he said when Church and Jansen popped up from behind the table and disappeared into the house.

Once Church was sure she was safe, he'd come looking for the shooter. It was time to rock and roll. Sirens sounded, getting louder by the second. Definitely time to haul ass. He jumped to the ground, gathered the shell casings, and ran to the road behind the Church property where Rex was waiting.

Who the hell was Kade Church? For the first time, fear crept in. Theo shook it off. The man wasn't some kind of superhero. The simple answer was that his senses were honed because of his special ops skills. Something to remember and prepare for.

"You get her?" Rex said the second Theo fell into the passenger seat.

"No. Time to go."

Rex had been waiting with the engine idling, and he put the car in gear and took off. "What happened?"

"They had a bit of luck is all. I'll get her next time." A soldier with an ego bigger than his brains wasn't going to get the best of Theo Watson.

Chapter Nineteen

"Hey. Can I come in?" Skylar said from the doorway of Tristan's bedroom.

"Sure." Harper eyed with regret the new clothes she'd gotten at Fanny's. They wouldn't fit into her duffel, so she was going to have to leave them behind.

Skylar sat on the edge of the bed. "Are you okay?"

"I'm alive. That's a good thing." She picked up the red leather jacket. If she wore it, she could take it with her.

"That's a beautiful jacket."

"Yeah. Fanny has some great stuff. I'm going to have to leave it all here, since everything won't fit in my duffel." Unless she could wear all her new things until she got to where she was going...wherever that was.

Skylar stood and disappeared into Tristan's closet. Harper hadn't peeked in there since it seemed like an invasion of his privacy. Skylar returned with a suitcase that she set on the bed.

"Take this."

"Oh, I can't." She wouldn't be coming back. Would Skylar take her to a bus station? Wouldn't she be happy to have Harper gone and the family safe? Harper couldn't forget the vision of Everly coming out to the deck when someone was shooting at them. Her stomach rolled at the thought of something happening to that precious little girl.

"Sure you can. You can return it when all this is over."

"I'm not coming back." She zipped up the duffel. "Will you take me to the bus station?"

"No." Skylar opened the suitcase and started putting the clothes in it that Harper had set aside. "Kade would kill me if I sent you off on your own." She laughed. "And believe me, he knows how to hide a body. You're not in this alone, Harper, and that man has talents we can only guess at."

"I could have gotten Everly killed today." She hated that her voice trembled.

"Were you the one pulling the trigger?"

"It doesn't matter. Those men are here because of me, Skylar. Or who knows, maybe just one of them came. And that's the problem, we don't know anything. Where will they show up next? In the middle of town where other people could get hurt?"

"You're not going to be hanging out in the middle of town, so not a problem. Kade's taking you to a cabin he owns in the middle of nowhere."

"He owns a cabin?"

"Yes, it's where he keeps his boat. Nothing fancy, but it's his place to go when he needs to be alone, to decompress. Usually for a day or two when he has leave, before coming home. You might as well give in. Even if you managed to sneak away, he'd just follow you."

Of course he would, and as much as she tried to convince herself that leaving was the right thing to do, relief poured through her that she wasn't going to be facing this alone.

"Do you like to fish?" Skylar asked.

"I don't know. I've never done it."

"Well, Kade loves to, but mostly he likes to take the boat out and then nap. He says on the lake is the one place he can really sleep. Get him to take you out on the boat."

"Okay." It almost sounded like they were going on vacation, and wouldn't that be great? But she'd landed herself in the middle of a deadly game, as evidenced by someone shooting at her. So a lazy day out on a boat wasn't in the cards.

"All packed. Let's go downstairs," Skylar said.

When they reached the kitchen, Parker was staring out the window, and Everly was sitting at the island eating a pickle. An iPad was in front of her, her attention on the screen.

"They still out there?" Skylar asked him.

Parker turned and leaned back against the counter. "Yeah. They've got Fuzz and Duke with them, hoping the dogs can pick up a trail. I'm guessing the bas..." He glanced at Everly. "The person had a car parked on the street behind us. Tristan sent two of your deputies to canvass the houses on that street, see who has a doorbell camera. Maybe we can find out what the man was driving."

"Good. Hopefully, we can also learn if he was alone or not." She went to the pantry, then glanced at Harper. "Kade wants to take Duke with you guys, so we need to pack up his food and stuff."

It had only been her and her father for as long as Harper could remember, and spending time with this family made her wish she'd had a bigger family, one as close as these people were. She longed to call her dad, but they'd agreed that she would only check in on Sundays at nine in the evening. Even though she had a burner phone, she didn't want to turn it on more than necessary.

She went over to Parker. "I'm really sorry that I brought trouble to your door. I would die before seeing Everly get hurt." Or worse, but she couldn't bring herself to say that.

He smiled, but she could see the tension in his eyes. "No one's going to die, Harper. I won't say that I wish you and Kade were staying here, not after today, but that's only because of my daughter. She's the one life I won't risk, and I know you agree. But know this. This family has your back, and you can count on help when needed from all of us, and that goes double for Kade. He'll keep you safe, and he'll send these people straight to hell if that's what it takes for this to be over."

"Thank you." Those two words didn't seem adequate considering what they were doing for her, but she didn't know how to tell him how much their actions meant to her.

"Do you want a pickle, Miss Harper?"

It seemed surreal that after getting shot at she was being offered a pickle. "I sure do." As she accepted the pickle Everly handed her, tears burned in Harper's eyes. This was the last time she'd ever get to share pickle time with this precious little girl. When she left today, it would be the last time she'd step foot in this house, a home and a family she was really going to miss.

And sooner than she'd be ready for, she would walk away from Kade, too. When she did, it would be with a broken heart.

Chapter Twenty

"He sat up there," Kade said. He pulled himself up to the lower limb of the tree. A small piece of gray fabric stuck to the rough bark caught his attention. "Hand me a rubber glove." They probably wouldn't be able to get fingerprints off a strip of material, but it might have some DNA on it. Tristan held up a glove and a baggie. Kade slipped the glove on, dropped the fabric in the baggie, then dropped it down to his brother.

Tristan gave it to his detective. "Here, Bentley. Looks like our shooter left a piece of his shirt behind. You get photos of the shoe prints?"

"Sure did, Chief."

Kade jumped down. The shooter had picked up the shell casings and taken them with him, which meant the man knew the police would love to have that evidence. Probably someone who watched a bunch of TV police shows. They had the bullets, though. What was left of them after they were embedded in the house.

He was still enraged that someone would dare shoot at a house where a child had been playing minutes before. Duke and Fuzz were running around the tree with their noses to the ground. Bentley was sliding the piece of material into an evidence bag, and Kade glanced from it to Duke.

"Let me have that back," he said.

Bentley's brows lifted, but he handed it to Kade.

This would be another good test for Duke. "Duke." The dog lifted his head. Kade opened the baggie and held it in front of Duke's nose. "Find him." Keeping the material inside was going to be a real test of Duke's tracking skills.

Duke sniffed inside the baggie, then Kade closed it before letting Duke have it. Duke lowered his nose back to the ground, zigzagged around the tree for a minute, then headed to the back of their property. He led them to the road behind their property where he made several circles, then stopped and looked up at Kade with a puzzled expression. Fuzz had followed them, and he walked to where Duke was standing. It seemed as if the two dogs were communicating, then both sat.

"He had his car parked here," Kade said, taking the evidence from Duke and giving it back to Bentley. "We need photos of those tire tracks."

"On it," Bentley said.

Their property bordered the road, and assuming the shooter had a car parked somewhere in this vicinity, Tristan had sent two of Skylar's deputies to go door-to-door to the houses on this street. Hopefully, someone would have seen something, and even better if someone had a doorbell camera that had caught something.

His phone chimed, Talon Security coming up on the screen. "Church here."

"This is Chase. Got something for you on those license plates."

"Great."

"Someone got into the DMV's files and deleted the original plate numbers. They no longer exist."

"That's possible?"

"Anything's possible if you got someone who's good at hacking."

"Like a black hat?"

"Yeah. I'd say that's what we have here, someone who's done stuff like this before. We don't have names yet because the plates don't exist anymore, but Nick's intrigued now, and he won't be happy until he gets to the bottom of it."

One possible scenario crossed Kade's mind. "What if they knew Harper had their plate numbers, so they destroyed those, got new plates, and their black hat guy created new files for the cars? Could this person do that?"

"I don't see why not if he or she is really good. I'll pass that idea on to Nick. That might help him know what to look for."

"Appreciate it. Things are escalating. Someone shot at Harper."

"Shit. She okay?"

"Yeah. I saw the glint of a rifle and managed to take her to the ground a second before he pulled the trigger, but it was damn close. I'm royally pissed, and not just about that. My five-year-old niece was playing in the yard just minutes before."

"Damn. Not cool, man."

"Roger that."

"What's your plan?"

Good question. "I'm working on a plan, but the priority is to make sure my family is out of the line of fire, so I'm going into hiding with Harper. After that, I'm not sure. I need to figure out who these bastards are, and how they found Harper."

"You're positive you weren't followed after you picked her up?"

"Definitely, so they're tracking her somehow. Once I figure out how, I can use that to bring them to me on my terms." Terms that were not going to be fun for these assholes.

"She bring any electronic equipment with her?"

"Her laptop and a burner phone she uses to call her father. She keeps the burner off, but I'm going to destroy it and get her a new one."

"Ship me the laptop. My brother will be able to find out if they're tracking her through that."

"Will do. Again, appreciate your help. Tell Nick I said thanks, too. If it is through the laptop, leave it as is so I can use it to bait a trap."

"Make sure it's powered off when you send it to me. Don't forget to include her password if she uses one."

"Copy that. I'm taking off with Harper in a few, so my brother will overnight it to you."

"Stay safe and keep in touch."

"I plan to, and I will."

"What am I overnighting?" Tristan asked after Kade slipped his phone back into his pocket.

"Harper's laptop. Talon Security is going to make sure it's clean."

"You think that's how they found her?"

Kade shrugged. "Don't know, but I'm positive I wasn't followed from Myrtle Beach, so they're tracking her somehow."

"I don't like this."

"You think I do?"

"She needs to go to the police."

Kade stopped walking and faced his brother. "She did, and they pretty much blew her off. She's got us now, and you are the police."

"It's not my jurisdiction, so there's not much I can do."

"So, someone shooting at our house doesn't count?"

"Of course it does, and believe me, I want the bastard who was on our property shooting at Harper and with a child living here. We catch him, I can throw him in jail for that, but the bigger part of this will have to be handled by the police in Fayetteville."

It didn't make Kade happy, but he got it. "Maybe she needs to try contacting that detective again, see if she can get him to take her seriously. But first let's get her laptop sent to Talon. I have a bad feeling about it." And his bad feelings were rarely wrong.

Bentley jogged up to them. "Skylar's deputies found three houses with doorbell cameras. They're getting copies of the videos and will meet us back at the house."

"Let's hope they show us something," Kade said.

The first two videos were to the south of where the car had been parked and showed nothing during the time they were looking at. On the third, a silver sedan passed some minutes after the shooting, going north. There was a male passenger, so two people were in the car, but they couldn't see the driver. They'd lucked out on the passenger, though. He'd turned his head toward the house as if looking at something, and although his features behind the closed car window weren't distinct, they were able to tell it was a male.

"I think that's him," Harper said. "The man who came to my dad's house."

Kade leaned over her shoulder to watch the video playing on Tristan's laptop. "But you can't be sure?"

She leaned back and peered up at him, and his gaze fell to her mouth, and he wanted nothing more than to kiss her again. He also wanted to spirit her away from men who dared to show up on her driveway and scare her, who came to her father's home where she should be safe and hurt her, who dared to shoot at her with the intent to kill her in his own damn backyard.

"I wish I was, but his face just isn't that clear. I know it's him, though."

He stepped back, annoyed with himself that he'd almost kissed her in front of his family and all the cops crowding around them in his home. "We need to get going."

She looked at him as if she couldn't figure him out. He wished her luck with that because he couldn't figure himself out.

"Okay, I'll get my things."

His eyes tracked her as she left the room. Was this attraction to her simply because they'd been thrown together in a dangerous situation? High-octane situations got tense, got the adrenaline going. If that was what this new wanting her was, adrenaline lust, then he'd cut off his arm before touching her. She was special and deserved more than… She just deserved more.

He slid his hand into his pocket and touched the hair tie he'd never given back to her. *What if she was the—*

He shut that *what if* thought right down. She was not the one. There was no denying a head doc would have a field day with him, from the time his father had walked away, then a few years later when his mother decided she'd rather be free than be a parent to her sons, and then his years as a special operator, experiences that would screw with any man's mind.

But he wasn't going to try to fix the unfixable. No head doc for him. He was just fine with his life and his acceptance that he'd always be alone. Sure, there would be hookups, but they'd forever be just that, a few fleeting hours when he lost himself in a woman's body and forget that he'd never have what his brothers did. He'd never see a woman wearing his engagement ring like Tristan with Skylar. He'd never have a beautiful daughter like Everly.

There'd never be *the one* for him.

"You look… I don't know, a little sad," Harper said, walking up to him with her duffel over her shoulder and rolling a suitcase behind her.

"Me sad? Never." There was nothing to be sad about.

Chapter Twenty-One

After all the cops left, Harper gave Tristan her laptop and password, then zipped her duffel bag back up. "I'm ready."

Kade held his hand out. "Give me your phone."

She pulled it from her pocket and handed it to him, curious why he needed it when he had his own phone.

He gave it to Tristan. "Destroy it."

"What? I need it." How was she supposed to make her scheduled calls to her dad?

"There's another one waiting for you." He picked up a small black device and trailed it over her duffel and then the suitcase. When he finished, he dropped it into his jacket pocket.

"You have a bug detector?"

"He has all kinds of toys," Tristan said. "Wait until you see all his goodies at his cabin."

Kade shrugged. "Hope for the best but prepare for the worst. Words to live by." He whistled. "Let's go, Duke."

Duke raced into the room, followed by Everly. "Where's Duke going, Uncle Kade?"

"With me and Miss Harper."

"No!" She wrapped her arms around Duke's neck. "He has to stay with me."

"Duke is Miss Harper's dog, Everly," Kade said, his voice gentle.

"But he loves me." She glared at Harper. "He doesn't love you."

Harper wasn't sure why Kade wanted Duke to come with them, especially if it was going to upset Everly. She glanced at Kade and raised her brows.

"He comes with us," Kade said with no room for argument in his voice.

"Sweetie." Harper kneeled in front of Everly. "I know he loves you so much, but he has to go to work now. You know, like when your daddy and uncles have to go to work. They might not want to, and I'm sure Duke wants to stay with you, but he has a job to do."

"Is it an important job like my daddy's?"

"So important. I promise you, though, that when he finishes his job, he'll come right home to you."

"Tomorrow?"

"Well, probably not tomorrow, but soon. Okay?"

Jellybean strolled into the room and let out a drawn-out meow.

Parker stepped to Everly and put his hand on the top of her head. "Why don't you go feed Jellybean, then we'll go to the Kitchen for dinner."

"And ice cream after?"

"Sure." Parker grinned as Everly ran to the kitchen.

"You're a pushover, Daddy," Skylar said. She glanced at Harper and smiled. "Actually, all three of them are softies where that little girl is concerned."

"Well, she is a hard one to say no to." Being around Everly—this family actually—only confirmed her wish to have a big family herself someday. The problem was, she was now picturing her children with Kade's eyes.

After saying their goodbyes, and getting hugs from Tristan, Parker, and Skylar, she and Kade loaded her things in his truck. Kade opened the back door, and Duke jumped in.

As they were pulling out of the driveway, Kade powered down one of the rear windows to halfway, and Duke stuck his head out. Tristan and Skylar, driving separate cars, left with them, Skylar in front, and Tristan behind them.

"Are they escorting us?"

"For a little while to make sure we're not being followed."

"I feel like I've caused everyone—"

"Don't. Not a one of us blames you or wishes you hadn't come to us for help."

Maybe so, but she had disrupted their lives, especially Kade's. It occurred to her that he hadn't brought a suitcase. "You aren't taking anything? Extra clothes or anything?"

"No, everything I need is at the cabin."

Except for the gun in the holster inside his jacket she'd noticed earlier. He probably had more weapons stashed on him. That was how those special ops guys rolled. How had she gotten into this mess? Well, she knew how, she just hadn't expected to have to run for her life. She would do it again to save Lisa, but she'd do it differently. She definitely wouldn't have gone inside that warehouse. If she hadn't done that, they would have never known about her. She just hoped "curiosity killed the cat" wasn't going to be true in her case.

Kade's attention was focused on the road and on the car's mirrors, and she didn't try to talk. Was this intensity Kade the operator? The danger aside, it fascinated her to observe him in action. She didn't know how she knew, but all his senses were on high alert, and all possibilities had been considered, as well as actions to be taken should one of those events occur.

"Why are you staring at me?"

How did he know? He hadn't even darted a glance at her. "I was just thinking that your intensity and awareness must be what you're like on an operation."

He did look at her then. "It's called staying alive." His eyes returned to the road and mirrors.

What she didn't tell him was that the power and confidence radiating from him was hot. What would he be like in bed? Her body heated just thinking about it. Maybe once they got to his cabin, away from his family, she could get him to do something about this chemistry between them.

A few miles outside of town, Kade followed Skylar a short way up a dirt road. Harper glanced back to see if Tristan was still behind them. He was, but he'd stopped and was turning his car around to face the road.

"What's going on?"

"Picking up groceries."

Huh? "There's a grocery store up here?"

"No, groceries are being delivered." He stopped his truck next to an SUV with the sheriff's department logo on it. "Don't want to go to a store and risk us being seen."

When had they planned all this?

"Stay here," he said, then hopped out of the truck.

Holy moly bologna. If she hadn't been impressed enough by Kade—and she really had been—what she was seeing was a special operator at work, a mission well planned. An expertly choreographed operation took place before her eyes. Kade and a deputy went to the rear of the SUV and moved five coolers to the bed of Kade's truck.

After the coolers were loaded, Kade stopped at the open window of Skylar's SUV. A few words were exchanged, and then he smiled at something she said. Harper knew this scene playing out didn't come close to the planning of a special operations mission, but it gave her an idea of how Kade prepared for all possibilities.

She didn't know when he'd arranged everything, and he hadn't asked her what food she wanted, so she was curious to see what was in those coolers. She was really looking forward to seeing his cabin, curious about the place where he was able to decompress.

When they reached the paved road again, their escorts turned in the opposite direction. There had been comfort in knowing they were being guarded by police officers, and now that they were alone, Harper couldn't help worrying a little, and she watched the road as intently as Kade.

After driving for a while, the lake appeared, then came and went as they traveled on the curvy road. The houses on the lake were big and expensive, and she couldn't imagine Kade owning one of them. Even if he had the money, they just weren't him. Then she lost sight of the lake altogether and they left the houses behind.

Her tension eased as traffic became sparse. If anyone tried to sneak up on them, they would be easy to see, and it helped that Kade seemed to relax, too. Eventually, he turned onto a gravel road, and she guessed they'd traveled about two miles before a small log cabin came into view. The covered porch looked out over the lake, and there was a dock with a boat on a lift. The cabin was isolated, not another house in sight.

Duke, who'd had his head out the window the entire trip, barked, and his tail furiously wagged.

"He loves it here," Kade said. "Watch. As soon as I open the door, he'll head straight for the lake." He got out, opened the door for Duke, and sure enough, the dog raced to the lake, down the dock, and took a flying leap off the end.

Funny that she was jealous of her dog for getting to spend time with him here. She could see why this was Kade's peace place. After exiting the truck, she took a deep breath of the fresh mountain air and smiled at Kade when he came around the truck and stopped next to her. "It's beautiful here."

"You think so?" Mischief flashed in his eyes. "You're only the third female I've brought here."

Seriously, Kade? She did not need to know that.

Chapter Twenty-Two

Kade hadn't missed her nose wrinkling—her tell when she didn't like something—and he chuckled as he headed for the cabin. He glanced over his shoulder. "You coming?" He jogged up the steps to the porch, and when she joined him, he said, "The other two were Skylar and Everly."

"Oh."

He shouldn't like that it mattered to her to know that. He unlocked the door, pushed it open, and held out his arm for her to enter. As soon as he deactivated the alarm, he leaned against the wall and watched her. What would she think of his home away from home, the place he was most at peace? He wasn't sure why it mattered, but he wanted her to like it here.

She stopped a few feet inside and looked around, then spread out her arms. "This is perfect. Not too rustic and not too fancy. Just perfect."

Pleasure expanded in his chest "Thanks." He scanned the room, trying to see it through her eyes. His cabin had two bedrooms and one bath, one more bedroom than he needed unless Everly was spending the weekend with him, which she did a few times during the summers.

Even though Skylar occasionally came over for the day to go out on the boat with him and fish, she never spent the night. Other than Everly, he'd never let anyone sleep over, not even his brothers. Guess Harper was now on his sleepover list. He'd wondered if he would feel antsy with her in his sanctuary, but he didn't. *Interesting*.

The living room, small area for a dining table, and kitchen were open...no walls. He didn't like walls. When he'd bought the place five years ago, it had been a fixer-upper the owner was almost paying someone to take off his hands. Every room had been walled in. Damn claustrophobic. It had taken the years since taking possession to complete his DIY project, only finishing last spring.

The original wood floors had thankfully only needed refinishing, the smoke-blackened floor-to-ceiling stone fireplace a lot of scrubbing, and the log walls a good clear coat. The kitchen had been his biggest project as it had to be gutted. It wasn't huge and hadn't needed oversize appliances, but he'd gone with the best, along with new cabinets and light gray soapstone countertops.

Everything had been done by his hands, and although some of it was by trial and error, the work had been therapeutic. His brothers had offered to help, but he'd declined. If they were here in his space, he'd have to talk. He loved them and would go after anyone who hurt them, but he didn't always want to talk to them...to anyone. Especially when coming right off a mission. He was almost sorry he didn't have more to do because working on this place kept his mind busy and off things he didn't want to think about.

For furniture, he'd gone basic but comfortable. A light brown leather couch and matching recliner, wood and steel coffee table and side tables, and, of course, a big-ass TV. A small two-people dining table, beds—king-size for his room, and twins for the second bedroom—and dressers. That was it.

As he took in the great room, seeing it through Harper's eyes, he decided he needed a few things to make it homier. A throw rug, maybe, something for the fireplace mantel, a picture or two for the walls. Parker would probably paint something for him, and thinking about it, he liked the idea of having some of Parker's art in his cabin. Some of Parker's art in the bedrooms, too.

"I'm surprised you don't live here," she said.

"A little too far out." That wasn't the full truth. He was afraid if he lived here, it would stop being special, would no longer feel like his place to find peace. "I'm going to unload the truck."

"I'll help."

"No need, but you can start putting the groceries away." He took the burner phone Skylar's deputy had given him out of his pocket. "Here you go. A replacement. It's safe to use."

"Oh, thanks."

Their fingers brushed together when he handed her the phone, and she lifted her eyes to his. The air crackled between them as their gazes held. Damn. He dropped his hand. It was going to be torture having her share his space and not touching her. He really wanted to touch her, wanted his mouth on hers again. Hell, there were a lot of places he wanted his mouth.

"I'll start bringing in the groceries." And try to cool down.

"What about Duke? Is he okay out there?"

"He's part fish. He'll come in when he's worn himself out."

"I don't have a bathing suit."

That stopped him in his tracks. Harper in a bathing suit—and his brain went straight to her in a bikini—would be his undoing. "It's too cold. Your lips would turn blue if you got in the lake right now." And here he was thinking about her mouth again. Not only did he want his mouth all over her, but he also wouldn't be averse to having her mouth all over him. Eff him. He should go jump in the lake himself before she noticed the way his pants were tenting.

As soon as he stepped outside, he blew out a breath, sent a curse into the air, and adjusted his jeans. She was a girl who deserved the man of her dreams, he reminded himself. He didn't know how to dream and sure as hell didn't know how to give someone else theirs.

What he knew how to do was kill bad guys, keep people safe, and use his muscles to carry in the food. Those were pretty much his specialties. He paused at the bottom of the steps to watch Duke playing in the lake, and he smiled at the silly dog. If only humans had the traits of a dog. Dogs loved unconditionally. They didn't care about skin color, or gender, or social status. They just loved.

Kade picked up a stick and threw it past Duke's bobbing head. Harper's dog barked a sound of joy as he swam after the stick. When this was over, she would leave and take her dog with her. Best to ignore this urge to find a way to keep them in his life.

He carried in two coolers, one stacked on top of the other. "Here's the first load." Two more trips and he had all the coolers, along with her suitcase and duffel bag in. He took her things to the second room. When he returned to the kitchen, Harper had put all the cold items in the fridge and was busy stocking the pantry.

"You got me yogurt with cherries on the bottom and

pepper Jack cheese." She came to him, lifted on her toes, and kissed his cheek. "Thank you for remembering."

"You're welcome." She'd always been easy to please, and he liked making her happy. He liked her kissing him, too, even if it was only on the cheek. Before he shared that little fact with her, he grabbed a bottle of water from the refrigerator, something to keep his mouth busy before words he shouldn't say slipped out.

"We should be friends with benefits while we're here."

His water went down wrong, and he choked. She had her back to him as she organized the pantry to her liking, and she'd said that no differently than if she'd said it was a nice day out. Maybe he'd heard her wrong. Maybe she'd said she wanted eggs Benedict.

She glanced over her shoulder. "You okay?"

No. He was far from okay. He hadn't heard her wrong, but he was going to pretend he hadn't heard her at all. "I'm going to get Duke out of the water. He'll stay in the lake all day if you let him."

"Okay."

Coward, he thought as he walked outside. Give him guns shooting at him any day of the week and he wouldn't blink twice, but his best friend offering something he desperately wanted, and he was running for cover.

He grabbed the towel he'd left draped over the railing the last time he was here, then walked to the lake. He whistled for Duke, and the dog swam to shore, shook so hard to displace the water on his coat that he fell off his feet. "You're ridiculous," Kade muttered with a chuckle. Duke got himself upright, then knowing the drill, raced to Kade.

"Man to man, what would you do if a girl you really liked wanted to be friends with benefits?" Kade snorted.

"Yeah, silly question to ask a dog. If you still had your balls, you wouldn't even have to think about it. Am I right?"

Could they be friends with benefits while they were here and still be best friends when this was over? If he was sure they could, he'd be all in. That was a big if, though, so unlike Duke, he'd do some hard thinking.

Finished drying Duke, Kade decided to take a walk around the perimeter of the cabin and do some of that thinking before he went inside and faced the big elephant that would be in the room now.

Chapter Twenty-Three

So, that was a mistake, offering herself up as a friend with benefits. Harper finished putting the groceries away after Kade pretended not to hear her and walked out. She wasn't sorry she'd put what she wanted out there. Why shouldn't she tell him what she wanted? Let him do with it what he would. If he came back inside and acted like she hadn't offered him her body without strings, then he better not kiss her again. His running hot and cold didn't work for her.

Movement outside the kitchen window caught her attention, and she moved to the sink where she could see better. Kade was standing at the tree line, looking up. At what? As if sensing she was watching him, he shifted his gaze to the kitchen window. He stared at her, and she stared back, then he walked out of sight with Duke at his heels.

She let out a breath when she couldn't see him anymore. The groceries were put away, so she went looking for her things. The first bedroom had a king-size bed and several items on the nightstand, including a few books. She wanted to check the titles but was afraid he'd come in and catch her snooping since this was obviously his bedroom.

In a smaller bedroom across the hall, her duffel bag

and suitcase were on one of the twin beds. She opened the dresser drawers, and finding them empty, put the clothes from the suitcase away. Although…she took back a pair of jeans, two T-shirts, two pairs of panties, and a bra. If those men found them, she and Kade might have to bug out in a hurry, and she meant to be prepared. After putting the spare clothes in the duffel, she set it next to the bedroom door where it would be easy to grab if necessary.

Duke raced into the bedroom—wet and rambunctious—and jumped on the bed and rubbed his body on the spread to dry his fur. Duke being in the house meant Kade was, too. Time to go see if things were going to be awkward between them.

She found him in the kitchen. "Hey."

"Getting settled in?"

"Not much to settle, but yes."

He took a loaf of bread out of the pantry. "How's sandwiches sound for dinner? Something simple for tonight since I doubt either one of us feels like cooking."

"Sounds good to me." She'd found the plates and silverware earlier, and when he got out the makings for the sandwiches, she opened the cabinet to get them.

"Why don't we make our sandwiches and take them out on the porch?"

"I'd like that."

He set out deli ham, roast beef, and turkey, put all three of the meats on his sandwich, and she went with the ham. After their sandwiches were made, she handed him a beer.

"No, thanks, I'll just have water. I don't drink when on an operation." He speared her with a look, what she thought of as his game face. "And make no mistake, we are on an operation."

"Gotcha." She wouldn't have thought anything of it if

he had a beer. He really did take his responsibilities seriously, and her respect for him grew. She got his water and a bottle of green tea for herself, something else he'd remembered. He grabbed a bag of chips, and loaded up, they headed for the porch.

"No, Duke, stay," he said when Duke tried to slip out the door with them. "If he goes out, he'll head right back to the lake, and it's getting dark. I don't like not being able to see him."

It hurt a little that he knew her dog better than she, but it was another reason to leave Duke with him when she left. Plus, Everly would hate her if she took Duke away, and even though Harper would never see the little girl again after that, she couldn't bear to think of Everly hating her.

They settled in the two rocking chairs on his porch. Although night had fallen, a big full moon had risen over the mountain peaks, outlining them in a deep purple and casting yellow ribbons of moonlight dancing on the lake. "I see why you can find peace here."

"This place speaks to me."

She was happy for him that he had somewhere like this, but she'd never had a place that spoke to her, and suddenly she wanted one. Somewhere like this where she could sit on her porch at night and be mesmerized by yellow ribbons frolicking on the lake and not think about men trying to kill her or a man she wanted as more than a best friend.

They'd finished eating, and he still hadn't said a word about what she said that she knew damn well he'd heard. Fine. His loss. She stood. "It's been a long day. I'm going to shower and then call it a night."

He wrapped his hand around her wrist when she tried to step around him to go inside. "Stay. Please."

"Why?"

"Because I want you to." He let go of her wrist. "But only stay because you want to."

There was something in his voice she'd never heard before. Vulnerability maybe? Kade Church was never vulnerable, so she must have imagined it. She sat back down. And because she had to know… "Why do you want me to stay?"

He didn't answer for a good minute, then, "When I come to the cabin, I always sit out here most of the night." He rested his head on the back of the chair and then turned his face to her. "I've always been good with being alone on those nights, prefer it actually. Not sure why, but you make me want to be with someone. Come to think of it, not just any someone. You."

There was that vulnerability again. Kade Church was lonely, and he didn't even know it. Or wouldn't admit it to himself. Or she was seeing things that weren't there. She decided to address his hearing what she'd said. "I know you heard what I said, and I'm sorry if I made you uncomfortable."

"Ah, she's going straight for the elephant in the room. Hard to miss that big old thing."

"We can pretend I never said that."

"Or I can tell you how tempting your offer is."

"But?"

He reached across the small table between them and wrapped his hand around hers. "The but is this. As hard as I'll try hard not to, I'll find a way to hurt you. Then you won't want to be my best friend, and that's the last thing I want to happen."

"How will you hurt me? I'm not wedding dress shopping. I have things to do, places to go." Well, she used to.

"Does that mean you're still planning to join the Peace Corps?"

"No, that's not for me anymore. I really wanted to, but now..." How did she explain the fear that shadowed her because of that man?

"Now you're thinking of the bad things that could happen."

"Yeah."

He squeezed her hand. "That risk was always there, Harper. You just never thought of anything bad happening to you, but now you know it can."

"I'm so angry about that. I want my courage back."

"The first special ops mission I went on, a sniper shot at me. Fortunately, he wasn't all that good because he missed. But it was close. I heard the bullet as it passed by my ear. Scared the shit out of me, and when we got back to base, I went to my team leader and told him I wasn't cut out for special ops. He was a big John Wayne fan and was always quoting the man and could mimic Wayne's voice perfectly. In John Wayne's voice, he said, 'Courage is being scared to death...and saddling up anyway.' Then he poked me in the chest. 'So grow a pair, son, and saddle the fuck up.'"

"So you're saying I need to grow a pair?"

"Hell no. That would just be too weird." He chuckled at his own joke. "Symbolically, though, yeah. It's good advice."

"Did it work?"

"Eventually I figured out that being scared was a good thing. When you're scared, you're hyperaware, and that awareness has saved my ass ten times over."

"The difference between us is that you're a trained warrior and I'm not. Finding housing for people doesn't do anything to develop your fighting skills."

"If the Peace Corps is something you really want to do, and only that fear is stopping you, I'll sign up and go with you, if they'll guarantee we can stay together."

"You'd do what?"

Chapter Twenty-Four

Harper was staring at him as if he'd lost his mind. Kade was tempted to go look in the mirror because he was sure he had the same expression on his face. The surprise was that he meant it. He didn't like the idea of her being in some country on her own where she might not be safe. He really should have thought it through, though, before saying anything. It would mean giving up the job with Talon Security. Was he willing to do that?

"I'm not going to let you disrupt your life like that. Besides, I gave notice a few weeks ago and missed training. So I need to rethink what I want to do."

"Any idea what that might be?"

"Not really. Everything's up in the air right now. Tell me about Talon Security. I assume they're IT experts since we sent my laptop to them?"

"They're more than that." He gave her a brief summary of the things they were involved in. "They've offered me a job."

"Yeah? Doing what?"

"I guess I'd be involved in all the things they do, but I'm particularly interested in their involvement in rescuing people who've been kidnapped, especially children." He realized he was still holding her hand, and that was something new between them. He didn't hold hands. That was an intimacy that he'd never wanted or been comfortable with. Yet, he liked holding hers, which in itself was a good reason to not do it. He eased his hand away.

He'd changed the subject when she'd said she wasn't shopping for a wedding dress to avoid agreeing or disagreeing to being friends with benefits. He'd never had a relationship like that before, and as much as he wanted to go for it, he couldn't decide if it was fair to her. He could walk away when the time came, but could she? Would they still be friends?

An alert notifying him that one of his security cameras had picked up motion chimed on his phone. "Let's go inside."

"Okay. It is getting chilly." She started picking up their paper plates.

"Now, Harper," he said when she didn't move fast enough. Apparently, she heard the urgency in his voice as she dropped the plates and drink bottles and headed inside. After she was safely inside the cabin, he paused, listened, and sensed nothing. He went in, locking the door behind him.

"What's going on?" She'd moved to the entrance to the hallway, and worry was etched on her face.

"Not sure. Probably nothing." He went to his bedroom and got the laptop he kept at the cabin.

She followed him into the room. "Kade?"

"Stand by." He sat on the bed and booted up the computer. There were six motion detector cameras mounted in the surrounding trees. On the fourth one he checked—the one that scanned part of the backyard—he found the culprit. It was what he hoped to find.

Harper sat next to him and peered over his shoulder. "Is that a deer?"

"Yeah." He brought all six camera views up on the screen. "I was going to show you this tomorrow but might as well do it now. There are six cameras surrounding the cabin. I'll leave my laptop on with this screen up while we're here, and if you think you hear or see anything, you can check the videos."

"I noticed when we arrived that there are no bushes or trees next to the cabin."

"Correct. I cut everything back a good thirty yards. Makes it hard for anyone to sneak up on me."

"Were you expecting someone to… I mean before me and the people looking for me?"

"No, but if there's one thing I've learned from my job, it's always prepare for the unexpected."

One of his previous Delta Force teammates who'd returned to civilian life a few years earlier had been tracked down by the brother of a drug dealer. Hank had been out of the Army for a year when the man who blamed him for his brother's death found him. He hadn't prepared for the unexpected, and he'd almost paid for that mistake with his life. Kade had no intention of making the same mistake. He'd started with the cabin because if any of his enemies came looking for him, he'd draw them here, away from his family. Beefing up security at home was next on his list, though.

In the meantime, he had a woman he didn't want to be attracted to leaning against his arm, and her coconut scent surrounded him. His head lowered before he realized what he was doing. His mouth was inches from hers when he caught himself and stilled. Her eyes were locked on his, their hazel color deepening to a darker green. "Beautiful," he murmured.

"Kiss me, Kade."

And if that didn't do something to him, her ordering him to kiss her instead of asking. He'd resented following orders when he'd first enlisted in the Army, but he could be a smart man when he wanted, and he'd eventually smartened up and learned that following orders made life easier.

"Yes, ma'am," he agreed because he wanted to keep being smart. He set his laptop aside, then wrapped his fingers around her neck and pulled her to him. "Kissing you now." He'd wanted his mouth on hers since the last time they'd kissed, and as their lips touched and their tongues tangled and tasted, and her sex-on-the-beach scent intoxicated him, he couldn't remember why he'd resisted.

He took her down on the bed with him, then slid his arm under her and pulled her on top of him. She came willingly. Spread over him, she pushed her hand under his shirt, and when her fingers traced the contour of his ribs, he feared he was going to embarrass himself just from her touching him.

He hadn't been with a woman since before his last mission, so that had to be the reason he was on the edge. When he'd returned home, it was to learn that Harper had died, and he'd had no desire to hook up with someone while mourning the loss of his best friend. And now a miracle had happened, and she was here in the flesh, in his arms.

Why was he fighting this attraction between them? He pulled away. "Harper."

"Mmm?" She blinked her eyes as if coming out of a trance.

Had he ever seen anything sexier than her beautiful

desire-filled eyes and lips plump and damp from his kiss? "Are you sure this is what you want?"

"You mean you and me naked?"

He chuckled. "Yeah, that."

"I'm sure."

"And you understand the rules?"

She held up her hand and lifted a finger. "No falling in love." Another finger went up. "No expectation for a future between us." Up went a third finger. "We stay best friends no matter what."

He covered her hand with his. "That pretty much covers it." Those were the rules he wanted, so why was he annoyed at hearing them?

"I have a rule, too."

"Hit me."

"As long as we're doing this, we're exclusive. Someone comes along you want to be with, we're done. Still besties, though."

"Damn straight it's an exclusive deal." Another first, this irritation coming at him when thinking of her with some other man. He didn't do jealousy. Also, he didn't like how easily she was agreeing to his rules.

"Okay, so we're doing this?"

"Yeah, we are." Her smile made him think of a cat that had gotten into the cream…rather pleased with herself. "But later. I need to let Duke out before we lock up for the night, and then I want a shower." He also wanted to think this through one more time before they did something that she would regret in the morning.

"I'll take my shower while you're doing that."

"Sounds like a plan." He kissed her. "Back in a few."

He slipped his gun into a jacket pocket, grabbed the flashlight that was mounted on the wall at the back door, then clipped Duke's leash on his collar. Outside, Kade walked around the tree line with the flashlight shining on the ground. There were no footprints or any signs of disturbance. Satisfied no one had been nosing around, he waited for Duke to do his business, then they walked down to the dock.

"No, you can't go in," he said when Duke pulled on the leash. Duke sighed, then dropped to his belly at the end of the dock.

The full moon was now covered by a cloud, and as he stood in the dark of night, Kade thought hard on Harper and what he wanted. He snorted. There was no doubt what he wanted, but would she end up regretting it if they went through with this friends-with-benefits thing? If she did, then he would have big regrets.

He'd learned to go with his instincts, and that was the reason he was hesitating. His instincts told him they were rushing into this too fast. He also didn't really know where her head was. What had changed with her? She'd never looked at him with eyes that were turned dark with desire before.

That's not true, dude. There had been that one time when they had a planned movie night. He'd gotten called out the week before, only returning in the early evening of their movie night. He'd texted her to let her know he was back, that he'd left the door unlocked for her, and to come on over. He'd thought he had time before she arrived to take a shower and get dressed. When he'd walked out wearing only a towel because he wasn't expecting her yet, she was already there. Her gaze had roamed over him, and then her eyes had lifted to his and they had been darker. Her cheeks had turned pink, and she'd stammered something, and then she'd gone to the couch, picked up the remote, and refused to look at him.

He hadn't thought much about it then, but now he wondered if she had always been attracted to him and had hidden it. If she did feel something for him, that was another reason to keep his hands off her. He reached into his pocket and brought out her hair tie. Why had he kept it? Why did he want to? He didn't have the answers, so he slipped it back into his pocket. But he did come to a decision. Harper wasn't going to like it, especially since he'd already agreed that sex was on the table.

"Up, Duke. Time to go inside."

When he returned to his bedroom, Harper was asleep in his bed. Her hair was spread out over one of his pillows and one bare leg was out of the covers, and he was pretty sure she was naked. He refused to be creepy and lift the covers for a peek. Seeing her in his bed, something possessive and primitive settled in his chest, followed by a longing the likes of which he'd never felt before. He wanted to slide into the bed behind her and curl around her so that their bodies touched from their heads to their toes.

Instead, he showered, and then he settled on the sofa with the TV on but no sound. Duke curled up next to him and was soon snoring. He spent the night considering different scenarios that might happen with the people after Harper and planned for each possibility.

Chapter Twenty-Five

Harper stretched her arms above her head as she opened her eyes. She'd slept better than she had in months. But wait… She stared up at a ceiling fan. This wasn't her room. She sat straight up and looked around. At seeing the log walls, she blew out a relieved breath. She was at Kade's cabin. In his bed.

The previous night came back to her, and the last thing she remembered was climbing into his bed while she waited for him to join her. The covers on the other side of the bed were undisturbed, and she frowned. He hadn't slept in here.

She hadn't brought clothes to put on into his room because she wasn't expecting to need any. Since he hadn't joined her and she didn't know why, she didn't want to go from his room to the second bedroom naked. His closet door was open, so she slid out of bed, grabbed a blue-and-black flannel shirt, and put it on. Since it fit him, it almost reached her knees.

Somewhat dressed, she went looking for Kade and found him on the sofa, sitting up with his bare feet on the floor, his head resting on the back, and asleep. The TV was on with the sound muted, and she picked up the remote from the coffee table and turned it off. Duke was snoozing next to him, and when she turned off the TV, he lifted his head, stretched his mouth in a wide yawn, then went back to sleep.

Why had Kade stayed out here? Had something happened during the night? He had on sweatpants and a long-sleeve Henley, and there was no getting around it, the man was mouthwateringly hot. Her gaze roamed over his face. He wasn't a classically handsome man or beautiful like some men were. His facial features were strong and rugged, the bump on his nose adding character to an already interesting face.

Both his brothers were handsomer if you compared their features one by one to Kade's, but Kade did it for her. He was also the biggest of the brothers, more muscled, too. He was the one who could clear a path through a crowd with just an intimidating look. He was the one she wanted.

Even in sleep, he didn't look peaceful, and she wanted to press her fingers to his face and smooth those worry lines. This was a man who'd lived on the edge, courting death for ten years, and when he should be walking away from danger and finally coming home to a safe life, she'd dumped more danger in his lap.

"Why are you staring at me?"

She jumped back. How did he know? His eyes were closed. "Why are you sleeping out here?"

"Not sleeping." He opened his eyes, and his gaze roamed over her, stopping on her bare legs, then he lazily perused his way back up her body. He smiled. "You're wearing my shirt."

"Aren't you the observant one? I waited for you."

His eyes shuttered, and he sighed. "We need to talk, but coffee first."

"I hate it when people say they need to talk. It's never good. You make the coffee, and I'll let Duke out," she said when Duke jumped off the sofa and scratched on the sliding door.

"On it, but you'll have to take him out on his leash, or he'll head straight for the lake. And the temperature dropped, so you might want to put pants and shoes on so you don't freeze."

"Fine, you take him out."

He winked as he walked by her, and she realized she'd just been tricked into doing what he wanted. She scowled at his retreating back.

When he returned from the bedroom with sneakers on, he had his gun in his hand. "I'm sure there's no one around, but I don't want you outside by yourself. Why don't you get dressed, and I'll made us coffee when I come back in?"

She dressed in a long-sleeve T-shirt and jeans, and because she liked his flannel shirt, she put it back on. She took the time to brush her teeth and hair and moisturize her face, and when she went to the kitchen, the coffee was brewing and Kade was putting down a bowl of food for Duke.

"Sleep okay?" Kade asked.

"Yep." She'd never offered herself up before for a fling, and his rejection hurt.

He darted a glance at her terse answer, then he sighed. "You're mad."

"A little, but even more, I'm confused."

"You have a right to be." He poured coffee into two mugs, then added cream and sugar just the way she liked it. He drank his coffee black. "It's too cold this morning to sit outside, so let's take these to the living room, and I'll start a fire."

She settled on the corner of the sofa and tucked her legs under her. He handed her one of the mugs, set his on the coffee table, and then went to the fireplace. There was something about a man building a fire that was…well, manly. Or maybe it was just the particular man doing it that had her wanting to sigh into her coffee.

Once he had the fire blazing to his satisfaction, he sat at the other end of the sofa. "About last night." He toed off his sneakers, shifted to face her, and put one foot on the cushion. He stared into his coffee for a moment before meeting her eyes. "I want you, Harper, like I've never wanted a woman before. Don't doubt that."

"So, the problem is?"

"Regrets. I don't want either one of us to have them, and if we do this friends-with-benefits thing, I think we might have them."

"I told you I wouldn't have any. I agreed to your rules."

"That's the thing, though. Two people who are attracted to each other shouldn't have to set out rules to be together."

"Okay. No rules then." Was she begging? It sounded a lot like she was, and she didn't like herself so much for that. She was attracted to him—always had been—more than any guy she'd dated, even more than her one serious boyfriend, but she had her pride. "You know what, forget it. I can't handle the way you run hot and cold."

His face turned to stone. "I'm not intentionally jerking you around. I don't know why things changed between us, but they did. As much as I want my mouth on yours, my mouth all over you to be honest, it can't lead to anything, and that's my problem. I don't want to lose my best friend, and I don't want to hurt you."

They'd gone over this last night, and she'd agreed to his rules, but maybe he was right. She didn't want regrets either, and she couldn't promise herself or him that she wouldn't have them. "Well, it's settled then, no hanky-panky." Now she just had to figure out how to put a stop to this attraction she had for him. She also hoped things weren't going to be awkward between them now.

"If we can't play hide the sausage, let's go shoot some guns."

She rolled her eyes. "You did not just say that."

"What, go shoot some guns?"

The mischief was back in his eyes, and there was his signature smirk. Maybe they were going to be okay. "Here? How close are your neighbors?"

"It's pretty spread out around here, but no, there's an outdoor shooting range about thirty minutes from here. We can stop for breakfast on the way. Did you bring your gun with you?"

"Yeah. It's in the bottom of my duffel bag."

"Great. Come with me first."

She followed him back to his bedroom and into his closet. He pushed aside some hanging shirts to reveal a mounted cabinet.

"Is that a gun safe?"

"Yes. If something happens, come here to hide." He read off the combination as he opened the cabinet. "The closet door locks from the inside, and you'll have weapons at your fingertips."

"I'd say." There were several handguns, a long gun, three wicked-looking knives, and… "What's that? Pepper spray?"

"Yep."

"Okay, you weren't kidding when you said you like being prepared." There was also a cell phone in a charger.

"A consequence of my job."

They were standing close, her arm pressed to his, and his scent—something fresh and woodsy—washed over her. Why did he have to smell so good? She ordered her feet to step away from him, but before they obeyed, she made the mistake of lifting her gaze to his. He was staring at her mouth, and she half expected to see flames dancing around them from the heat blazing in his eyes.

"Kade?"

He blinked, then shifted so they weren't touching anymore. "Ah, you remember the combination?"

"Uh-huh." What just happened? If she was going to get rid of this attraction to him, he couldn't look at her like he wanted to devour her. Although… She smiled to herself at the thought running through her mind. Maybe he deserved to get a little taste of his own medicine after giving her whiplash with his running hot and cold. Something to think about, and how to go about doing it. She'd never tried to seduce a man before.

"Ready to go get some breakfast?"

"Sure." She was blocking his exit from the closet, so he couldn't move until she did. Should she? Why not? As she turned to leave, she *accidently* brushed her bottom against the zipper of his jeans. Oops. Her back was to him, so he didn't see her smile when he grunted.

Take that, Mr. Hot and Cold.

Chapter Twenty-Six

Harper was being weird, like she knew a secret he wasn't privy to. He hadn't missed the side eyes she was giving him or her pleased-with-herself smile when she thought he wasn't paying attention.

It was not the attitude he'd braced for after he'd told her he'd changed his mind. He should have been happy she didn't seem upset. He was not. He was irritated. It appeared that her friends-with-benefits offer was no more than that, that she didn't have feelings for him like he'd thought. That was what he wanted, so why was he cranky?

At the outdoor shooting range, she used her SIG Sauer for target practice. For a noncombatant soldier, her accuracy impressed him. "Do you practice a lot?" They'd never gone to a range together before, so he'd never seen her shoot.

"I grew up shooting. My dad was on the US men's shooting team during the Summer Games in Barcelona. It was something we did together from the time he deemed me old enough to handle a gun."

"You never told me that. That's cool. Did his team win a medal?"

"A silver."

"You don't think of a doctor as being an expert shooter."

"What can I say? My dad's a cool dude."

So was his daughter. What other things about her didn't he know? He called her his best friend, but their time together had mostly been spent watching movies, going out with their friends for a beer, or playing with Duke in the yard. The dog could spend all day catching a Frisbee or attempting to steal it when he and Harper tried to throw one to each other. They rarely talked about their pasts, and that was mostly his doing.

She put her gun away. "Can I shoot the long gun?"

"If you want." He'd brought his Glock and the rifle, and he took the rifle out of its case. "You ever shoot one before?"

"Yep."

That was a smug look on her face, so he knew he was going to be impressed again. He put his ear protectors back on, then stood and observed. When she finished, she glanced at him and shrugged, as if it wasn't a big deal that once she had a few practice shots to learn the gun, she hit the bull's-eye every time. Damn if she didn't handle the long gun like a pro. A woman who knew how to shoot like that was hot. Who knew?

She put her hand on his arm. "Thanks for bringing me here. I had fun."

There she went, touching him again. She'd been doing that a lot this morning. "We'll do it again sometime." But would they? Once it was safe for her to go home, she'd leave. He wasn't liking the idea of that so much. There had never been another woman he'd felt as comfortable with as Harper, and not one he wanted as much as her.

"We can have a shooting competition."

Now, that was definitely hot. Why did she have to be his best friend, a woman he'd cut off his arm before hurting? "Ready to head back to the cabin?" Before he decided it would be a good idea to back her up against the wall and show her the effect she was having on him.

She dropped her ear protectors and bent over to pick them up, drawing his eyes to her ass, and he almost groaned. Because he didn't trust his hands to behave, he stuffed them in his pockets.

She had one of those secretive smiles on her face, and he narrowed his eyes. The little witch knew exactly what she was doing. Should he pretend he wasn't onto her, or... Two could play this game. He'd spent the past ten years planning every move of an operation, and before he decided which direction to go, he needed to think and plan. But he couldn't resist toying with her a little.

He took his shirt off.

"What are you doing?"

"It's hot in here."

"No, it's not. Put your shirt back on."

Funny how she was demanding he put his shirt on when her gaze was locked on his chest. He draped his shirt and the jacket he'd worn to the range over his arm, then gathered up his gun cases. "You coming?" As he walked away, he resisted the temptation to glance back to see her face.

She ran in front of him, forcing him to stop. "What's wrong with you?"

That was a loaded question. "You got a few days?" He wanted to laugh. *Still having fun with this game you're playing, Harper?*

"Put your damn shirt on," she literally growled.

Since he'd made his point—not that he was sure exactly what his point was—he let out an exaggerated sigh. He did like how her eyes went right back to his chest. Something to keep in mind. "Sure, babe. All you had to do was ask."

"Do. Not. Call. Me. Babe."

He laughed. He knew that would rile her up. When was the last time he'd had this much fun? Answer, never. "Hold these." He dumped his gun cases in her arms. "Commence putting shirt on." Was that regret in her eyes when his chest was covered? He was pretty sure it was. "Happy?" He raised his brows.

"So happy," she said, then pushed his gun cases back into his hands.

He grinned at her back when she marched away. She'd probably slap him if he told her how cute she was when she got all pissy. One of the things he'd always liked about her was how she could get him out of his head. That was one reason she was the first person he wanted to see after returning from a mission. He'd come home, shower, eat, sleep, and then he'd call her for a movie night or to go out for a beer. No matter what had gone down on the operation, a few hours with her and he'd feel human again.

After they climbed in his truck, his phone vibrated, Chase Talon's name on the screen.

"Hey, Chase."

"Your girl's laptop has a bug. I'm putting Nick on to explain it since I don't understand a word he's saying."

Kade wasn't sure he'd understand any better than Chase. All he knew about the man was that he was a computer geek, a coder, and a gamer.

"Kade?" Nick asked.

"You got me. I'm with Harper. Okay if I put the call on speaker?"

"This concerns her, so definitely," Nick replied.

"On speaker." Kade held his phone toward Harper. "Say hi to Nick Talon."

"Um, hello, Nick."

"Harper. Got some bad news for you. Someone who knows their stuff embedded Wi-Fi tracking in your laptop."

"Oh my God. How?"

"Pretty simple, actually. It happened when you clicked on the link in Detective Johnson's email."

"Why would a detective do that?"

"Because he's a fake identity. There is no such person."

"How can that be? I sent an email to the police department, and he responded."

"Someone responded, so the odds are good that it was a cop, but he doesn't want you to know who he actually is. Every time you turn on your laptop, he can track your location."

"That answers the question of how they knew she was at my house," Kade said. Harper was looking a little green, and he put his hand over hers and squeezed.

"Whoever it is, they're good, but I'm better. It's going to take me a little time to trace the link back, but I will."

"Since you've had her laptop on, do they think she's at your location?" Kade asked.

Nick snorted. "Didn't I just tell you I was good? They don't know I've had it on. Chase said you believe there's more than one person involved. Here's what I think. We at least have a bad cop who got lucky and managed to get her email before someone else and then we have a competent hacker. Once we trace the link, do we go after them?"

Kade thought for a moment. "Depending on what you find out, that could mean having to infiltrate multiple locations to weed them out in areas we don't have law enforcement connections like we do here. I would rather be able to control the location, one where there won't be innocents who could get caught in the cross fire. So, we can use her laptop to set a trap at our chosen time and place. How long before you think you can trace the link to these people?"

"Depending on how good our hacker is, a day, two at the most."

"That's good. It'll give me time to plan. Don't take the tracker off. When you're finished, send Harper's laptop back to my brother."

"Will do. Any other questions?"

"Have they been able to see me when I turn on my laptop?" Harper said.

"No. They don't have eyes."

"Well, that's something anyway. That would be really creepy. Not like I'm not already creeped out."

"Understandable."

"Any way of determining who the cop is?" Kade asked.

"Unless our hacker is emailing him or her, no. My guess is they aren't because they're smart enough not to put anything on record. If you don't have anything else, Chase wants to talk to you."

"Thanks, Nick. Harper and I really appreciate you taking the time to help."

"No thanks necessary. Nothing I hate more than men who think it's their right to hurt a woman. We're going to find these people, Harper, and they're going to wish they'd stayed under the rock they crawled out from under. That's my promise to you."

"That means a lot, Nick," Harper said. "When this is over, I'll treat you and Chase to a steak-and-lobster dinner."

"It's a date. Here's Chase."

"I just want to say that I know this is upsetting, Harper, but the good news is that by putting a tracker in your laptop, they've given us the means to find them, and we will," Chase said.

"Thank you more than I can say. I told your brother that I'm treating you both to dinner when this is over."

"I never refuse dinner. Kade, whatever you need from me, you got."

"Appreciate it. Let me come up with a plan, and I'll get back to you."

"Okay. Just don't leave us out of your plan. We want in on teaching these assholes a lesson."

"Copy that." Kade disconnected, then shifted in his seat to face Harper. "You okay?" Some color had returned to her cheeks, but of course she wasn't okay. "Hey, you're safe. I'm not going to let anything happen to you."

"I'm never going to be able to use a computer again. It's my fault they know where you live, where your brothers and your—"

"None of that. No blaming yourself for any of this." The thought of someone shooting at her enraged him. Especially when it was at his home, and where Everly had been playing only moments before. These people were going down.

"If I hadn't come here, none of—"

"Hush. You're right where you need to be." He didn't even want to think about what could have happened to her if she hadn't come to him. They needed to make a mission plan, but more than that, she needed a few hours of downtime, and he knew just the thing.

Chapter Twenty-Seven

Harper turned her face up to the wind and sun as Kade throttled up his boat. When they'd arrived back at the cabin, she'd wanted to close herself up in the guest bedroom and brood. She never clicked on links from people she didn't know, not in emails and not on social media. It hadn't occurred to her that she couldn't trust a cop. It really creeped her out that someone had put a bug in her computer so they could find her no matter how well she hid. Then there were the trust issues. She didn't think she'd ever be able to trust anyone again unless she knew them inside and out.

Kade had practically bullied her onto his boat, refusing to let her hide in her room and feel sorry for herself. Now, she was glad he had. It was hard to be depressed and angry at the world when breathing fresh mountain air, and the sun was warm on her face as the boat raced across the water. She couldn't help but smile at Duke holding his nose up to the wind, his trademark goofy grin on his face.

"Cold?" Kade asked.

"Not at all." The afternoon was a bit brisk, but with a sweater and her leather jacket, she was comfortable. Kade wore an Army sweatshirt, and had the sleeves pushed up to his elbows. There was something about a man's forearms that was arousing, and Kade's were downright sexy. His muscles flexed as he steered the boat across the lake, and she wanted to wrap her fingers around his arm and feel the strength under her palm.

"Want to drive?"

"Yes!"

He stepped back from the wheel but kept one hand on it. "Come here."

"Should I sit or stand?"

"It'll be easier for you to see over the bow if you stand. Have you ever driven a boat before?"

"Nope. You'd think living on the Gulf I would have, but my dad gets seasick, so we were never into boating."

He pulled the throttle back a little, slowing their speed somewhat. "Just don't jerk the wheel hard to the left or right. She's all yours." When she took the wheel, he stepped up on the seat and sat behind her on the top of the backrest.

That put him within reach, and it eased her mind that he would be there for her if she did something wrong. It also meant that she was nearly standing between his legs, and that, she was very aware of. Another boat passed them off to the right, and when their wake reached them, he pressed his knees against the outside of her thighs to keep her steady. She scanned around her, looking for more boats to send a wake their way so he'd do that again.

Her life was a mess, and men were after her, which was as serious as it could get, but the reprieve from thinking about the trouble she'd gotten herself into for a few hours was a blessing. Somehow Kade had known it would be, had known just what she needed.

She glanced over her shoulder. "Thank you."

"For?"

"This." She waved a hand around. "For knowing what I needed today." For being there for her when she didn't know who else to turn to. For putting his life on hold for her, maybe even risking it before this was over. For being a friend she could count on. Even for taking her dog when she'd asked.

Damn tears burning her eyes. Those tears were for her, for the bone-deep loss she felt at knowing he was a man she could love to the end of her days but who would never be hers. She'd never cried over a man before, and she didn't much like doing it now.

"Watch it!"

Startled, she jerked her gaze to the front of the boat. "Shit." Two Jet Skis had raced around the back of another boat, putting them in the path of Kade's boat. The men on them were paying attention to each other and not their surroundings as they sped across the lake. Forgetting Kade's warning, she yanked the wheel to the left, then promptly lost her footing.

"I've got you." Kade wrapped his arms around her to take the wheel and keep her from face-planting on deck. He righted the boat.

"That was way too close for comfort." Her heart was hammering in her chest.

"Fools. They're going to get themselves killed."

As reckless as they were on those Jet Skis, it could happen. She was grateful she hadn't run over them. Kade's arms were still around her, and when he rested his chin on the top of her head, she leaned back against his chest.

She expected him to move away, but surprising her, he moved his mouth to her ear.

"You smell so damn good, H, like the beach on a summer day. A beautiful girl in a bikini, her skin glistening in the sunshine from her coconut suntan lotion, is the picture you put in my mind. I'm trying really hard to do the right thing, but you're making that difficult."

She turned to face him, and because he still had his arms around her and his hands on the wheel, they were breast to chest. The leather jacket was in the way of getting closer to him, and she wanted to tear it off. "The right thing for who?"

"You." He throttled down the boat to let it idle. Even though they were now drifting, he kept his hands on the wheel, which kept his arms around her.

"I think I get to say what's right for me." His eyes were locked on hers, and she wondered if he could see how much she wanted him. "Kiss me, Kade."

He made a strangled sound as he glanced off to the side. "We should talk first."

"Talking's overrated." What was there to talk about? She was good with his rules, had told him so.

Duke whined, and Kade chuckled as he shifted his gaze to Duke. "Your dog is half fish."

"What's his problem?" Hers was that he wasn't kissing her.

"He wants in the water." Kade let go of the wheel with one hand and waved it at Duke. "Go."

Duke let out an excited yelp as he jumped into the lake. They both watched him for a minute, then she decided to take the decision out of Kade's hands. If he'd told her he wasn't interested, she wouldn't do what she was about to, but he'd admitted he was, so...she kissed him.

He stilled, his lips not moving against hers, and she panicked. She'd read him all wrong, and now she was assaulting him. Embarrassed, she tore her mouth away. He slipped his hand around the back of her neck and brought her mouth back to his.

"I surrender," he murmured against her lips.

She slid her eyes closed on a soft sigh, and all there was in the world was the two of them. He kept the hand behind her neck in place and put his other one on her lower back, pulling her tight against him. She pressed her palm to his chest, and even through his sweatshirt, she could feel the rapid beat of his heart. She was lost in him and his kisses.

His mouth left hers, and she whimpered a protest, but then his mouth traveled down her neck, and when he gently nipped at her skin just above the collar of her jacket, she forgot her complaint. Amazing how kissing him made the world rock. But no, it was the wake from another boat rocking them, and he held her tight, keeping her on her feet.

He lifted his head and pressed his forehead to hers. "How about we head back to the cabin to continue this?"

She nodded in agreement because speech was beyond her ability. If his kisses did this to her, he was going to wreck her when they made it to his bed. But she would be a happy wreck.

"I need you to let go of me for a minute so I can get Duke in the boat."

She hadn't realized she had the hem of his sweatshirt fisted in her hands, and she reluctantly let go.

It took him a few minutes to get Duke in, and then he

returned and sat at the wheel. He patted the seat. "Next to me, snookums."

"Snookums? Really?"

"Sugar pea? You like that one better?" He shot her a grin as he throttled up the boat. "I've never called a girl a pet name before, so I'm testing some out. What do you think of cutie patootie?"

"If you call me that, I'll punch you where it hurts the most." She'd never admit how much she loved hearing there'd never been someone he liked enough to give a pet name.

"Ouch." He covered the zipper of his jeans with his hand. "Okay, cutie patootie's definitely out. Candy pants, toots, cuddly-wuddly, butter biscuit…any of those catch your fancy?"

"Call me any of those, and I'll call you hottie pants."

He laughed. "You think I'm hot?"

Well, duh. "I think you're silly." She'd always loved this playful side of him. Kade Church was a complicated mix of funny, deadly serious, charming, intense, insecure, and sometimes…lost boy. Everyone who knew him thought he was an extrovert. He really wasn't. That was a front he'd perfected to hide his vulnerabilities.

She was his best friend because he felt safe with her. His teammates were his brothers, and he was as close to them as unrelated men could be. He'd die for any one of them. But they only knew the Kade he showed them, the one willing to walk into danger without blinking an eye, the one who they never doubted had their backs. He ate with them, drank with them, joked with them, but he never let them see the real Kade.

As for his blood family, his love for them was bone

deep, and he'd give his life for his two brothers, his niece, and now Skylar without a second thought. But she didn't think they really knew him, that he kept his true self hidden from them, too. She found that sad. If there was anyone who could convince him he was worthy, it was his brothers.

In the year she'd known him—become close friends with him—she'd been an observant student of Kade Church, snatching up the crumbs he unintentionally dropped, giving her teasing tidbits of who he was. She'd studied the man with the fascination of an archaeologist digging for a rare artifact. He'd only given her glimpses of that lost little boy who lived inside him, the one who didn't believe he was lovable. She'd always wanted to tell him he was wrong, but if she'd even hinted that she was figuring him out, he would have disappeared from her life. That was a loss she wasn't willing to risk, so she'd kept her observations to herself.

Another thing she kept to herself—she could love him if he'd only let her.

"I got one," he said, snapping her out of her thoughts. "Foxy lady. I like it, so you have to."

"I do, huh?" She did like it.

"Yep. Now you need one for me, and it's not hottie pants."

"Okay. How about stud muffin?"

He snorted. "Try again."

"Sugar lips?"

"Nope, but just sugar's good, though. I've always wanted to be someone's sugar."

"You have not." The last thing this man wanted was to be in a committed relationship. She knew that going in, so she knew to protect her heart.

"Maybe I want to be a foxy lady's sugar."

"Fine, but I want it on record that I vote for stud muffin."

"Noted." He leaned over and put his mouth to her ear. "You can call me stud muffin when I'm buried deep inside you."

Heaven help her.

Chapter Twenty-Eight

After sending Harper inside, Kade secured the boat, then with Duke at his side, he walked the tree line around the cabin. There weren't any footprints that didn't belong, and nothing was disturbed. He hadn't received an alert on his phone that the cameras had picked up any activity, but he'd watch the security feeds later just to be sure.

Duke's favorite squirrel raced halfway down a tree, chattering away at the dog. Duke let out a happy bark at seeing his nemesis and jumped up, trying to reach the squirrel. The rodent loved to torment the dog, always staying just out of reach.

While the two of them played, Kade called Tristan, updated him on what Nick had learned, and arranged to meet after his brother received Harper's laptop. When he finished his call, he whistled for Duke.

"Let's go, bud. There's a foxy lady waiting for me." He was over running hot and cold as she'd accused him of, but the soldier in him couldn't turn off the need to make a reconnoitering walk around the property. If he didn't, he wouldn't be able to give Harper the attention she deserved.

They'd both needed a few hours away from thinking or talking about what was coming at them. The silly business with pet names had added laughter to their afternoon. He'd always had fun with her, and he never wanted that to change.

If she hadn't kissed him, he wouldn't have surrendered. But she had, and he had, and now she was waiting for him. With each step he took toward the cabin, the faster he walked.

The shower was running when he came inside, and he thought about joining her. He shook his head to rid his mind of an image of Harper slick and wet, her skin soapy and smelling like the coconut body wash she used. Yes, he'd sniffed it when he'd showered last night.

Instead of shedding his clothes and slipping in behind her, he checked that the doors and windows were locked. After setting the alarm, he fed Duke, then leaned back against the hallway wall while Duke chowed down. He slipped his hand into his pocket and pulled out the hair tie and stared at it. He still didn't understand why he was keeping it, other than now that he'd been carrying it around in his pocket for a few days, it felt like it belonged with him.

The shower shut off, and he put the tie back in his pocket. The bathroom door opened, and a vision wrapped in a towel walked out of the steam. She stilled at seeing him, and when she smiled, his long dormant heart woke up and banged around in his chest. That had never happened before, and he wished it would go back to sleep.

"Hi," she whispered in a sultry voice he'd never heard from her before.

"Hi, yourself." His feet took over, and he stepped in front of her. "Are you sure about this?" He pointed a finger at her then back at him. "Us?"

"Yes."

One simple word uttered without a doubt in her mind. "You won't let me hurt you?"

"No."

Another simple word full of conviction, the eyes looking back at him filled with trust. "Promise me."

"I promise." She put her hand on the towel where it was tucked in to keep it from falling. "Stop worrying, sugar." A giggled escaped her. Then she pulled the towel apart and let it fall to the floor.

"Fuck me," he muttered. "I've tried so hard to be good, but you don't play fair."

"Good boys are boring. Be bad for me, Kade."

"How have you hidden this side of you from me for so long?"

"You weren't ready for me. Now you are."

"I am?" When she nodded, he put his hands on her hips. Her skin felt like silk under his fingers. "Okay, then. Bed. Now."

He was going to make love to her from one end of his bed to the other. *Make love.* He only fucked…but this girl! She put words in his head he'd never had there before. And her coconut scent had his mouth eager to taste her, to run his tongue all over her, to explore her curves and feel her soft skin under his hands.

As he followed behind her, he pulled his shirt off, and dropped it on the floor. She took a running jump and landed on the bed on her stomach. Foxy lady indeed. He unzipped his jeans and stepped out of them but left his boxer briefs on. He sat on the edge of the mattress and skimmed his hand down her, starting from her neck, then over her spine, to her ass. When she tried to turn over, he pressed his hand down. "Stay."

She looked over her shoulder at him, a soft smile on her

face, and desire shimmering in her eyes. "I want to touch you, Kade."

"You will. Just be patient and let me play with you a little." Had he ever been this aroused? He loved sex in all the ways…slow and easy, fast and hard, and occasionally he wanted it a little dirty.

When he was younger, he liked it hard and fast, down and dirty best, but since becoming a special operator, his preference was for slow and easy. That was something he'd wondered about, and he'd concluded that it was because of the violence that came with his job. Losing himself in a woman's soft body—taking his time to give both of them pleasure—soothed him, calmed the chaos that sometimes clouded his mind after an operation.

"I'm going to worship this beautiful body of yours all night long." He sat on the mattress again, leaned over, and peppered kisses across her shoulders. "Don't even try to rush me. There's something else you need to know about me. I like having control, but occasionally, I need to be controlled."

"How will I know?"

"Because I'll tell you what I like, what I want. I want that from you, too. If something feels good, tell me. If it doesn't, tell me. I talk a lot during sex. That doesn't mean you should if that's not your thing, but if you don't let me know when I'm doing something you like, I won't know to keep doing it."

"I don't talk much during sex."

"That's fine, but…" He danced his fingers down her spine, smiling when she shivered. "How did my fingers feel skimming over your skin?"

"Good."

"See how easy that was?" But he wanted more than

one-word answers from her. He'd always found it a turn-on when a woman talked to him during sex, telling him how something he was doing felt while he was pleasuring her. Without Harper even being aware of it, he would teach her to talk to him. He moved his hand to the inside of her thighs. "Spread your legs apart." When she did, he cupped her sex. "What do you want my hand to do? Or do you want my fingers to do something?"

"I want them to touch me."

"They are touching you, both my hand and my fingers. Tell me exactly what you want them to do." He wasn't trying to embarrass her, but he wanted her to be comfortable with asking for what she wanted. "Do you like sex, Harper?"

Chapter Twenty-Nine

How to answer his question? Sex was good, but Harper had never had mind-blowing sex, the kind that was so incredible that her bones turned to jelly and stars danced in front of her eyes. Going out, meeting a man in a bar, and going home with him had never been her thing. She had to know the guy and like him before she slept with him. There hadn't been that many she'd liked enough to take her clothes off for, and the ones she had…well, she'd enjoyed her time with them, but her mind had never been blown.

"Do you like sex?" he asked again.

She wished he'd stop talking and get down to business. She squirmed against his hand, hoping that would encourage him to do something. Although, the things he was saying, and the hand cupping her, were making her antsy in a way she'd never felt before.

He chuckled. "You can wiggle all you want, but nothing's going to happen until you answer."

"Sex is good, okay!"

"I see."

What did he see?

"Good is something you say about toast. Toast isn't awful and it isn't great, but a talented chef can do magic with toast. You want great toast?" He brushed the hair away from her neck, then leaned down and scraped his teeth across her skin. "Do you want the magic?"

A moan escaped her. "Yes." Dear God, he'd barely touched her, yet every nerve ending was tingling with anticipation.

"Then talk to me. What do you want my fingers to do?" He used one finger to put a little pressure on her clit, and she almost came out of her skin.

"More of that." When he released the pressure and didn't do anything more, she growled. Really, she was growling now? "I want you to put a finger inside me. I want you to make me come."

"Thank you for telling me," he whispered.

She buried her face in the pillow as he did exactly what she'd asked for. She'd never asked for what she wanted during sex. For one thing, she hadn't wanted to make her partner think he wasn't satisfying her, even though sometimes he wasn't. The other reason was because she didn't want to come across as someone who was loose, who knew her way around a bedroom, and wasn't that just ridiculous? She didn't have a lot of sex, but so what if she did? That wouldn't make her a bad person.

He did exactly what she'd asked for, and as her climax sent shock waves hurtling through her, she lost all feeling of weight and thought she might float up to outer space. And he'd done that to her while she was on her stomach and not looking at him or touching him. *You've ruined me for any other, and we've only just begun*, she wanted to tell him, but that was information that would scare him off. She did not want to scare him off, so she pressed her lips together to keep the words from escaping.

"Turn over and look at me."

The rasp in his voice and his words… How was she supposed to survive this night? "I don't think I have the strength to roll over."

"Not even for me to taste you?"

"Why didn't you say so?"

He chuckled when she quickly flipped over. "Thought that might do it." His eyes, darkened with desire, roamed over her. "Where do you want me to start?" He brushed his thumb over her bottom lip. "Here?" Then he trailed his fingers down her neck to a breast and flicked a finger over the nipple. "Or here? Those are your two choices."

Her skin was electrified, and everywhere he touched, the sensation was almost too much. They hadn't gotten to the good part yet, and if it was this amazing so far, she was going to die, but she'd go out happy.

"What do you want, Harper?"

Her gaze fell to the tent in his boxer briefs. "I want to see you. Take them off."

"Not until you tell me where you want me to start."

"My breasts, now take them off." When he stood, then dropped his boxer briefs to the floor, she uttered an awe-struck "Oh" and maybe even drooled a little. Well, she didn't think she had, but when one gazed upon a man that beautiful and fit and with a very impressive erection, surely drooling was acceptable.

"Like what you see?"

She shrugged. "You'll do."

He laughed. "That's what I like about you. You keep me from getting a big head." He smirked as he looked down at himself. "Or maybe not."

"I see what you did there." Funny man.

"That's because you're a smart foxy lady." He put his knees on the bed, then crawled between her legs. His eyes stayed locked on hers as he lowered his body over hers, then his lashes dropped as he gazed down at her. "Look at these pretty pink nipples that I'm about to taste. Which one first, hmm?"

She was learning something new…that these pauses of his that built her anticipation, the things he said, was foreplay and more arousing than anything she'd ever experienced. He should give workshops to other men.

"I think this one's calling to me," he said, then swirled his tongue around the nipple of her left breast. Before she could sink into a sensual haze, he stopped, and his gaze lifted to hers again. "Or maybe this one needs my tongue more."

He gave the other breast a few seconds of attention, then he moved his mouth back to the first one, and all the while, his hands were skimming over her, touching her in places she didn't know were erotic zones for her. Or maybe it was the magic he'd talked about.

Magic mouth, magic hands, so much magic he created in his touches and his words. By the time he brought her to another climax with his tongue, she couldn't have told him her name.

He crawled up her body, and when he hovered over her, his gaze searched hers. "Do you want me inside you?"

She nodded.

"Words. Give me the words."

At least he hadn't asked her name. "More than I've wanted anything in a long time, so yes, please."

He smiled. "Thank you."

That was another thing, the way he often looked into her eyes as if to gauge her reaction, to make sure he was pleasing her. In her experience, guys didn't make eye contact during sex. They didn't make the effort to see her, to make sure she was as into the experience as they were. Kade saw her.

This time with him was a temporary thing, she knew that and accepted it, but he was sure setting the bar high for any man after him. Although she couldn't imagine wanting another man after Kade.

He reached over to the nightstand drawer. Her heart did a little dance of happiness that the box of condoms was full. *Don't go being possessive of him, Harper. He's not yours.*

"I want to return the favor," she said.

He paused with a condom half on, and his eyes locked on hers. "What favor?"

The only word she could think of to describe the gleam in his eyes was devilish. "You know."

"How can I if you don't say the words?"

Oh, he knew what she meant, but he was going to make her tell him. Why was she reluctant to say it? It was ridiculous that she was embarrassed. He was a sneaky bastard, teaching her to tell him what she wanted by using the words. Were other women like her, both embarrassed to ask for what they wanted and clueless how to even ask?

"Smoke's coming out of your ears. Stop thinking so hard. What you want matters, so never be afraid ask for it…whatever it is."

"I want to taste you. Like you tasted me." And wasn't that just awesome, that she was telling him what she wanted?

His gaze locked on hers as he finished rolling the condom on. "Thank you for telling me. I do want that, very much, but later. Right now, I want to be inside you. I have to be, Harper."

It was strange what his thank-yous were doing for her,

how she wanted to hear them. Also, his *have to be* had sounded desperate. That this incredible man was desperate for her was empowering.

She put her hands on his arms and tugged. "Then be inside me. That's what I want, too."

"There is a God." As he eased into her, he kept his eyes on her in that way of his. When hers closed, he took her hands, raised them above her head, and pinned them to the edge of the pillow with one of his. "Eyes on me. Look at me while I'm inside you."

Her eyes snapped open, and if the heat in his didn't singe her, it would be a miracle.

"Do you know what you feel like to me when I'm inside you?

"How could I?" Already, she was talking more during sex than she ever had, and it only added to the pleasure skyrocketing in places she'd barely paid attention to. "Tell me."

His hand tightened around hers where he held them captive. "You're so fucking wet and so hot. And the way you're clenching around me, it's taking everything ounce of control I have not to come. But I'm not going to, not for hours. Not until you're begging for mercy."

And even when she begged for mercy, he refused to relent. Each time she reached the edge, he would pull her back from the brink, change positions, and whisper more dirty words in her ear. He would make her tell him what things he did to her felt good, and soon, she'd reached the point where she was telling him what she liked without his asking. When he finally let her come, he was under her as she straddled him. She had no memory of how she'd gotten in that position.

"My turn," he said.

His gaze locked on hers, his lips parted, and his hands tightened on her hips as he helped her ride him. Just watching him reach for his own pleasure sent her over the edge again.

"I'm a cooked noodle," she gasped as she tried to catch her breath. She dropped on top of him, and he wrapped his arms around her back, holding her close.

He nuzzled her neck, right under her ear. "Better than good?"

"Mmm?"

"You said sex was good. Was that better than good?"

"How can you even ask that?" She could now say she'd had mind-blowing sex, and wasn't that awesome?

"Was it?" He flipped them over, then stared down at her.

"How soon can we do it again?"

Oh, that smile of his. The feeling of empowerment filling her mind was amazing, and Kade had given her that. A gift she would treasure. She would never again hesitate to ask for what she wanted, to tell a guy what she liked and what she didn't. If she wished that guy would always be Kade, that was her secret.

Chapter Thirty

Theo slammed his fist on the table. "Where the hell is she?"

"Don't know," Rex said. "But keep it down. You're getting attention."

They should have met somewhere besides a diner during the breakfast hour when it would be crowded. He lowered his voice. "Can't you do something to trace her computer?"

"Not until she turns it on. I've explained this to you already."

"And you're sure she's not still at the Church house?"

Rex sighed. "No, but there's no sign of her or Kade Church. After your screw-up, it makes sense that he'd go into hiding with her."

Theo was seconds away from putting a fist through his cousin's face.

Rex pulled out a twenty and dropped it on the table. "Since she hasn't followed up with your fake detective about what she thinks she knows, it looks like she wants everything to go away. That means we don't have to worry about her. Stockton's talking about kidnapping the kid to trade for her, and that's a no-go for me."

Stockton's idea would be worth considering if they weren't dealing with a Special Forces soldier, a police chief, and a sheriff. That was too much heat to bring down on their heads. He'd really like to get his hands on Harper Jansen. Not only did the bitch need to be taught a lesson, but she knew where Lisa was. He'd gotten impatient when he'd decided to kill her. He wouldn't make that mistake again.

Rex stood, put both hands on the table, and leaned his face close to Theo's. "I'm going home. You've gone way past thinking of this as strictly business, and you're all over the place. One minute wanting to kill her, the next wanting to kidnap her to teach her a lesson. They don't know who we are, so we should just halt filming for a few months, let things blow over, then we pick up where we left off."

"You just worry about finding Jansen." She might have muscle on her side, but he was smarter than them all put together. Some bitch of a woman wasn't going to bring them down. They had a moneymaking enterprise going, one that was putting more dollars in his pocket than his job ever could, and they weren't going to put a halt to it. He was meant for bigger things than arresting lowlifes who were thicker than a brick.

The twenty Rex had left on the table would cover their breakfast with little change left over. Theo shrugged as he walked out, not adding anything for a decent tip. What did he care about some nobody waitress in a two-bit town with the ridiculous name of Marsville?

Outside the diner, a police car across the street caught his attention. He recognized Tristan Church from the photos his cousin had shown him. The police chief was standing with an old woman who was banging her cane on the street. Next to them, a turquoise Cadillac that had to be from the sixties was parked, taking up two spaces.

Looked like the old bat didn't take kindly to being told she needed to park between the lines.

Theo didn't want to catch the chief's attention. Small-town police were always suspicious of strangers. He'd never admit it to Rex, but they shouldn't have met at the town's diner. He walked to his car while the man's attention was still on the old lady.

As he drove to the cabin outside of town that he'd rented for the week of vacation his captain thought he was on, an idea came to him, and he grinned. It was a brilliant plan.

Chapter Thirty-One

Kade held the binoculars to his eyes as he scanned the lake. He stopped on the boat headed their way, identified the occupants, then watched to see if it was being followed. "They're on the way."

"No one's following them?"

He lowered the binos and glanced at Harper. "Nope." They were drifting in the middle of the lake on his boat, the safest place he could think of to meet his brother and Skylar. They were coming from a marina on the opposite side where they'd rented a small boat. He whistled for Duke to come back on board so he didn't get run over.

When Tristan and Skylar reached them, Kade tied ropes around the cleats to hold the boats together. At seeing Tristan and Skylar, Duke barked his excitement and leaped into their boat, then bounced between the two of them, showering them with face licks.

"Your dog's a dork," he said to Harper as he took a seat next to her.

"But a lovable one."

"I'll give you that." He was still processing what had happened between them last night, maybe the best night of his life. Correction. No *maybe* about it. And that was his dilemma. He didn't do relationships. He'd tried twice, once in high school, and the second time his first year in the Army. He'd been told by one that she couldn't be with him because he didn't share his feelings. He didn't even know what his feelings were, so what was there to share? The other one had broken up with him because she claimed he didn't let her in, whatever that meant. So he'd learned how to please a woman in bed since that was going to be the only time he spent with one.

Then along came Harper. Somehow, she'd become his best friend. He shared more with her than he had with anyone, including his brothers. She leaned against him, and he wanted to put his arm around her and tuck her next to him. He'd slipped out of bed early this morning after watching her sleep for a good twenty minutes and wishing she was his. She wasn't.

Amazing sex with an incredible woman didn't mean he was in love. But when she smiled up at him, sharing her amusement over Duke's exuberance at seeing two of his favorite people, he cursed his treacherous heart for wanting more. More of her smiles, more of her hand on his leg, like she was doing now, and especially more nights with her in his bed. He'd get over wishing he was a different man—one who could be what she needed—as soon as he made sure she was safe and she left to live her life.

"You're wet," Skylar said, laughing as she tried to hide her face from Duke.

"Duke!" Kade snapped his fingers. "Go swimming." The dog didn't have to be told twice.

"Here's Harper's laptop," Tristan said, handing over a canvas tote.

"I don't want it." She looked at the tote the way one would a rattlesnake.

Kade took it and set it on the bench next to him. "Have

you seen anyone around the house or town who doesn't belong?"

Tristan shook his head. "No, but we're keeping an eye out. Katie said two strangers had breakfast at the Kitchen yesterday morning. She said it looked like they were arguing, but whenever she approached the table, they stopped talking."

"You doing okay?" Skylar asked Harper.

"As good as I can be considering. I just want this over with."

"Understandable," Tristan said. "What's the plan, brother? I know you have one."

"I'm going to use Harper's laptop to bring them to me."

"To us," Tristan said.

"No. I'm not involving you and Skylar." He glanced at his future sister-in-law. "I won't risk my family."

"You need to let the police handle this," his brother said.

"No offense, but your cops and deputies don't have the skills I do. We don't know who these people are, how many there are, how connected they are, or what kind of weapons they'll bring to the party."

"I don't like it. We're not leaving you unprotected."

"I won't be. I'm bringing in a team, the kind that knows how to fight dirty then disappear. We'll have weapons your people can only dream about." There could be only two coming for Harper, or there could be twenty. Because he didn't know who they were dealing with, he didn't know what kind of resources they had. He'd rather err on the side of overkill by bringing in a team than be sorry he hadn't.

"I still don't like it."

"Same," Skylar said. "We're not Barney Fife, Kade."

"Never thought you were, but this is the way it's going

to be. Besides, the cabin is out of your jurisdiction, Tristan, and out of your county, Skylar. You'd have to involve Sheriff Lamorne, and you really want to do that?" He chuckled at the expression of horror on her face. "Yeah, not a good idea." The man was full of himself without the skills to back up his attitude. Kade would take Barney Fife any day over Lamorne.

"What I want from you two is to be our eyes when these people start arriving." He turned to Harper. "When the time comes, I want you to take the boat to the other side of the lake, where Tristan will have one of his cops pick you up."

"No." She narrowed her eyes. "This was my doing, and I'm not hiding from these bastards."

He knew she'd say that, but it was worth a try. He was the planner in his Delta Force team, and he always had plans A, B, C, and D, so plan B it was. "Then you're our sniper." She was as good a shot as him, even with a long gun, and in the sniper role he could stash her in a hidey hole.

"You're not going to try to talk me out of being involved?"

"Would it do any good? Because if so, I'll give it a try."

"No, but I thought I'd have to throw a tantrum."

"I can think of better ways to get your way." At the sound of a chuckle, he glanced at his brother and Skylar, both looking at them with amusement. "What?"

His brother opened his mouth to say something, but when Skylar elbowed him, he snapped it shut.

Kade scowled. He probably didn't want to hear whatever it was, anyway. "Back to the plan. Once Harper logs into her laptop, our bad guys will be able to pinpoint our location. I'll call when she does so both of you and your cops and deputies can watch for them to head my way and give me updates. I'll also want you to mess with them a little. Pull them over for going too fast or too slow, anything you can think of. That'll throw them off their game a little."

Tristan frowned. "You're bringing them to the cabin?"

"I know this area inside and out and have cameras all over the place, so I can track them when they look for us."

Kade's phone buzzed, Parker's name coming up on the screen. "What's up, baby brother?" He frowned at what Parker was telling him. "Hold up. I'm with Tris and Skylar. Let me put you on speaker. Okay, start over."

"Two US Marshals just left. They're looking for Harper as a person of interest in a murder."

"What?" Harper shrieked. "I didn't murder anyone."

"I told them that. I also told them that you'd been here for a short visit but had left a few days ago, and I didn't know where you were going from here. Don't think they believed me, but there wasn't much they could do."

"Who was she supposed to have killed?" Kade asked.

"A woman by the name of Abby Warton."

Kade exchanged a look with his brother. "The game just got dirty."

"That's the woman you saw at the warehouse?" Tristan said.

Harper nodded. "Yes. She was alive when I saw her. I only knew she'd died when I saw her picture in the paper, and I was at my dad's when it happened, so they can't put that on me. The paper quoted the police as saying it was a drug overdose. She'd looked drugged the night I saw her."

"Did the marshals have a warrant?" Skylar asked.

"No, they only said that the police wanted to talk to her as a person of interest."

"That's interesting," Tristan said. "Usually, the marshals

have an arrest warrant when they come looking for someone. My money's on a cop calling in a favor."

"A dirty cop." Kade was going to take the dude down.

Harper grabbed his hand. "I didn't kill anyone."

"We know that, H."

"I'll call the police there, find out what the deal is," Skylar said.

Kade shook his head. "No, not yet. Nick Talon apparently has a talent for getting into places with a computer, and he's following the trail of the email Harper got from the fake Detective Johnson. Let's give Nick another day to see what he can dig up. I'd rather not alert our bad cop that we're onto him."

"Keep me updated," Parker said. "If the marshals return, I'll keep up the clueless act. By the way, Everly wants her dog back."

"Tell Ev that he'll be home soon." His niece was a trip.

"She means he needs to be back today, but I'll give her extra pickles in exchange for being patient."

Kade disconnected. If only everyone's problems could be solved with extra pickles.

Chapter Thirty-Two

"You're in charge of the boat," Kade said after Tristan and Skylar motored off.

"Why?" Harper did not want to be in charge of the boat. She did not want to be in charge of anything. What she did want was a magic wand she could wave that would send her back in time while knowing what she knew now. If she could make that happen, she would have never called Kade, begging for his help. But she had, and here she was.

"If you need to escape and all other options have been taken away from you, go to the boat. I'll leave it ready for you, so you need to practice." He whistled for Duke, and when her dog was aboard, Kade stepped to the other side of her. "She's all yours, Captain."

This was her second time driving Kade's boat, and she hadn't been sure she'd like boating since it was something she'd never done. She loved it and wished her life was normal and she and Kade were out for a day of fun instead of planning for battle.

"You're doing great," Kade said. "Give her a little more speed."

She pushed thoughts of what was to come out of her mind as they sped over the lake. For the time it took to return to the cabin, she was going to enjoy herself. Duke had his face in the air, snapping at the wind. She grinned at Kade, and he grinned back, and so much joy filled her heart that she didn't know what to do with the feeling.

No, no, no! Don't go and fall in love with him.

Wise words, but she was afraid that she was halfway there. She didn't have experience with protecting her heart since no man before him had been a threat to that organ, but she needed to figure out how to do it before it was too late.

She wanted a happily ever after, a man who loved her the way she loved him, a big family, a dog. Duke was the first step in her life plan, but even he wasn't hers anymore. No matter how much she might want that happily ever after with Kade and all that came with it, it was never going to happen. She wasn't upset with him because of that. He'd been honest with her on what he could and couldn't be for her. It made her sad for him more than anything. She'd seen him with Everly, and the man could deny it all he wanted, but he'd make a great father.

There was no use wishing for something that would never be, so she would cherish her time with him, and as soon as this was over, she'd leave. Hopefully with her heart intact. They were approaching the dock, and she eyed it with trepidation. "You should probably take over now."

Instead of taking the wheel, he moved behind her. "You can do it." He put his hands on her shoulders. "Ease back on the throttle. You got this, H."

"If I crash your boat, I'm blaming you, sugar lips." He had his chest pressed to her back, and his chuckle vibrated through her.

"I'll show you sugar lips," he murmured into her ear, then leaned around her and covered her mouth with his.

He didn't linger, only left her wanting more. She tried not to think what it would be like to live this life, days of being out on the boat with him and their dog, stolen kisses, smiles exchanged. She tried not to want that.

"Ease the port side of the boat up to the dock." He left her to put the bumpers out. "You're doing good."

"Oops," she said when she hit the dock instead of easing up to it. Thank goodness for rubber bumpers.

"No harm done. Shut down the motor." He jumped out, and Duke jumped in the lake.

"You'd think he would have had enough of swimming."

"He's a fish. He'll never get enough." He tied off the boat, then held out his hand to help her onto the dock.

When he pulled her up, he tugged her against him and slid his hand down her back to the curve of her bottom. "You up for some playtime before things get serious?"

"Thought you'd never ask."

"Good. I need to get Duke out of the lake, then walk the perimeter." He kissed her, and then gave her butt a little smack.

She couldn't resist putting her hand on his tush and giving it a squeeze. "Don't be long."

"Ten minutes."

"Oh, the laptop."

"I'll bring it in."

Good. She had no desire to even touch it again. When she reached the bedroom, she dropped her jacket on a chair, then stripped. She grabbed panties and the flannel shirt she'd swiped from Kade, and then headed for the shower. She'd just finished washing her hair when Kade slipped in behind her.

"Mind if I join you?"

"I've never had shower sex." Why had she blurted that out?

His lips lifted in a predatory grin. "Then let me show you what you've been missing."

Shower sex…boy, had she been missing out. An hour later, and she was still floating on air. If Kade wasn't placing a FaceTime call to Chase and Nick Talon, she'd go roll around in the dirt so she'd need another shower.

"What are you smiling about over there, H?"

"Um, I was—" The Talon brothers' faces appeared on the screen, and she snapped her mouth closed.

"Kade," one of the brothers said, nodding at him, then he looked at her. "You must be Harper. I'm Chase, and the ugly one here is my brother, Nick."

"She's got eyes, bro, and can clearly see who's the ugly one, and it ain't me." Nick winked.

Harper liked them already. She waved. "Nice to meet you, Chase and Nick." They were both good-looking guys, and she tried to find similarities between them. There weren't any that she could see. They even had different-colored eyes, one had brown and one had blue. She never would have guessed they were brothers, and she wondered if there was a story there.

"Wish it was under better circumstances," Nick said. "Let's get to it. I've identified our black hat."

Next to her, Kade tensed. "Name?"

"Rex Sorenson. Works in IT for a bank. He's good, but I'm better."

She didn't hear any boasting in the way Nick said that, only a statement of fact. "Do you know what he looks like?"

Was he one of the men she saw at the warehouse that night or the man who'd hurt her?

The screen changed from a view of the brothers to that of a man she'd never seen before. "He's not the man I saw at the warehouse or the man who showed up at my dad's."

"So we have at least three people," Kade said.

Nick nodded. "I should know who the other two are, and if there are more, by tomorrow."

"What's your plan?" Chase asked.

"Still working out the details, but two of my teammates are headed this way tomorrow. The mission objective is to draw our bad guys here. As soon as we know who the others are and we're set up for them, we'll turn on Harper's laptop, letting them know where we are."

"I want in on this," Chase said. "You got room in that cabin for one more?"

"Never going to turn town experienced help. I've only got one guest bedroom, so bring a sleeping bag."

"You got any security cameras set up there?" Nick asked.

"Got them all around the cabin."

"That's good. I'm not a combat soldier like you and Chase, but I can be your eye in the sky. Give me the link and password, and I'll connect to them. What about comms? You have them?"

"My teammates are bringing them."

"How about we use ours so I can be connected to everyone?"

"That works." Kade squeezed her leg. "Anything you want to say or ask, Harper?"

Actually, there was something she'd been thinking about while they talked. "Do you have a recording device, something I could wear that wouldn't be obvious?"

Kade narrowed his eyes. "Exactly what are you needing that for?"

He wasn't going to like her answer, but he'd have to get over it. "For a confession. I want that man who hurt me to admit it. I want him, or one of them, to admit they killed that poor girl."

"No. You won't be getting close to him, to any of them."

"I'm a part of this. You agreed."

"And you will be. We'll go over the plan later."

"A confession would be helpful," Nick said. "It won't be admissible in court because we won't have his consent to record it, but it wouldn't hurt to have it, and we do actually have a wire that looks like a necklace she can wear. Chase will bring it with him."

Kade glared at the screen. "She is not getting near these people."

"You're not the boss of me," she muttered.

"We'll just see about that," he muttered back.

Both the brothers chuckled. "I think this is where we'll fade out," Chase said. "Send me the location of the cabin, and I'll see you two tomorrow."

"Thank you both for everything," she told them. "The steak-and-lobster dinner's on as soon as this is over. And don't forget that necklace."

Kade logged off, then turned what she was sure he thought was an intimidating stare on her. It was impossible to be intimidated by a man who'd worshiped her body while shower water rained down on them.

Because she couldn't resist messing with him, and because she wanted a repeat even if she was already squeaky clean, she tapped his nose. "If you need me, I'll be in the shower." As she walked away, she pulled her T-shirt over her head and tossed it behind her.

"Come back here. I wasn't finished with you," he growled.

She sure hoped not. She smiled when she heard his boots hitting the floor as he came after her. To make sure he didn't lose interest, she dropped her bra, leaving him a trail to follow.

Chapter Thirty-Three

There was no way Kade was letting Harper within a hundred yards of their targets. He didn't give a damn if the men crowded shoulder-to-shoulder in the living room of his cabin agreed with Harper that they needed a confession. Fine, he wasn't against that. It was her insistence that she was the one who could get it that was a negative. No. Not happening. Not on his watch.

He glared at them all—Tristan, Parker (and why was he here?), Viper, Cupcake, and Chase. His team. The team that was watching him pace in front of them. Why hadn't he bought a bigger cabin, one with some damn pacing room?

And then there was Harper, squeezed in between his brothers, as if they were her protectors. That was his role. If they didn't get those smirks off their faces, he'd do it for them. He scowled at the necklace as he passed her, the one she'd put on as soon as Chase gave it to her.

"You're making me dizzy, dude, and I'm not even there."

Right, Nick was here, too. Kade was tempted to slam down the lid of his laptop. What the devil was wrong with him? He'd never been batshit bonkers because of a woman before. He stopped in front of her. "You're our sniper." He had a spot for her in mind, although he'd locate her in the next county if he could get away with it. "You bring her a long gun?" he asked Viper.

"You told me to, so yeah."

There was too much amusement in Viper's and Cupcake's eyes. When this was over, he was taking them both down. "Take her outside, set up some targets, and let her get used to the rifle."

Viper stood, bowed, and held out his hand to Harper. "My beautiful lady, shall we?"

"Cut it out, Rafe." He was surrounded by jokers. When she put her hand in Viper's, Kade wanted to snatch her away from his teammate. He hadn't thought this through. Viper, aka Rafael Alejandro Luis De La Fuente, a descendant from Spanish royalty that the family could trace back for centuries, was a shameless flirt. He loved women and they loved him.

As Viper passed him, still holding Harper's hand, he smirked. Kade sent him a you-mess-with-her-and-you-die look. Viper laughed.

He snapped his fingers at Duke. "Go with them." *And bite Viper's ass if he so much as smiles wrong at Harper.* The men watching this little drama play out chuckled. He scowled at them.

Harper, oblivious to the undercurrents in the room, waved. "See you guys later."

"I like her," Cupcake said.

When Colton Rhodes had joined the team, he was dating a girl who said he was as sweet as a cupcake. The name had stuck, even though Colton swore he wasn't sweet. He actually was. He could also make anything out of nothing, a MacGyver on steroids. That skill set had proven valuable many times.

Chase stretched his legs out. "Let's hear your plan, Ace."

For the next hour, they went over the plan, finessing the details until they were all satisfied with it. Kade eyed the men sitting in his living room. They were the best of the best, his blood brothers and his brothers in arms, including the man joining them via FaceTime.

He fisted his hand, then held it out. "Brothers, appreciate you being here for Harper." Because that was why they had come when asked, to keep her safe. Each man bumped a fist against his.

"Listen up, people," Nick said.

Everyone turned their attention to Kade's laptop screen. "Got something?" Kade said.

Nick nodded. "Got a name. Your fake detective is a real one, Detective Theo Watson, cousin to Rex Sorenson, the IT guy. My guess, he got lucky and saw Harper's email to the police before anyone else. There's a third person they've referred to as Stockton. Don't know yet if that's a first or last name, but I've got a number both men have called frequently. Stand by a minute."

"Nothing I hate more than a dirty cop," Tristan said.

Nods and words of agreement came from all the men. The cop was going to wish he'd never heard Harper's name. Kade was going to make sure of it. It burned that she'd tried to do the right thing by notifying the police, and the result was a beating and now the man was trying to kill her.

"Here we go," Nick said. "Stockton Rawls, owner of three strip clubs. He was arrested six years ago for assault and battery. One of his dancers claimed they'd had an affair, but when she tried to end it, he beat her. She later changed her story, said it had just been a verbal fight even though there were photos on file of her battered face and the bruises on her body. She refused to testify against him, and eventually the charges were dropped."

"He got to her," Kade said.

Nick nodded. "No doubt."

"You got photos you can send me of these three? I want to see if Harper recognizes any of them."

"Sending them now. I'm going to ask Tristan and Parker to step outside for a few minutes. As officers of the law, it's better that you have deniability."

Tristan frowned. "Deniability of what?"

Nick chuckled. "If I told you that, then you wouldn't have that deniability, would you? It's nothing big, just something I'm going to suggest that normally you'd need authorization for. Why don't you let me talk to your brother, and he can tell me if it's something you'd want to know or that you'd be adamantly against."

"If it helps keep Harper safe, I'm good not knowing," Parker said as he stood.

"Put that way, it's probably something I can live with. Kade will know." Tristan followed Parker out to the porch.

After the door closed behind them, Kade turned his attention to his laptop screen. "What's on your mind?"

"Legally, you need a warrant to listen in on phone conversations, but we don't have time to make that happen. Illegally, I can do it. It's up to you, but it could give us a real advantage if they discuss their plans over their phones."

"Do it." These shitheads were playing dirty and would kill Harper given half a chance. He had no qualms about getting down in the dirt with them, not if it would give his team an advantage and keep her safe."

"Anyone else in this room have a problem with it?"

"Not me," Cupcake said.

"Or me." Chase met Kade's gaze. "These assholes lost

any right to have a fair fight when they hurt Harper. Not to mention that they probably had a hand in Abby Warton's death."

"And how many women have they drugged like Lisa to force them to make porn movies? These people need to be stopped. My brothers wouldn't object to you listening to those conversations, but they could lose their jobs if it ever came out we did this and they knew, so this stays between us."

"Understand that this is only to keep tabs on them, not collect evidence since anything we learn this way wouldn't be admissible in court," Nick said. When they all said they understood, Nick nodded. "I'll let you know if I learn anything more."

Chase stood, stretched his arms above is head, then walked into the kitchen. "Got any coffee?"

"Yeah. I'll make a pot."

"I could use a cup, too," Cupcake said.

Chase opened a cabinet. "Just tell me where it…ah, here it is. I'll make it."

Where was Harper? She and Viper should be finished by now. He walked to the window. Harper was standing with Viper at the end of the dock with a wet dog staring up at him in anticipation. Viper threw a stick, and Duke jumped into the lake.

Kade walked out to the porch. "You can come in now."

"Anything we should know?" Tristan asked.

"Nope. The plan hasn't changed. The only question is what time they'll arrive."

"We're going to head out. Text me before you log on to Harper's computer so I'll know to start keeping an eye out. Skye and I will talk to our people and fill them in."

He gave Kade a hug. "Be safe, brother."

"Always."

Parker hugged him. "Be safe and be badass. Keep our girl safe."

"That's the plan."

He followed them down to the dock, and after they were in the rental boat, he pushed it off, then he walked to the end, stopping next to Harper. "You comfortable with the rifle?"

"She's a pro," Viper said. "Hit the bull's-eye every time once she got the feel of it."

Kade smiled at her. "That's my girl." But she wasn't his girl, was she? He needed to stop saying things like that before either one of them started thinking they might have something going. "Why don't you come inside? I have some photos for you to look at."

"Let me get Duke out of the water." She called him, but he ignored her.

He whistled. "Duke, out!" The dog swam to shore, then raced down the dock. When he reached them, he shook, spraying them with water.

"That dog sure loves the water," Viper said.

"He's a fish," he and Harper said at the same time, then grinned at each other.

"We have a pot of coffee brewing if you want some, Viper. The guys can fill you in on the plan." He wanted a few minutes alone with Harper. Duke gathered his legs under him to jump back in the lake, and Kade grabbed his collar. "Take Duke with you," he told Viper.

Once Viper and Duke were walking up the steps to the cabin, he took Harper's hand. "Come with me."

He took her to a tree on the far side of the property that had a view of the gravel road leading to the property as well as a view of the lake, dock, and back porch. It was an easy tree to climb, and the reason he'd debated over it. She could easily get up there, but so could a bad guy. He had no intention of letting any of those men anywhere near her.

"Tomorrow morning, I'm going to nail a section of plywood to that limb about twelve feet above us. That's where you're going to be. You won't have a spotter, but it's not like your targets will be a mile away. After I have your perch in place, I want you to go up there, practice shooting from it, get used to it."

She studied the tree, then lowered her gaze to his. "Thank you for including me."

"I'd be much happier if you'd leave. Go stay with Parker and Everly." He sighed when she gave him a look that said *not happening*.

"The problem I see, if I'm up there, how am I going to get a confession?"

Chapter Thirty-Four

If Harper didn't know him, didn't know that Kade wasn't as scary as the face he was giving her right now, she might have fainted dead away. Boy, he could sure look intimidating. She wanted to laugh and tell him nice try, but she decided not to provoke him more than she already was.

"Well?" she said when he stayed mute.

He wrapped his hand around the necklace Chase had given her. "I should take this away from you. You. Are. Not. Getting close enough to any of these men to get a confession. Tristan can get that when we turn them over to the cops."

She slapped his hand away. "Leave my necklace alone. I'm not about to put myself in their line of fire, but if I get a chance at getting a confession, I'm taking it. Got it?"

"You're making me bonkers, woman."

Before she could respond to that ridiculous statement, his mouth crashed down on hers. She'd had a response, but dang if she remembered what it was. His tongue traced the seam of her lips, and she opened them, welcoming him in. As he kissed the ever-loving daylights out of her, she slid her hands under his sweatshirt. She dragged her hands down his chest, and his muscles rippled under her palms.

He rocked his body hard against hers and speaking of

hard...his erection announced its presence where it pressed on her belly. A moan escaped her, and she rolled her hips against his. She wanted more of him. That was her mistake because as soon as she made a sound, he moved away from her.

"Why can't I keep my hands off you?" he said, breathing hard and sounding more like he was asking himself that question and not her.

"You don't have to." She'd accepted that when this was over that it would be the end of them, but until then, she wanted his hands on her. She didn't think that there'd be a man after him who would...who *could* make her feel the way he did. Until then, she wanted his touches and kisses and all that followed.

"Let's go inside. We've got things to talk about."

When they walked into the cabin, the guys were drinking coffee, watching a baseball playoff game, and arguing over which was the better team. If she didn't know better and what was ahead of them, she wouldn't be able to guess that they were warriors, here to fight for her.

"Viper was bragging about your shooting," Cupcake said. "A pretty girl who can shoot with the best of us... will you marry me?" He held up a finger. "Wait. Before you answer that, can you cook?"

"Only when I feel like it."

"Well, honey, let me think about it. That might be a deal breaker."

She laughed when Viper thumped his head. She'd been around him and Viper back at Fort Bragg, had gone out for beers with them and Kade when they'd been there. Cupcake was adorable and sweet, but she'd never tell him she thought of him like that. He bristled whenever someone told him he was sweet. He was from California and a surfer, and he had the appearance of a very cute one with his blond hair, blue eyes, and boy-next-door looks. If you didn't know him, you'd never guess he was a soldier, much less a Delta Force operator.

Viper, though, before she got to know him, she thought he was downright scary. He was the biggest man in the room, all muscle, with sleeves of tats on both arms, and she guessed that he was covered with them under his shirt. If he didn't like you, his black eyes could pin you in place with a laser glare. He was the only man in the room who had an actual beard instead of the stubble the others went for, and his beard was as black as his hair. She'd never been a big fan of beards, but on Viper, it worked. The man was hot, a shameless flirt, and an unapologetic horndog, but he was respectful and attentive to any woman he was with.

She hadn't formed an opinion on Chase Talon. He was friendly enough, but there was an aloofness about him. He observed a lot, and she had the feeling he didn't miss anything. There was intelligence in his gray eyes. Not that the others here weren't intelligent, but she sensed that his brain worked on a higher level than most humans. He sure was handsome, almost pretty.

It was Kade, though, who made her heart beat fast, who made her want to sigh when she looked at him, probably with hearts in her eyes. If she wasn't careful, he was going to realize she was falling for him. That would scare him off.

"Come look at these photos," Kade said. He'd taken a seat at the table.

She sat in the chair next to him. "What are we looking at?"

"Some pictures Nick sent over." His laptop screen came

to life. "This is Rex Sorenson, their hacker. What about this one?"

She squinted at the second photo. "It was dark and shadowy, but I'm pretty sure that's the man I saw with Abby Warton."

"He's not the man who came to your house?"

"No."

"He's Stockton Rawls. Owns some strip clubs around the base."

A cold chill traveled down her spine when the third photograph appeared on the screen. "That's him, the one who hurt me."

"Detective Theo Watson, Rex Sorenson's cousin."

She gasped. "He really is a cop?" She was so hoping they'd been wrong about that. It was hard to believe a police officer would hurt a woman the way he had.

The guys had come over and were standing behind her as Kade showed her the photos. Cupcake put his hand on her shoulder. "They're going to learn that they messed with the wrong people."

She wanted justice for Abby Warton and for what they'd done to Lisa, and she wanted to stop being afraid. She wanted her father to be able to return home and not fear one of these men showing up at his house. The men surrounding her were going to help her make that happen. How was she ever supposed to thank them? A lobster-and-steak dinner—which she'd include all of them in—seemed inadequate.

What would it have cost if she'd actually hired them? However much, it would be an amount she never could have afforded. She shifted in her chair and met each of their eyes. "Thank you. The past two months have been a living hell. I didn't see how my dad and I could make all this go away. If anything had happened to him because of me…" Her throat closed up on her. She swallowed past the burn. "When this is over, send me a bill for your time." It might take her a decade to pay those bills, but it was the least she could do.

A chorus of snorts sounded around her. "Stop talking silly, H," Kade said. "There's not a one of us who'd be here if we didn't want to be." Grunts of agreement filled the air. He took her hands in his. "Nothing gets us more excited than taking down scumbags like these people. We'd pay you to let us play." He lifted his chin at the guys, and they melted away.

When it was just the two of them, he smiled. "There might be one thing that gets me more excited, but that's none of their business. We can revisit that later tonight. You okay?"

"Better now. Thanks. It's just all a little overwhelming. I've gotten so used to being afraid, and it's hard to believe it might be over soon."

"Not *might*. It *will* be over."

"I need to call my dad."

"Why don't you do that while the guys and I walk the property? I want them to get the lay of the land before it gets dark."

"Okay." She wanted to rest her head on his shoulder, to snuggle into his arms and just be. No worries about tomorrow, no bad men coming for her.

Chapter Thirty-Five

In the morning Harper was a bundle of nerves, so Kade got everyone together for a game of volleyball before lunch. He hoped some fun and the exercise would take her mind off what was coming. After they ate, she would log on to her laptop. How long it would take their targets to arrive was anyone's guess. They had a pool going on that, which Harper thought was ridiculous, but she'd ended up playing.

Viper and Cupcake had taken the twin beds in the guest room, Chase had spent the night in his sleeping bag in the living room, and that had left his bed for Harper. He'd thought she might balk at sleeping with him since they had company, but he hadn't even had to tell her that was where she was sleeping. After dinner, she'd said she was tired, and had left him to spend time with the guys. She'd gone to the guest room, collected her stuff, and moved everything to his room. By the time he'd come to bed, she was asleep. He'd showered, then eased into bed, wrapped his arms around her, and had slept through the night. Something he never did.

He'd awoken to the best thing ever, her kissing her way down his chest, and when her mouth had wrapped around his erection, he was sure he'd died and gone to heaven.

When he could take no more, he'd pulled her up and made love to her.

Made love to. He loved thinking of their time together like that, but it wasn't him. Not long term. No matter how much he might wish otherwise. He'd left her in bed when she'd fallen back asleep. He'd told himself he needed to get up because he had a lot to do, but in truth…he didn't know how to handle these feelings for her that were growing inside him. He didn't want them.

By the time she appeared, all sleepy-eyed and beautiful, he and the guys had everything ready for their trap. Her sniper stand was in place, all sorts of weapons were stashed inside and outside the cabin and in the woods, and they'd gone over the plan several times. Now all they could do was wait and play volleyball.

He, Harper, and Duke were playing against Viper, Cupcake, and Chase. Yes, Duke. The dog had watched for a few minutes, and then when both he and Harper had missed the ball, Duke had bounced it back up in the air with his nose for Harper to hit it back over the net. He was faster than the humans playing, and anytime the ball sailed over Kade's and Harper's heads, he was under it, bouncing it back to them. The only problem was he didn't understand out-of-bounds.

"It's really not fair that you have super-dog on your team," Cupcake said. "I'll trade you Viper and two cases of beer for him."

"Hey!" Viper thumped Cupcake's head.

Cupcake tackled Viper, and both went down. Duke thought that was a great new game, and he joined in the wrestling match.

"How old are they, anyway?" Harper asked with laughter in her voice.

"Thirty going on twelve would be my guess." He slung an arm around her shoulders as they watched the show.

Chase ducked under the net and came to stand next to him. "You have an unusual dog."

"Not my dog," Kade said. "He's Harper's."

She shook her head. "Was."

"What do you mean?"

"How can I take him away from everything he loves? The lake, you, Everly. She'd never forgive me if I took Duke with me when I leave."

That was true, but the thought of Harper alone somewhere without even her dog sat heavy in his chest. He knew she'd be leaving, but it was something he'd pushed to the back of his mind to deal with when it happened. The idea of not having his best friend in his life made him want to…what? Keep her? How could he? He'd never been able to see himself married with kids. He didn't have what it took for that kind of life.

Even if he tried, he'd screw it up somehow, and he'd cut off his right arm before he'd hurt her. No, he had to let her leave when the time came. And if…when, she found someone, got married, had those children she wanted, he'd be happy for her even if it killed him.

"I'm going in, get lunch started."

"I'll come help," she said.

"No, I got it. When the kids finish playing, tell them to come in for lunch." He needed a little time to get his head back on straight. To remind himself all the reasons why he couldn't keep her.

"Go ahead. Log on," he told Harper.

She sucked her bottom lip between her teeth as her

fingers hovered over the keyboard. "I feel like I'm about to touch a rattlesnake."

"We'll protect you, cariña," Viper said. "Snakes are our specialty."

Cupcake nodded. "That's true. They see us coming, they just roll over and die 'cause they know they're gonna die anyway."

Kade was standing behind her, and he squeezed her shoulders. "All you have to do is log on, nothing else." He glanced at his laptop monitor, open beside hers on the table. "Right, Nick?"

"That's right. Leave it on for about twenty minutes. If I don't see any activity from them, I'll have you log on again in a few hours."

She blew out a breath, then brought her laptop to life. "So it begins," she whispered.

"The sooner it does, the sooner it's over." The muscles in her shoulders were tight knots. He needed to distract her again. "Guys, there's a playoff game on. Why don't you watch that while Harper and I take Duke out in the boat for a little while?"

"Sounds like a plan," Chase said.

When none of them said they wanted to go, too, Kade knew they understood she needed a time-out. "We won't go far. Call me if you hear anything from Nick."

Harper grabbed her jacket, and he hooked Duke's leash to his collar to keep him from running straight into the lake as soon as he made it outside. As they walked down the yard to the dock, he tossed Harper the boat keys. "She's all yours, Captain."

The smile she shot him as she snatched the keys out of the air confirmed his hunch that this was what she needed.

He and Duke followed her into the boat, then he untied the ropes and brought the bumpers in.

"Where to?"

He shrugged. "You're the captain." In a small way, he was giving her control, something she hadn't had since a dirty cop had made her a target.

She grinned. "All right, matey. Hold on to your hat."

For about twenty minutes, she raced the boat over the lake, and her laughter wrapped around him. There, that was his best friend, the girl who laughed easily, who'd always been able to make him feel good. Who had a joy for life until it was taken from her. He would give that back to her by removing the people threatening her.

The plan was to capture them, then turn them over to the law, preferably the feds if they could get the FBI interested in the case. Tristan and Nick thought that was a sure thing considering they were dealing with a dirty cop in the business of making porno movies, drugging the women involved, and that a detective had traveled across state lines for the purpose of beating a witness.

Harper would be a prime witness, and she thought Lisa would testify against them once it was safe to do so. Nick was also digging into their lives and gathering all the dirt he could find on them. Not that what he was collecting could be used to convict them, but Nick knew someone in the bureau who could use the information as the groundwork for an investigation.

The mission objective was to keep Harper safe, and after that, capture their targets without killing them. A lot fewer questions that way, but if it came to a choice between those dirtbags and Harper, he wouldn't hesitate to take them out. Nor would any of his team. He hoped it wouldn't come to that.

"Let's drift for a little, give Duke some water time," he said, raising his voice to be heard over the wind.

She throttled down the boat, and when she shut the engine off, he said, "Duke, go." The goofball dog gave him a silly grin, then took a flying leap into the lake. "He's smarter than he wants you to think he is."

"Maybe he intentionally flunked out of military dog school because he was clever enough to know that he didn't want to be a soldier."

Kade chuckled. "I wouldn't put it past him." He rested his arm on the seat behind her. "Talk to me. What are you worried about?"

"You. The other guys." She picked at the denim covering her knee. "If anyone gets hurt, I don't think I could live with myself."

He'd thought that was part of it. "That's not going to happen, but if it did, it wouldn't be your fault."

"I should have never gone in that warehouse."

"Not gonna argue with that, but you can't undo it. That still doesn't make any of this your fault. Don't take responsibility for the evil these men are up to. What you need to remember is that you did a good thing getting Lisa away before she got hurt or worse. A lot of people would have ignored their misgivings in a situation like that simply because they didn't want to get involved. Because of you, these men aren't going to hurt anyone else. We're going to make sure of it."

"Damn straight." She raised her fist, and he bumped his against it. "Thanks, I guess I needed to hear that. I made a mistake going in the warehouse, but I did get Lisa away from them, and that's what counts."

"Damn straight," he said, giving her words back to her. "Wanna make out?" She laughed, which was his intention.

She straddled him and smiled. "Give me those sugar lips."

"Yes, ma'am." Every time she gave him one of those special smiles meant only for him another layer of ice surrounding his heart melted. Being with her felt like stepping out of a cold winter day and into the sunshine of summer. And now he was a poet. He internally chuckled at his absurd thoughts.

They were just a guy and a girl enjoying each other's company while they could. He put his hands on her hips and gave himself over to the feel of her tongue dueling with his. Just when she slid her hands under his sweat-shirt, his phone chimed. He wanted to ignore it, to see how far she would go, here in the middle of the lake in view of anyone passing by, but it could be one of the guys.

She lifted her head and gave him a rueful smile. "Guess you better get that."

"Yeah." He pulled his phone out to see Viper's name on the screen. "Talk to me."

"You need to come in. Nick's got news."

Chapter Thirty-Six

Theo glared at his cousin. "What the hell's wrong with you? We know where she is now. We can proceed with the plan."

"Why did she turn her computer on after days of keeping it off?"

"Don't know. Don't care. You better not get squirrely on me now, Rex. She's the only thing standing in the way of our putting some big bucks in our bank accounts. Pull that location up on Google Maps."

He and Rex lived in the house Rex had inherited after his mother died. It was a three/two ranch in a middle-class neighborhood. Theo hated it. He was meant for better things. A penthouse overlooking the ocean in South Beach Miami, beautiful women sharing his bed, and his nights spent at the hottest nightclubs as a VIP...that was the life he deserved. Then he could thumb his nose at the old man, a father who'd said from the time his son could understand words that he'd never amount to anything. Didn't matter that Harold Watson was dead—*thank you, Jesus*—Theo knew the old man was watching from hell, just waiting to gloat that his son had turned out to be the loser he'd expected.

When Theo had it all—everything the old man had

wanted for himself but had been too stupid to figure out how to get, the man who couldn't even make a success at petty crimes—Theo was going to go to the bastard's gravesite and spit on the ground. *Showed you, fucker*, he was going to say.

"Gotcha," he said as he studied the satellite view of a small cabin on a lake. The surrounding woods would make it easy to sneak up to the place.

No one walked away from him, a lesson Lisa needed to learn. Yes, he'd had a lapse in judgment when he'd tried to kill Jansen, had let his anger take over. But he was back in control and things would go the way he wanted them to. He needed to wrap this situation up because his vacation time was nearing an end. One more year as a detective dealing with shit that was below him and then he'd have the life he deserved.

He called Stockton. "We got her location," he said when Stockton answered. "You line up some muscle?"

"I've got five. Two of my bouncers, both meaner than a rabid dog, and three more from the Road Killers motorcycle club. Boys you don't want on your bad side."

"Great. Set it up to leave tomorrow after lunch. It's about a three-hour drive, so we'll get there and in place before it gets dark. When their lights go out and they think they're safe for the night, we strike."

"We all leaving together? That don't sound like a good idea."

That don't sound like? Did this man even go to school? Theo tried not to feel superior to the people he came in contact with, but it was damn hard sometimes. "Of course not. Your people will get there first. I'll text you the location. Tell them to set up in the woods. You, me, and Rex will arrive an hour after them. I'm not expecting trouble from one man and a woman but tell your men to come well-armed and to answer their damn phones if we have to call."

After tomorrow night, this problem would be gone. He'd know where Lisa was, he could get back to putting big money in his bank account, and this time next year, he'd be living in a South Beach penthouse, surrounded by beautiful women.

Chapter Thirty-Seven

Nick's intel was good. They now knew who and how many to expect. Based on the conversation between Watson and Rawls, they knew the men thought it was just him and Harper at the cabin. That was also good. These dirtbags weren't going to know what hit them.

Kade faced Harper and slid his hand behind her neck. "Everyone's in place except you. You ready to climb a tree?"

Tristan had called thirty minutes ago to tell them that three bikers wearing the colors of the Road Killers Motorcycle Club were riding through town. A black SUV had been following them, the occupants two beefy men. That had to be the two bouncers. They would reach the area in about twenty minutes. The assumption was that they'd park where they could stash the bikes and car and then come in on foot, thinking they could hide until the bosses arrived. Fools.

"Did I ever tell you how much I love climbing trees?" Harper said.

"I think you failed to mention that." She was nervous but trying to pretend she wasn't. "There's still time to take the boat to the other side of the lake." He wished she would more than he'd ever wished for anything. That thought caused his heart to skip a beat, then two.

Damn him. He was falling for her…like in love. He almost looked up to the top of the trees to see if that evil mythical creature Cupid was up there shooting arrows straight through his heart. Instead, he lowered his gaze to the ground, giving him time to get any sign of his feelings for her out of his eyes and off his face before she saw it. He didn't want her to hope for something he couldn't give her.

But his world had just been rocked off its axis. He wasn't a man who fell in love, hadn't thought so anyway. The joke was on him, but he wasn't laughing. He also wouldn't tell her he was in love with her because it didn't matter. Even being in love her, he'd still find a way to mess it up, and the day would come when she'd hate him. That wasn't acceptable.

She rolled her eyes. "Not happening."

"What's not happening?" Somewhere, he'd lost the thread of their conversation.

She tilted her head and frowned at him. "That I'm not taking a boat to the other side of the lake? Are you okay?"

Negative. He was having an earth-shattering moment. "I'm fine," he lied.

"Good. Give me a kiss before I show you what a badass tree climber I am."

"Be happy to." He pulled her to him, and when their lips met, he closed his eyes and memorized the taste and feel of her. After they'd slayed her dragons tonight, she'd be free to go, and all he'd have left of her was his memories. He forced himself to let her go. "Remember, we don't want any injured or dead if we can help it. Too much paperwork."

"They're safe from me as long as you or one of the guys aren't in danger." She gave him a cheeky grin. "That happens, all bets are off."

As she climbed the tree, he fisted his hands at his sides to keep from pulling her back down, putting her in his boat, and spiriting her away. He ordered his feet to walk, and although it took a few seconds, they finally obeyed. He jogged up the steps to the porch. Duke had his nose pressed against the screen door, and Kade picked up the leash he'd left on the railing.

Duke didn't understand why he was on the leash if they were just going to sit on the porch. He kept trying to go out in the yard and from there he'd go straight to the lake. "Dude, get with the program. We're undercover here." Kade pulled him back from the steps. "Sit." Duke plopped down on his belly with a sigh. Kade rolled his eyes. "I think you intentionally do the opposite of what I tell you."

The first wave of their visitors would try to get eyes on the cabin, and Kade wanted them to report back to Watson and friends that the cabin's occupants didn't suspect anything. He settled in one of the Adirondack chairs, picked up the magazine he'd put on the table, and opened it. There were two beer bottles, one empty, on the table, another prop that added to a picture of a man passing time on the porch of his cabin.

What couldn't be seen was the gun tucked under his sweatshirt, a second gun on the table, hidden by the towel dropped over it, his long gun behind his chair, and the various knives tucked in his clothes and boots. Then there were his teammates, also loaded down with weapons, who their targets would never see until they wanted to be seen.

Kade checked his watch after he had everyone test their comms. Their targets should be close by now, probably hiding their SUV and motorcycles. He let his gaze go to Harper's tree one last time, nodding in satisfaction when he couldn't see any part of her. "You doing okay, foxy lady?"

"Roger dodger, sugar lips."

"Sugar lips?" Viper said.

"From the bottom of my heart, thank you for that one, foxy," Cupcake said. "Ace is officially retired, replaced by sugar lips."

She giggled. "Oops. Forgot the guys were listening in."

"I got movement," Chase said, cutting in. "Stand by."

"And so it begins," Kade murmured. They were going to let the advance crew get eyes on him and report back before taking them out of play. Kade slipped on his sunglasses to hide his eyes. Anyone watching would think he was reading the magazine instead of watching them back.

"Two gorilla-size men passed," Chase said. "They're not wearing biker colors, so those would be the bouncers. The one in a light blue hoodie is carrying an assault rifle and the other, wearing a bright red pullover of all things, has a semiautomatic pistol with a second gun in a holster at his waist. Cupcake, they'll pass you in five." Chase chuckled. "Never thought I'd be saying the word *cupcake* on an operation."

"Hey, it's a good name. Manly," Cupcake replied.

Based on Nick's eavesdropping, the men were under orders to stay out of sight and observe only, so Kade wasn't too concerned that they'd decide to shoot him. He put his feet up on the railing and continued to flip through the pages of the magazine.

"Bikers in the house," Viper said. He was in the woods

on the opposite side of the cabin from Chase and Cupcake. "The three are sticking together and sound like a herd of elephants. They're not even trying to keep their voices down. All three are carrying sawed-off shotguns. I'm thinking this is nothing more than a lark to them."

Kade snorted. "It's amateur night at the circus." He darted a glance at Harper's tree. She was still keeping her head down. *Good girl.*

"Send in the clowns," Cupcake sang. A minute went by then, "My boys will have eyes on you in three…two…one."

Duke lifted his head, ears perked forward, his gaze on the tree line. "Settle down, boy, nothing out there you need to be concerned about." Kade picked up the beer and pretended to drink while he scanned the area that held Duke's attention. There, a flash of red. Duke growled. "Easy, boy."

Kade set the magazine and beer bottle aside, stood, and went to the screen door. He opened it and stuck his head inside. "You decide what you want for dinner, babe?" He let thirty seconds go by. "So I don't need to get the grill ready? Works for me." He'd raised his voice just enough for it to be heard across the yard. Back in his chair with the magazine in his hands, he waited for a report. It wasn't long in coming.

"Blue hoodie is calling someone on his phone," Cupcake said, whispering now, which meant he was breathing down the fools' necks and they didn't even know it. "He's telling them that you're sitting on the porch getting drunk and that the woman is inside the cabin."

"Perfect," Kade said without moving his lips.

"He's off the phone now."

Kade pretended to take a long drink of beer, then stood,

stretched his arms over his head, and loudly belched. He opened the cabin door and as soon as Duke followed him inside, he closed it behind them, and then leaving Duke in the cabin, he went out the back. From there, he slipped into the woods, coming up behind Cupcake. Expecting him, his teammate didn't flinch when Kade put his hand on Cupcake's shoulder to let him know he was here.

"Party time," he quietly said.

Like a well-oiled machine, they came up behind the two bouncers without making a sound. Believing Kade was inside the cabin they just had to keep an eye on, the two fools were talking about a new stripper at the club, arguing over whether her tits were real or fake.

Kade and Cupcake exchanged eye rolls, then Kade nodded. As though enacting a choreographed maneuver, they materialized in front of the bouncers, their weapons aimed at the men before either of them could react.

"One sound, and it will be the last one you make," Kade said. "You." Kade looked at the man on the right with the assault rifle. "Slow and easy, set your gun on the ground, then slide it toward to me. One wrong move, and I will shoot you." Once his order was obeyed, he said, "Lock your hands behind your head." He shifted his gaze to the other man. "Now you. The gun in your hand and the one at your waist, then hands locked behind your head. Same warning."

When both the men's guns were on the ground close to him, he said, "My teammate's going to search you. You know the drill. Spread your feet and keep your hands where they are. I'm not joking around when I say I will kill you if you try anything." He nodded at Cupcake.

Cupcake moved behind them, stuck his gun in his waistband, patted one down, then the other. He found an ankle gun on both of them.

"You," he said to the one on the right again. "Hands behind your back." When that one's hands were secured with zip ties, he repeated the command to the other one.

Once their prisoners were locked down, Kade picked up their weapons. "Follow me. My teammate will be walking behind you. He'd love to shoot you as much as I would, so try anything, utter a sound for any reason, and you won't live to see tomorrow. That's a fact."

He glanced at Cupcake, almost laughing at the disappointment on Cupcake's face that these two bozos had folded faster than a hand of bad cards.

Kade led them deeper into the woods to where Chase was waiting for them. "They're all yours, brother."

Chase would guard them while he and Cupcake went to help Viper round up the bikers. He knew that Chase would give anything to be in on the takedowns, but Chase understood that Kade, Viper, and Cupcake had years behind them of working as a team.

"Welcome to my accommodations, gentlemen," Chase said with an evil grin.

Kade laughed as he walked away. As planned, they'd left the cell phones on the two men for now. Chase would make sure the phones stayed in their pockets.

"Headed your way, Viper."

"Can't miss me. Just head for all the racket these jokers are making."

"Foxy lady, you good?"

"Affirmative. Ready to kick some ass."

He chuckled. "That's my girl." Next to him, Cupcake smirked, and Kade scowled at him. "Just a figure of speech."

"Uh-huh."

He ignored that. To protest would only invite more smirks. They crossed the yard and entered the woods on the other side of the cabin. "Viper, your location?"

Viper gave them his coordinates. "These dumbasses are lost. First they went the wrong way and now they're going in circles."

That explained why the coordinates were a surprise. "We'll double-time it and catch up with you in ten."

A shot rang out about seven minutes later. "That wasn't Viper's gun," Cupcake said.

"I know. Viper, sitrep."

"Fucking clowns. One of them tripped over a log and his shotgun went off."

God save them from fools. "We can hear them yelling at each other now, so we're close." These jokers weren't trying to keep their voices down. "Where are you in relation to them?"

"The east side, between them and you."

"Good. See you in about three." When he and Cupcake reached Viper, the bikers were stationary, arguing over which way to go. "Let's surround them before they get on the move again."

"They stopped and shared a joint a while back, and then one of them handed out some pills, so they're not going to be thinking straight," Viper said.

Cupcake grunted. "They'll be trigger-happy."

"The sooner we got those weapons out of their hands the better." Kade raised a fist, and his teammates bumped theirs to his, then they spread out and surrounded the bikers.

Their argument over which way to go was heating up, their tempers flaring. Much longer and they'd start shooting at each other. Cupcake was right, they were going to be trigger-happy.

"You both in place?" He got affirmatives from his two teammates. "Hey, assholes," he yelled from his cover behind a tree. "You're surrounded. Drop your weapons and put your hands in—" A bullet hit a tree near him. Kade sighed. "Your turn, Viper." The bikers needed to realize they really were surrounded.

"Dudes, you're pissing us off. Do what the man said and drop your weapons." Another shot sounded. "Missed me, dirtbag."

"You should listen to him," Cupcake yelled. "He only has so much patience."

The three fools started wildly shooting in all directions. Kade peered around his tree, picked the man facing in Viper's direction because his shotgun was not in front of him from Kade's point of view, took aim, and put a bullet through the stock.

Splinters of wood hit the man's face, and he screamed as he dropped the gun. "I've been shot!"

"What a big baby," Cupcake said, then did the same thing and took out a second man's weapon.

That man, after dropping his shotgun, took off running. Unfortunately for him, he ran right at Kade, and as he was running past, Kade stuck out his leg and tripped the man. When he was facedown on the ground, Kade stuck his gun to the side of the biker's head. "Freeze, motherfucker." The man froze.

The sounds of weapons firing ended, and a few minutes later, Viper and Cupcake appeared, each pushing a biker in front of them.

"Most fun I've had in a long time," Viper said cheerfully.

Kade laughed. "You're not right in the head, man."

They zip-tied the bikers' hands behind them, and while he and Viper walked their prisoners to the cabin, Cupcake went back to collect their shotguns.

"You can bring your boys out, Chase," Kade said into his comm when they reached the cabin's yard.

When the two bouncers and the bikers met up in the yard, Kade laughed at the shock on their faces. "Something to remember for the future, boys. Never mess with a Delta man."

"Or a SEAL," Chase said.

Kade grinned. "Just had to get that in there, eh?"

"Yeah, I did. Can't let Army take all the credit."

Cupcake and Viper carried all the weapons they'd collected inside the cabin while Kade confiscated one of the men's phones. He asked the man his name. Not surprisingly, the man balked with a brave "Fuck you," but he was prepared for that.

"Cut his ties, partner," he told Chase, who already knew what was going to happen.

By this time, his teammates had returned from stashing the weapons. He held out his hand, and Viper gave him a pair of pruning shears. When the ties were cut, Chase trained his gun on the man while Cupcake and Viper forced their victim's arm out.

"I'll do you a favor, pal. I'll let you keep the important fingers and just take your pinkie." The man tried to pull his hand away, but he was no match for Cupcake and Viper. For a moment, when the man stayed mute, even with the shears biting into his skin, Kade worried that the ruse wasn't going to work. He had no intention of cutting off anyone's fingers, but they needed the names that belonged to the phones.

"Frankie," the man blurted just when Kade was about to pull the shears away.

With a Sharpie, Cupcake wrote the name on the back of the man's phone. "You like dogs, Frankie?" Cupcake said.

Frankie's eyebrows scrunched together. "Who doesn't like dogs? Why?"

"Just wondered." Duke had run out behind Cupcake and Viper and joined them. He sniffed the strangers' legs. Cupcake glanced down at him. "That's good, though. Duke here only bites people who don't like dogs, so you're safe."

He chatted with Frankie for another minute, then moved to the next man and asked that one if he liked cats. He went down the line, getting each man to talk to him by asking silly questions as he wrote names on the back of phones. With the threat of the pruning shears, no one gave them any more trouble.

Kade shared an amused look with Viper. Only Cupcake could get the enemy to chat with him as if they were suddenly besties. That talent had come in handy over the years. There was a reason for getting the men to talk, though. Cupcake could mimic any voice with only a few sentences from his mark. If Watson or one of the other men with him called one of the phones, Cupcake would answer it. Since an incoming call on cell phones could be answered without a password, all they needed to know was who belonged to each one.

"Come with me, gentlemen," Chase said after the five phones were identified with the owner's names.

They loaded them into Kade's boat, and when they were all seated, Viper hog-tied their legs together. Chase would take them to the marina across the lake where Skylar and some of her deputies were waiting for them. That left him, Viper, and Cupcake to deal with Watson and friends. Three against three. Not at all a fair fight for the incoming second wave of clowns.

"You guys got to have all the fun," Harper said over the comms. "I'm bored."

He figured he had about twenty minutes to go steal some kisses before it was game on again. He'd managed to keep Duke out of the lake and had retrieved and clipped on his leash while Cupcake was doing his phone thing. He handed the leash to Viper. "Don't let Duke go in the lake."

Viper smirked. "And where might you be going, sugar lips?"

"My woman's bored. Enough said." He walked away from the laughter of his teammates.

But...*my woman*? Stuff like that had to stop coming out of his mouth.

Chapter Thirty-Eight

Theo couldn't be happier with the way his plan was unfolding. He had five men already on-site who'd just as soon shoot you if you said hello wrong. Kade Church was halfway to drunk, and Harper Jansen, the bitch, was inside the cabin without a clue he was coming for her. They were going to be in and out before anyone could stop them or know who they were.

Harper Jansen had to be rattled by the appearance of US Marshals showing up, looking for her. That had been a brilliant move on his part.

Then there was Rex's surprise. He glanced over his shoulder, to the back seat of Stockton's Hummer. Someday, he was going to have a hot shit Hummer. "I can't believe you got us a drone, cuz. Why didn't you tell me?"

Rex shrugged. "I wasn't sure it would get here in time."

"What the hell is this?" Stockton growled.

"Is what?" Theo faced forward. In the middle of Marsville's Main Street, there was a turquoise Cadillac, nose to the back bumper of a rusted-out pickup that had to be older than the Caddy. The car and truck blocked both lanes through town. The old lady he'd seen talking to the police chief was whopping an older man on the back of his legs with her cane, while a goat chewed on the hem of her dress. The old man looked like he was doing a jig. Any other time, it would be funny, but not today.

"There another way around this hick town?" Stockton said from the driver's seat.

"I'd think so." Theo looked behind them. Even if there was another way, they were now blocked in by the traffic behind them. Theo rolled down his window to yell at them to move their damn vehicles to the side, but the police chief, who he now knew was Kade Church's brother, walked around the Caddy and headed toward them. Theo powered his window up.

The chief stopped at the driver's window and tapped on it. "Roll it down," Theo said when Stockton shot him a what-the-hell-do-I-do-now look. The police chief had never seen them before, so they just had to be cool and not give him a reason to search the Hummer.

"Good afternoon, gentlemen," the police chief said after Stockton lowered his window. He poked his head in and his gaze landed on each of their faces. "Sorry about this. Hope you're not in a hurry."

Stockton grunted.

Theo wanted to strangle him. He leaned around Stockton. "We're good, but you've got a bit of a traffic jam going now. Maybe they could move their vehicles to the side of the road while they duke it out?" Some humor would probably help, so he said, "Might want to pull the goat away from the old broad before the public gets a view of her skinny fanny." He laughed. The chief didn't. Behind him, Rex groaned, and Stockton frowned at him. Nobody had a sense of humor these days.

The chief walked back to the fighting couple, talked to them for a few minutes, and the old woman glanced at them. She gave the man another whack with her cane, then she stomped their way with the goat hopping behind her, still chewing on her dress. Stockton's window was open, and she leaned her arms on the door.

"Chief Church…" She tilted her head as if thinking. "That sounds funny, Chief Church. We don't call him that. He's just Chief to us, but if I just said Chief, you wouldn't know who I meant. The Chief said we're inconveniencing you, and as a member of the town's founding family, I reckon it's my duty to apologize to you boys." She pulled what looked like tickets from inside the neck of her dress. "Welcome to Marsville, the home of the Marsville UFO Museum. These are good for twenty percent off admission." She handed Stockton the coupons.

The old man she'd been arguing with walked up behind her. "Give me Billy back, Miss Mabel."

"I don't have your goat, Earl. You need to keep that menace to the town locked up."

"You got him right behind you, Miss Mabel. Give him back."

She turned, and the goat hopped around behind her. "See, no goat. Maybe you should go have a lie down, old man."

The old man reached down and wrapped his arms around the goat. "Come on, Billy. It's dinnertime. Let's go home." He pulled the goat away, and a swath of dress tore off. The goat chewed on the material as the two walked away.

The police chief returned. "Miss Mabel, you leave those men alone. We need to get your car moved out of the road."

"And you need to tell Earl to stop making sudden stops in front of me if he doesn't want me to run into him." She tapped on Stockton's shoulder. "You boys make sure to visit the museum."

"What just happened?" Stockton said as the woman marched away. He dropped the discount coupons in the cup holder.

"They really do have a UFO museum," Rex said. "I'd like to see it." When Theo glanced back, Rex turned his laptop around to show the picture on the screen of the museum. "Cool, huh?"

Theo rolled his eyes. "Sure." What he wanted was to get to that cabin. "Call one of your men," he told Stockton. "Make sure everything's still quiet over there."

"Call Frankie," Stockton said to his Bluetooth.

"Yo," a man said. "What's up, boss?"

"Anything changed since I last talked to you?"

"Nah. Dude's still sitting on his porch with his dog, drinking beer. Ain't seen the woman, but he goes to the door and talks to her off and on."

"Keep your eyes open, and if something does change, call me." Stockton disconnected. "This is gonna be a piece of cake."

If they ever got there. Theo put his hand on the door handle, intending to get out and lend his help in getting the road cleared. But the chief got in the Caddy, started it, and backed it to the curb, so Theo settled back in his seat. As Stockton slowly drove past the Caddy, the police chief waved. Theo lifted two fingers to his forehead in a salute. What he'd like to do was give the man, and the whole damn town, the finger for putting them almost thirty minutes behind schedule.

"If you ask me, that was weird," Rex said.

Theo ignored his worrywart cousin. He also stopped listening to Stockton talk about his latest squeeze and her many talents in bed. The man had no class. When he had enough money to move to South Beach, Theo decided he was going to find classier friends.

"Start looking for a place to hide the Hummer," he said when they were a few miles from the cabin. About a half mile from the gravel road that led to the cabin they found a break in the trees that was big enough to drive the Hummer into. "Stick the keys under the floor mat."

"Why?" Stockton said.

"In case one of us needs to move it to another location." Or should he, Theo, need a fast getaway.

"Either one of you decides it's a good idea to take off without me, I will hunt you down," Stockton said.

"We're all in this together. No one's bailing on the others." Except him, if it came to saving his neck. "You know the plan, Stockton. Go find your men. Rex will meet up with the bikers. When we have the cabin surrounded, we come out of the woods with weapons drawn. Even if Church is armed, he won't dare fire his gun being this outnumbered."

"What if he's inside by the time we get there?" Stockton said.

"Simple. We order him to come out. Once he's neutralized, we take the woman. You brought ski masks like I told you, right?" They both showed him their masks. "Good. Go find your men. I'll call you when it's time to make an appearance."

The best plans were kept simple, and his was about as simple as it could get. Church wouldn't dare try anything with eight men pointing guns at him.

"What are we going to do with Church?" Rex asked after Stockton left. "I don't want any part of killing."

"Tie him up and leave him breathing. He has no idea who

we are, and with the masks, he won't be able to describe us. Before you go find the bikers, let's take a look-see with your drone. It'll help to know if Church is still on his porch."

Turned out Rex's drone came in mighty handy. Without it, he never would have found Harper Jansen hiding in a tree. "Change of plans."

"We're taking off?" Rex said hopefully.

"Yeah, as soon as I get Jansen."

"Damn it, Theo. Why do you think she's in that tree with a rifle? Because they're expecting us."

"You go wait in the Hummer. I'll be there in fifteen minutes with the woman. Stockton and his men can find their own way home."

"Tell me you're kidding. Stockton already said he'd hunt you down if you left without him."

"Not kidding. Go get the Hummer ready to leave." His cousin knew his way around computers, for sure, but he thought small. It was time for Theo to strike out on his own. He'd just have to move up his timeline for heading south. Harper Jansen just got promoted to a starring role in his movies.

Because he was brilliant, he worked out the details in his head for leaving immediately with enough cash to seed his new business. Stockton was going to be beyond pissed, not only because his Hummer would be gone, but when he finally made it back to his office and looked in his safe, the pile of cash he kept in there would be missing. Wasn't his fault Stockton had let him watch the man open his safe several times. Theo grinned as he slipped through the woods to retrieve his star, then it was off to the new life that awaited him. What should his new name be? Definitely something cool.

* * *

Rex retrieved his drone, packed it back into its travel case, then loaded it in the Hummer. His cousin had lost touch with reality. Theo had always had a big ego and an even bigger sense of entitlement. Rex had gone along with Theo's schemes because his cousin really was smart. If only he'd use those brains of his for schemes that weren't going to get them killed. He was crossing a line today that Rex wasn't willing to follow.

Rex had worried this day would come, the day he finally accepted that Theo was too far gone to save. If he didn't get away from his cousin, he'd either end up in prison or dead. Neither appealed, so he'd prepared for it.

There was a passport with his new identity, along with money he'd been saving the past year, in a locker at his gym. In three hours, he'd be back in Fayetteville, putting his contingency plan into action. He had his laptop with him, so he wouldn't even go home. As soon as he picked up the bag he'd stashed in the locker, he'd take a cab to the bus station where he'd make sure the agent noticed him when he bought a ticket to New York. Then he'd walk a mile or so from the bus station before catching a taxi to the airport, where he'd purchase a ticket with his new identity. If his cousin was still alive after today, Theo would never think to look for him in Thailand.

"Sorry, cousin," he said as he backed the Hummer out of its hiding place. It didn't have to come down to this, but the blame was all on Theo. As Rex drove away in Stockton Rawls's Hummer, excitement for his new adventure grew with each mile he put behind him.

Chapter Thirty-Nine

Harper had a new appreciation for military snipers. She was bored, this piece of plywood was as hard as a rock, her muscles were screaming for her to move around, and she really had to pee. How did combat soldiers stay in positions like this on uncomfortable surfaces for hours at a time?

She stretched one leg and then the other. There hadn't been any communication from the guys since Chase left with those men and the team had returned to their assigned places. She wanted to talk to them, but it would only be to relieve her boredom, and that would distract them from their jobs.

"You still doing okay, foxy lady?"

She grinned. It was like Kade was reading her mind. "Just bored. Other than that, I'm great." Except for her sore muscles and needing the bathroom, but he didn't need to worry about her. She leaned around the trunk of the tree to see him and panicked a little when he wasn't on the porch where he was supposed to be. "Where are you?"

"At the side of the house with Viper. We caught us another snake."

"That's good. Only two more to go, right?"

"Yeah, and it's only a matter of minutes before we have them, too."

"Ace, the Hummer that these jokers arrived in took off down the road," Cupcake said over the comms.

"You see who was in it?"

"Negative. Just caught the back of it headed down the road."

"Looks like your friends left you hanging in the wind, Mr. Rawls," Kade said.

"Don't know what you're talking about. I was just doing a little deer hunting."

Harper noted that the man ignored the fact that Kade knew his name. But it was over. Well, until they somehow caught up with Theo Watson and his cousin. She wasn't going to give up on that happening.

As she listened to Kade and Viper question Rawls, she picked up the rifle, then climbed down the tree. One foot had fallen asleep, and it felt like thousands of needles were attacking it. She set the rifle on the ground so she could massage her foot. "I'm going to the cabin." Before she peed in her pants.

"No! Stay in place until—"

She didn't hear the rest because her comms were ripped out of her ears before Kade finished what he was saying. A hand wrapped around her mouth, a body pressed against her back, and cold metal dug into her cheek. She froze.

"Hello, love. Miss me?"

That voice. She'd never forget it.

"I'm going to remove my hand, but you call out to your boyfriend, and I'll shoot you."

"He's going to kill you, Theo." Who left in the Hummer?

"Ah, so you learned my name. Shows you care. Here's what's going to happen. We're going to walk away. If you open your mouth for any reason, it will be the last thing you ever do."

"Did you not hear what I said? You should go while you can."

He pressed the gun so hard into her cheek that tears stung her eyes. "I'll forgive you that one, but only that one. Do not speak, or I will shoot you. Doubt me, and you die. Start walking." He dropped her comms to the ground and stomped on them. "Walk."

He picked up the rifle, put his handgun to her back, then pushed her forward with the barrel. She believed him and didn't see she had a choice. The only thing that kept her from having a meltdown was knowing Kade would find her. She'd made a possibly deadly mistake leaving her perch in the tree before Kade said it was safe to do so. He wasn't going to be happy with her. And she still had to pee.

They came to a clearing, and he put a hand on her shoulder, pulling her to a stop. She could see a road, but she wasn't sure if it was the road to the cabin. Even if she could break away from him, she wouldn't know which direction to go.

"I'm going to kill Rex when I find him," her captor snarled.

Cupcake had said he'd seen the Hummer that the men had arrived in leaving, so Theo's cousin had taken off and left him behind? She'd laugh if there wasn't a gun poking into her back. By now, Kade would know she was missing, and the guys would be looking for her.

"Change of plans," he said. "Move."

They crossed the road and entered the woods on the other side. She guessed it was five minutes later when they came to a shallow creek. The sound of the water almost made her say the hell with it and pee in her pants. "I have to pee." It killed her to even say that to him, but she couldn't wait much longer.

"Don't care. Think your boyfriend will use that dog to try to find you?" Without waiting for an answer, he pushed her. "Walk down the middle of the creek."

She turned to face him for the first time since he'd taken her hostage, this man who'd become a recurring nightmare in her life. She intended to explain to him that she really had to pee, but the change in him since she'd last seen him was so shocking that she forgot what she was going to say.

The man who'd shown up at her home in Fayetteville and then at her father's house had been scary enough with his threats and cold eyes. The man standing in front of her now was still scary, but in a whole other way. His eyes were dead pools. There was nothing human left in them.

She was officially frightened out of her mind. Because she couldn't look into those zombie eyes another second without losing all hope that she'd survive this monster, she turned away from him and walked down the middle of the creek.

Chapter Forty

"No! Stay in place until I come for you." Kade expected an immediate response from Harper. It didn't come. "Foxy lady?" Nothing. "Harper, report in." Nothing again. Her comms must have stopped working. "You got this asshole?" he asked Viper.

"Yup. Go get your lady."

The minute he let go of Rawls, the man made a run for it. Both he and Viper tackled him before he got two feet away. Kade rolled away, stood, put his foot on Rawls's back, and pressed down hard. "Don't try that again." He nodded at Viper, then headed around the cabin to get Harper.

"Ace, you need to get to Harper's tree."

There was urgency in Cupcake's voice, and Kade ran to the tree. The first thing he saw were her smashed comms. "Where is she?" She wouldn't have destroyed the comms, which meant either Watson or Sorenson had her. Unless an unknown had left in the Hummer, leaving Watson and Sorenson behind, which would mean both men had her.

Cupcake scowled at the destroyed comms. "I don't know. After I saw the Hummer leave, I walked down the road to come back. I didn't pass anyone."

"You couldn't tell how many people were in the car?"

It was startling how calm his voice sounded considering he was a raging volcano inside.

"No, it was too far away, but she had to still be here because she talked to us after I told you the Hummer was gone."

Okay, that was good. She was nearby. He prayed that was true. "Tell Viper to tie Rawls to a tree or something, then both of you start searching." He took out his phone and called his brother.

"Was about to call you," Tristan said on answering. "Your three bad actors just passed through town. Miss Mabel ran into the back of Earl's truck again, and—"

"Harper's missing. Send someone to pick up Stockton Rawls. I need you and anyone else you can pull off duty to come here so we can form search teams. We're as sure as we can be that she's still in the area."

"Stand by." Tristan barked orders to someone, then came back on the line. "My people are on the way. Skye's at the jail booking your prisoners in. Chase is with me, and we're both coming to you. Do you know what happened?"

"All I know is that one or both of those walking dead men have her. Call me when you get here." He disconnected.

"Dude's trussed up like a Thanksgiving turkey," Viper said, joining them. "What's the plan?"

"The fucking plan is to find her." He blew out a breath. "Sorry, but I'm a volcano about to blow."

Cupcake put his hand on Kade's shoulder. "We're gonna get our girl back. That's the only option."

"Damn straight. Tristan's sending help to search. When his people get here, pick one of them to take Rawls to the jail. If I put eyes on him again, I might kill him." He glanced at his watch. "Whoever took her has a ten-minute head start on us, but we're counting on them still being in the area since the Hummer must have left without one of them… Watson or Sorenson." From what they'd learned of the men, he'd prefer it to be Sorenson, but he had a bad feeling it was Watson.

"We gonna split up to look for her?" Viper asked.

"Affirmative, at least until we get a clue of their direction. You take the north side of the cabin, Cupcake, take the south. I'm going to walk along the road in case they crossed over it somewhere. Let me know if you find anything."

His two teammates took off in opposite directions, and Kade headed for the cabin to get Duke and something of Harper's. She kept her dirty clothes in a white cloth bag in the bathroom. He dumped the contents on the floor, grabbed a sock, then raced back outside, taking Duke to Harper's tree.

He held the sock in front of Duke's nose. "Find Harper." This had to work. "Duke, find Harper. Don't let me down, boy."

Duke snatched the sock away, then put his nose to the ground. For a few minutes, he made circles around the tree as if the scents confused him, and Kade thought he might be having a heart attack. What if Duke couldn't track her? After running around the tree many times, Duke veered toward the road, and with his nose and Harper's sock dragging on the ground, he took off.

"Viper, on me. Duke's picked up her scent." He hoped to hell that was what Duke was tracking. "Cupcake, when my brother gets here tell him to have one of his men take Rawls to the jail and then you and the rest of his people start searching in case Duke's wrong."

"Headed to you," Viper said.

"Copy that," Cupcake said.

Please, dog. Do your thing.

Chapter Forty-One

Harper guessed they'd been walking down the middle of the creek for almost a mile. Her Chuck Taylors and socks were soaked, and her feet were freezing. Walking through the water wasn't helping her problem. "Please, can we stop a minute so I can go behind a tree and pee?" Maybe she could manage to get far enough away to run.

His sigh sounded angry. "You can go right here."

She hadn't turned around to ask because she didn't want to see those dead eyes again, but she did now. "That's not happening, asshole." There was a good-size tree to her left, and to hell with him. She marched out of the creek, heading for that tree. He could shoot her if he wanted, although he wouldn't. She'd already figured out that she was his ticket out of this mess. Or so he thought, but he hadn't factored in Kade and his teammates. Or her determination that he was going to answer for his crimes.

"Stop right there."

"Go to hell." When she reached the tree, she looked back at him. "You stop right there. If you keep following me, I'll just go to the next tree and the next one and the next one."

He glared at her, but he stopped. "You have one minute."

"Aren't you generous?" She shouldn't be goading him, but he was making her angry.

"You have a mouth on you, Harper," he said as she walked behind the tree. "It's not attractive."

She really hated hearing her name come out of his mouth. Partially hidden from view, she did her business. As she pulled her jeans back up, she scanned the area around her. There was a thicket of rhododendron bushes about twenty feet from her. If she could make it to them before he caught her, she had a good chance of getting away.

"Don't even think about it."

How had he sneaked up on her like that, and how had he known she planned to make a run for it? She flinched—darn it—at seeing his gun inches from her face. "Think about what?" She was proud of her voice for not trembling. That was something, anyway. As she glanced down at her jeans to button them closed, she noticed the necklace Chase had given her. She'd forgotten about it, being a hostage and all.

Okay, new objective. Get him to admit to what he'd done to Lisa, but more importantly, his involvement in Abby Warton's death. With his gun pointed at her, she had no choice but to walk back down to the creek. She used to love creeks, but he'd ruined that for her. Another thing to never forgive him for.

They traveled another ten or so minutes, while she mentally ran through things to say that would have him confessing the crimes that would send him to prison for the remainder of his rotten life.

"What's that?" he said, interrupting her mentally planning his demise. "Go up there."

She looked up to where he was pushing her. A structure that appeared to be nothing more than someone's hunting shack was halfway up the hill. Her closet was bigger, and she shuddered at the thought of being in tight quarters with this creep.

He poked her with the gun. "Move."

There was a tiny stem on the necklace that Chase had told her would activate it. While her back was to the creepo, she reached up and pushed in the stem. She sure hoped this worked. When they reached the shack, he kicked his foot at the door to open it, startling her, and she yelped.

"In."

He pushed her, and she stumbled in. The two windows, one on each side of the shack, were so dirty that they hardly let any light in. It didn't smell so great, and she wrinkled her nose. There was a paper-thin mattress on a rusted metal frame, a small table, two metal folding chairs, and that was about it. Whoever stayed here must have used the woods for a bathroom and the creek for water.

"Sit."

Although tempted to give him a snarky salute, she turned her back on him instead and went to one of the chairs. She wasn't about to sit on that filthy mattress. He pulled the other chair to the opposite wall, turned it to face her, and sat. Before she could decide how to get him to talk, he dropped the rifle and his handgun on the mattress, pulled out his phone, angrily punched the screen, and then put it to his ear.

"Answer the fucking phone, Rex. Damn it. Call me back."

"Trouble in paradise?" she said when he slammed his phone down on his leg.

"Shut up."

"You should believe me when I tell you that Kade Church is going to kill you."

He laughed. "You think a blockhead soldier is smarter than me?"

Sure, he could go ahead and laugh, but she'd seen the flash of fear in his eyes. It was the first sign of life she'd seen in them.

"Where's Lisa?" he said, staring at her with those zombie eyes.

"Beats me. She and Abby Warton decided it was in their best interest to remove themselves from your reach, so they took off to wherever they went." She shrugged. "They said I was better off not knowing." It was a risk putting Abby's name out there, but she hoped to make him angry enough to let something slip…like how he or one of his partners had supplied the drugs that killed Abby.

He reared up, strode to her, and wrapped his hand around her neck. "Stop lying. Abby Warton's dead."

"Because you killed her. Are you going to kill me, too?" She knew it wasn't smart to taunt a man who was coming unhinged right in front of her eyes, but she had to get him to say something that would implicate him in Abby death.

"It might come to that if you don't shut up." He let go of her, stepped back, and stared at her. "But since you're my new star, I'll probably keep you alive. Maybe I should test the merchandise, make sure it's up to my standards."

He giggled, and it was such a weird and creepy sound that Harper shivered. And when his gaze roamed over her, she slid her hands under her legs to keep from crossing her arms over her breasts. Whatever she did, she couldn't show him any weakness.

"Star for what?" Oh, she knew, but she needed him to say it so she'd have it on record. He also hadn't denied that he'd killed Abby.

"My movies. Lift your shirt up. Show me your tits. Need to make sure you're porno material."

Not in this lifetime, creepo. She forced herself not to glance at the guns he'd left on the mattress, not to clue him in that she was aware of them. Could she get to one of them before him? Just as she decided to go for it, his phone chimed, and he moved back to the chair, taking away her chance.

He frowned as he stared at the screen, then he stuck his phone back in his pocket. "That was my captain. He probably wants me to cut my vacation short. I'm his best detective. You know why?"

She shook her head, hoping he'd keep talking, maybe say something incriminating. And the more he talked, the more time that gave Kade to find them.

"Because I close all my cases. No cold files because of me."

"That's not always possible." She didn't think it was, anyway.

"Sure it is, as long as all the evidence to close a case is there."

Was he saying… "You plant the evidence you need to do that?"

"I do what I have to do to be the best."

"Like you did with Abby Warton?"

A sly smile crossed his face. "Wouldn't you like to know?"

Yes, she would. But he'd as good as admitted it. She hoped the device in the necklace was working and was recording this conversation.

His phone dinged with a message alert, and he took it back out. As he listened, he lifted rage-filled eyes to her. Like he'd done before, he slammed his phone down on his leg. "Skylar Morgan. She's the sheriff, right?"

He looked like he was seconds from going on a murderous rage. "Yes, why?"

"The bitch called my captain, told him he needed to take another look at Abby Warton's death. That it wasn't an accidental overdose. Do you know what I had to do to make it look like that?"

She shook her head again. The good stuff was finally coming, but her fear of this man was growing by the minute.

"Doesn't matter. I won't be going back. We need to go."

Go where and how? Did he think he could just walk his way out of this mess? She needed to get to those weapons. He snapped his fingers. "Right. We don't have a car." He took out his phone and made another call.

"Damn it, Rex, you better call me back. If you try to pull a fast one on me, I'll kill you. I swear I will." He threw his phone. It hit the wall, then bounced onto the bed. His gaze landed on her. "You see any men sneaking around? There should be a couple of motorcycles and another car somewhere around here."

"No." It probably wasn't a good idea to tell him the men were all sitting in a jail now. It was possible that the motorcycles and the car were still nearby since she doubted Kade and his teammates had taken the time to deal with those instead of looking for her.

"By now my friends will have your boyfriend taken care of. Get up."

It was now or never. She stood, took a step, and pretended to trip. The room was so small that her upper body fell onto the bed. She grabbed his gun and managed to get her finger on the trigger before he landed on her back.

They fought over the weapon, and although he was stronger than her, rage fueled her, and she felt like she had superhuman strength…until he fisted his hand and hit her above her right eye. Something sharp sliced her skin, and blood flowed into her eye. White stars danced in her vision and pain burst through her head. She reflexively let go of the gun and brought her hands to her face.

"I should kill you right now, bitch." He straddled her and traced the shell of her ear with the barrel of the gun. "But lucky you. My new star gets to live another day. Pull another trick like that, and I don't care how perfect your tits are, I'll put a bullet through your brain."

She tried to buck him off her back, but he just laughed. She'd never in her life thought she'd want to kill someone, but she could murder him and still sleep at night. Blind in one eye because of the blood, and with a skull that felt like it was going to explode, she gave up and let her body go limp. She wanted to cry over her failed attempt and the pain in her head, but she refused to give him the satisfaction.

He moved off her. "If you don't want my fist in your face again, get up."

When she pushed up, she noticed the ring with a black stone he wore. The ring was what had cut her when he'd hit her, and that stone had to be his dried-up evil black heart.

He grabbed the rifle from the floor, then waved the hand holding the revolver at the door. "Walk."

She swiped the sleeve of her hoodie across her eye, trying to clear the blood away. "You won't get away with this."

"I already have. You should be thanking me. I'm taking you to South Beach, where the rich and famous play. Think outside of your boring little box, Harper. Yours can be the name every man fantasizes about when they wrap their hand around their cock while they watch one of your movies."

"You're a disgusting pig."

"We need to come up with a sexy name for you," he went on as if she hadn't just called him a pig. "Maybe we'll go with just one name, you know, like Cher does. Cherry? What about Kitty? Yeah, I like that one. Kitty. Pussy. Get it?" He laughed, amused with himself.

Kade was going to find them before they ever reached South Beach, but if this sick pervert managed to evade him, he had to sleep at some point, and when he did, one way or another, she was going to kill him.

Chapter Forty-Two

"Can dogs track through water?" Viper asked when they came to a shallow creek.

"I don't know." Duke crossed the creek, sniffed the ground on the other side, then turned around and came to a stop in the middle of the water. He looked up at Kade as if asking, *What now?*

"Find Harper." Kade didn't know what else to say. Obviously, whoever had Harper had used the creek to throw them off the scent. Which way did they go, though? Up or down it? Duke lowered his head, and after a few seconds, he headed up the creek, dragging the sock through the water. "Hope he knows what he's doing."

"Why don't I go the other way?" Viper said. "In case he's wrong."

"Yeah, good idea."

They'd been following the creek for about ten minutes when Duke left the water. Nose to the ground, he trotted to a large tree. There were footprints both going and coming. One pair was larger than the other, and Kade hoped the smaller pair belonged to Harper.

Duke went to the back of the tree and whined. Kade studied the footprints. The larger ones stopped a few feet from the tree, and the smaller ones stopped where Duke was standing. The leaves on the ground were wet, and he realized that Harper had hid behind the tree to go to the bathroom while her captor waited only a few feet from her. Rage burned his blood that she'd been humiliated like that.

At least he now knew they'd come this way. "Come, Duke. This was just a pit stop." Duke didn't want to leave, so Kade picked him up and returned to the creek. To make sure Duke didn't try to go back to the tree, he carried the dog a few yards through the water before putting him down.

How long had they walked in this creek? Harper's feet had to be freezing. Whoever had her—he didn't care if it was one man or a hundred—was going to pay for both humiliating her and torturing her, even if that was only for the cold feet. He tried raising Viper on the comms, but he was too far away now and didn't respond.

When his phone rang with the ringtone he'd assigned Tristan, Kade answered, but kept walking. "You here?"

"Yes. Colton—sorry, but I just can't refer to a man with muscles the size of a tree trunk as Cupcake. Colton's sending my men out to search in a grid pattern. Where are you?"

Kade pulled up his coordinates on his smartwatch and gave them to Tristan. "Duke's following her scent. I hope that's what he's following. We think either Watson or Sorenson has her, but it could be both."

"I'll leave Colton to organizing my men to search, and I'll come catch up with you. Colton told us about the Hummer leaving, so Chase is on the phone with his brother. Nick's trying to find the Hummer."

"Good. I don't want any of these people getting away."

Duke still seemed to be following a scent, but Kade couldn't image they'd walked through the creek for much longer. He should have put a tracker on Harper. That had to have been them at the tree, though, so he'd keep going. But what if they'd doubled back, and Duke had missed finding where they left the creek?

He'd never been indecisive on an operation, but he was questioning his every step now. At this point, he was trusting a dog that had flunked out of military dog school because everything was a game.

"Duke!" When Duke glanced over his shoulder at him, Kade said, "Tell me you know what you're doing." His imagination was running away with him because he could have sworn that Duke rolled his eyes before facing forward and continuing up the creek.

Another five minutes passed, and Kade was seriously considering turning around when Duke stopped and circled back a few feet. All this time, he hadn't let go of Harper's sock, and with it hanging from his mouth, he lifted his head and stared up the hill. Kade followed the dog's gaze and saw a shack that looked like it could collapse any second. Duke whined and ran to the end of his leash.

"Hush. Sit." Duke obeyed both commands, which was a miracle since the dog always did the opposite of what he was told. Kade had the brief thought that Harper was right, that he'd intentionally failed every test the military had given him. Something to think about and laugh over with Harper later. Because there would be a later.

"Come," he said, pulling Duke's leash to the opposite side of the creek from the shack. Time to do what Ace did best, and that was to plan a rescue mission. In his career as a Delta Force operator, he'd only lost two hostages, on an operation that had gone south almost from the start because of bad intel. He was not going to add to that number.

He might not be boyfriend material, and he was no way, no how the man for Harper, but she wasn't going to die on his watch. She was the best person he knew, and she deserved to have her dreams of a man who could give her what she needed and all those kids she wanted. Never mind that he wanted to tell the man to go find some other woman, and if the dude dared to mistreat her, he'd be hearing from Kade.

"You need to stay here," he told Duke as he tied the end of the leash to a tree branch. "I'm going to go get your girl so you can give her the sock. You did good." When Duke whined, Kade wrapped his hand around the dog's muzzle. "Quiet."

With his gun ready in his hand, he faded into the woods and made his way up the hill to the shack. When he was even with the building, he crouched next to a tree. Were they even in there? The one visible window was impossible to see through because of the grime that covered it. There was probably a window on the other side, but it would be as dirty as this one.

Watson or Sorenson, whichever had her, was armed with at least Harper's rifle, but probably with a handgun, too. They wouldn't have come for her without being armed. He'd give his left nut to be able to see in that window. If he barged in, and the man with her had a gun in his hand, he could shoot her before Kade got to him. That was not going to happen.

He thought for a minute, then made a decision. The first thing he needed was intel, and for that, he was going to have to get next to the door. It was broken near the bottom, and Kade guessed that it had been kicked open. Because of the damage, there was a gap between the door and the frame where he could get a visual on the inside of the shack.

"Viper, you copy?" he said, trying one more time to reach his teammate. No response. Tristan was on the way, but it could take another twenty or so minutes for him to get here, and not knowing what might be happening to Harper inside that place, he wasn't waiting.

He was on his own. *It's a go.* He'd taken two steps when the cabin door opened, so he eased back behind the tree. Harper walked out, and was that blood running down her face? Whoever hurt her was dead and just didn't know it. Theo Watson stepped out behind her. He had Harper's rifle slung over one shoulder and a handgun pressed against her back.

That would be a big mistake on Watson's part if it was Kade or any one of his teammates. That close, they'd have possession of that gun before Watson knew what was happening. Unfortunately, Harper hadn't been trained in that kind of warfare. Watson's finger was on the trigger, and that left Kade with few options. Even if he fired, killing Watson instantly, the man could involuntarily fire the gun. So Kade would have to follow them and watch for the opportunity to rid the world of a monster who preyed on women.

No one else exited the cabin, so it was just Watson, which was good news. Kade melted back into the woods to call his brother. The last thing he needed was for Tristan to stumble on the pair unprepared.

"I've found Harper," he said when Tristan answered. "Watson has her, and he's armed. I want you to stop wherever you are now and find a place out of sight where you can still see the creek. If they come your way, do not try to stop them. I've got this."

"Can't think of a better man for the job."

That was it, all Tristan said before he disconnected. Damn but he loved his brother. Before Kade joined the Army, he'd been a punk with an attitude, and even then, Tristan had had faith in him. He still needed to thank his brother for that.

As he pocketed his phone, a shot rang out, and a dog yelped. He ran back to the tree he'd hidden behind, his gaze first searching for Harper. Watson was behind her with his gun pointed at her back as he had been before.

Movement on the other side of the creek caught his attention, and he frowned at seeing Duke racing toward the woods, his leash trailing behind him. A leash that was shorter than it should be. The cunning dog had chewed it in half to free himself. He must have tried to get to Harper, and Watson had shot at him. Harper had told him that one of Duke's problems when the military was trying to train him was that he freaked out every time he heard a gun fired, that they never could get him used to it.

There was nothing Kade could do about Duke at the moment, so he turned his attention back to Watson and Harper. She was yelling at him for shooting at the dog, and Kade wanted to tell her not to provoke the man. Watson's gaze was darting around him. He correctly assumed that if a dog dragging a leash was in the area, so was the owner. Did Watson know who that owner was? Kade hoped not.

Duke had disappeared into the woods and would probably head back to the cabin, where he'd consider it safe. But Kade had missed the perfect opportunity to take Watson out. If he hadn't been on the phone with his brother and had been watching when Watson turned his gun to Duke, Kade would have had the perfect shot. Regret was a waste of energy, and he dismissed the missed opportunity from his mind.

"Show yourself," Watson yelled. "Come out and drop your weapon."

The man was delusional if he thought that was going to happen. If only Harper would drop to the ground, but Kade had no way of telling her to do that. It could very well come down to risking a shot in the hopes Watson didn't pull the trigger.

Movement from above caught his attention. What the hell was Duke doing? The dog came out of the woods behind Watson and Harper, slowly and soundlessly creeping up to them. As he neared them, he lowered his belly almost to the ground, and Kade was reminded of a wolf stalking his prey.

The game had just changed, and now he had a dog on a mission to factor into the equation. *What are you going to do, Duke?* There was nothing Kade could do but be ready for whatever happened.

Watson was still stopped and still had his gun pressed to Harper's back as his gaze searched the woods on one side and then the other. "I'll shoot her if you don't show yourself. Come out with your hands above your head."

"You need to worry about what's coming at your back, pal," Kade quietly said as he stepped into view. "You shoot her, I shoot you. Let her go and you get to live."

Duke was about ten feet from them now, and Kade raised his gun and aimed it at Watson's forehead, the only part of him visible as he stood behind Harper. He estimated he was forty yards—give or take—from them, close to the Glock's maximum range. It would be the most critical shot of his life with a variable he couldn't predict…a dog.

Chapter Forty-Three

Had Kade turned Duke loose? Harper couldn't imagine he'd do that, not with Theo having a gun. Thank God Theo had missed when he'd shot at Duke. Hopefully, Duke would stay out of sight. She'd noticed his shortened leash and wondered what that was about.

She'd yelled at Theo when he'd shot at Duke, and she'd been too concerned about Duke to realize she should have done something...like spin around and knee him in the balls while he was distracted. If she'd done that, he probably would have dropped the gun. She wouldn't have hesitated to shoot him if she could have gotten ahold of it. Before Theo Watson, she couldn't imagine aiming a weapon at a person and pulling the trigger, but she sure could now.

Duke was proof that Kade was around somewhere, though, and knowing that was a relief beyond imagination. She didn't know how he'd found her, but she had never doubted he would. She wished she still had her comms so he could tell her what he wanted her to do.

Should she try to do something, and if so, what? Or would Kade not want her to do anything that would interfere with whatever he intended? Kade would never be this indecisive, he'd see what needed to be done and then he'd do it. She needed to think like him. She inwardly snorted. Like that was possible. He'd had years of training that made him the elite warrior he was. All she knew how to do was find housing for military personnel and their families.

The best thing she could do was nothing and trust that Kade would do what he did best, that he'd rescue her like he had so many others in situations even worse than hers. And she did trust him...with her life. A calmness settled over her for the first time since Theo had put his hand over her mouth back at the tree.

"I'll shoot her if you don't show yourself. Come out with your hands above your head," Theo yelled.

Harper almost laughed. He was a fool if he thought Kade would walk out of the woods with his hands in the air. Theo Watson, if he was smart, would drop to his knees and beg for mercy.

He poked her with the gun barrel. "Tell him to come out."

"You think it's just him in the woods? His entire Delta Force team is here. You're surrounded by men who eat cowards like you for breakfast." Of course, she didn't know if Cupcake and Viper were out there, too, but it was likely.

"Shut the fuck up. One of them tries to—"

"You shoot her, I shoot you. Let her go and you get to live," Kade said, stepping into view. He raised his gun and pointed it at them.

A low growl sounded behind them, and without thinking, she turned to see what was happening. Theo had turned, too, and they both froze at seeing Duke, his teeth bared, flying through the air at them.

At the same moment Duke's teeth latched on to Theo's arm, a shot rang out. Not knowing where it came from,

Harper dropped to the ground, but when she saw Theo's gun land a few feet from her, she scrambled over to it. She grabbed it, then rolled over and aimed it at him. Duke had his teeth in Theo's arm and was shaking it for all he was worth. Theo was punching the dog in his throat and on his face, despite all the blood spewing from where half of Theo's ear was missing.

"You hit my dog one more time, and I'm going to—"

"I got this," Kade said from behind her as he reached over and took the gun away from her.

She looked up into the eyes of the man she hadn't been sure she'd ever see again, and she'd never been so happy in her life. She waved her fingers at him. "Hi."

He grinned. "Hi."

Don't ever leave me, she wanted to say, but she didn't. He wasn't hers to keep. She sat up and watched in amazement as Kade ordered Duke to stand down, and the dog instantly obeyed. "Is Duke okay?"

Kade kicked away her rifle, then grabbed Theo's arm and pulled him to his feet with the ease of a puppet master. "I'm pissed," he said. He tapped his finger between Theo's eyes. "I was aiming for right there, but you moved, so you only lost half your ear. My vote, you bleed out before medical help gets here." Kade glanced at her and winked.

What was up with these operators that they could be winky when her heart was jackhammering because this was just too much of a near-death experience for a normal person?

Kade walked Theo a few feet away. "Sit."

"I'm a detective. This woman is wanted for questioning in a murder."

"Shut it." Kade snapped his fingers at Duke, and the dog trotted to him. After running his hands over Duke's face and neck, he glanced at her. "He's fine." Then he patted Duke's back. "Watch him."

Duke sat in front of Theo, slitted his eyes, and growled.

"Who is that dog, and what did you do with Duke?" she said when Kade came and squatted in front of her.

He glanced at Duke and chuckled. "I'm wondering that myself." He gently touched a finger next to her cut. "What'd he do?"

"Cut me with his ring when he hit me." The bleeding had stopped, and her eye had cleared up, but it still hurt.

"We need to get it looked at. You might need stitches. I should kill him, but I promised my brother that I wouldn't kill any of these dirtbags."

"I'm glad you didn't. I wouldn't want you to have to live with that. And I'm fine. Really." Mostly. She glanced at Theo Watson, who had his hand pressed against his ear, then back at Kade. "So, you meant to shoot his ear off?"

"That's what I meant to do, and I only nicked it." He grinned. "Pierced it for him free of charge."

She snorted.

"You're making a mistake," Theo called. "She's a suspect in a murder, and I'm a police officer. You're interfering in an investigation."

Kade stood and pointed at Theo. "One more word out of you, and I'll let the dog do what he's dying to do…chew you to pieces."

As if agreeing, Duke growled again.

Two men walked out of the woods, and Harper grinned, happy to see Tristan and Viper. "You start the party without me, Ace?" Viper said when he and Tristan reached them.

Kade bumped fists with Viper. "'Fraid so, man. You can blame Duke for that, though."

"Sounds like a story there," Tristan said.

Harper eyed Duke. "Why's half his leash missing?"

"I tied him to a tree so he'd stay put while I came for you," Kade said. "Next thing I know, he's stalking dirtbag over there. He had to have chewed his leash in half to escape. About the time I decided I was going to have to shoot a cop, Duke attacked. I had to settle for shooting his ear."

Viper high-fived Kade. "Dude, you're so going to get free beers off that story."

"Won't turn those down." He bumped Tristan's shoulder. "What was that about Miss Mabel running into the back of Earl's truck? How many times does that make now?"

"I stopped counting. I think she does it on purpose just to get his goat."

The two brothers looked at each other, then burst out laughing. Harper exchanged a glance with Viper, and they both shrugged. She didn't get what was so funny to the brothers, but she loved seeing Kade laugh.

Tristan told them what had happened when Theo and cohorts drove through town, and by the time he finished the story, she and Viper were laughing, too.

"You assholes laugh now while you can," Theo said. "I'm going to throw every charge I can think of at all of you."

"Thought I told you to shut up." Kade stepped next to her, touching his arm to hers. "Why don't you two get this douchebag out of here?" he said to Tristan and Viper. "He probably needs to see a doctor. Harper and I will be right behind you."

Tristan and Viper hauled Theo up by his arms, and as they walked away with him, Theo was yelling threats about what he was going to charge them all with. Duke started to follow, then stopped and looked back.

Kade waved a hand at him. "Go on. You know you want to."

After giving them a bark, Duke caught up with the three men and nipped at Theo's heels.

"I think he considers Watson his prisoner," Kade said, sitting next to her. "You want to rest a little before we head back?"

"No, but I wish you could poof me back." It was at least a thirty-minute walk, and she wasn't sure she had that much energy left.

"I'll carry you."

She rolled her eyes. "You will not."

"Up you go then." He stood, then held out his hand.

When she was on her feet, she forced her legs not to show him how rubbery they were as they started walking. What she wouldn't give for a warm bath, a glass of wine, and then a bed. "How'd you find me?"

"I didn't. Duke did." He wrapped an arm around her waist. "Wish we'd reached you sooner, before Watson hurt you. Did he say anything about his activities or Abby Warton?"

"Oh, he sort of admitted he had something to do with Abby's death. I really hope the necklace Chase gave me is working because my mind's a little fuzzy on everything he said." The arm Kade had around her was all that was holding her up, and she was sure he knew that.

When he'd appeared and she'd waved hi, what she'd really wanted to do was jump in his arms and for him to kiss the ever-loving daylights out of her because he was so happy to see her. Other than a grin and a wink, she hadn't gotten any emotion from him. Pretty much what a best friend of his would get. She wasn't surprised, but she'd hoped she was more than a BFF by now.

She didn't have to be a rocket scientist to figure out that their time was over. But she couldn't think about that right now or she'd cry in front of him, and that, she refused to do. He'd been up front with her, hadn't made her promises he wasn't going to keep. If she'd fallen in love with him and wished for a lifetime with him, that was her secret. And, suddenly, she wanted nothing more than to be home with her dad. He would hold her while she cried and told him about a man she loved.

And someday, it wouldn't hurt anymore. She had to believe that.

Chapter Forty-Four

Kade walked out of his cabin after his interview with the North Carolina State Bureau of Investigation. The SBI had arrived and taken over his cabin, bringing him, Harper, Viper, and Cupcake in for separate interviews. Harper had gone in first, and then him. Thankfully, the necklace had worked and recorded what Watson said to her. Kade thought the SBI would be able to collect enough evidence without the recording to charge Watson and his cohorts with some serious crimes, but the recording was the icing on the cake. They felt they could use it to get confessions from those involved. The SBI told him they were bringing in the FBI.

One of the SBI agents and Tristan had taken Watson to the hospital to get his ear and dog bite treated, then they'd take him to the Horace County jail where Rawls and his muscle were being held until the SBI transported them to wherever. Kade didn't really care. It was over and Harper was safe. That was all that mattered.

Where was she? She'd refused to go to the hospital to have her cut looked at, but Cupcake, the team's medic, had cleaned it and put a butterfly bandage on it. A bark and then a splash caught Kade's attention, and he shook his head. The hero of the day was Duke, and if he wanted to grow gills and be a fish for the rest of his life, that was fine with Kade. It was the woman sitting at the end of the dock, watching Duke play in the water, that he wanted.

"I called my dad to let him know it's over," Harper said when he sat next to her.

"That had to make him happy."

She laughed. "Understatement of the year. He's coming to get me."

Did someone just stab him in the heart with an ice pick? She was looking at him as if waiting for…he didn't know what. "When will he get here?"

"He's leaving now and driving all night, so in the morning."

It wasn't an ice pick. It was a damn sledgehammer. He rubbed his chest. "Stay with me tonight." He'd always known she'd leave when this was over, but he wasn't ready to let her go yet.

"Not sure that's a good idea."

It was the best idea. She had her arms wrapped around her knees, as if protecting herself. From him? He'd never hurt her. That was why he wasn't trying to stop her from leaving. "Please stay." He'd never begged a woman before, and he wasn't sure why he was now. He filed that away to examine later. "After everyone's gone, we'll grill a couple of steaks, sit on the porch while they're cooking, and have a beer or two, and then some you-and-me time."

She lowered her face, resting it on her knees. "Okay."

The word was whispered so quietly that he barely heard her, but he had. He could count on one hand the times in his life he'd truly been happy, and this one moved to the top. "Good." *Good?* That was the best he could do when a girl had just given him what he wanted more than anything?

"How's your head?"

"It's fine."

He wanted to touch her, but since making it back to his cabin, she'd seemed distant, as if she already had one foot out the door. This urge to wrap his arms around her and not let her leave was only because he liked having his best friend around.

Yeah, keep telling yourself that's the only reason. He'd already accepted that he was falling in love with her, and since he still didn't know what to do with that revelation, he'd wish her the best and send her on her way. But for tonight, she was his.

After their steak dinner, Kade sat on the porch drinking a beer, his eyes on Harper as she stood in the yard talking to her dad. He'd stopped to eat somewhere in Georgia and was returning her call so she could tell him where she'd meet him.

The easiest place to meet up was the Kitchen, and Kade would take her there in the morning. They'd promised to stay in touch, so he should be good with how everything had turned out. *Should be* were the operative words because he wasn't feeling so good. Maybe he was coming down with the flu.

"I'm going to miss her," he told Duke. The dog tried to lick his face. "Sit." Duke rolled over. "So, you're back to pretending you were absent when the brains were passed out? Sorry, bud, won't work. I'm onto you now."

"Okay, Dad will meet us at nine at the Kitchen," she said, returning to the porch.

"Come here." He took her hand and pulled her onto his lap. She leaned her head on his shoulder, and he wrapped an arm around her back. "What are you going to do when you get home?"

"I don't know, and I don't want to think about it right now."

"Hmm. What do you want to think about?"

"This." She kissed him.

He loved everything about this woman—how soft her lips were on his, her coconut scent, how her body fit his, the way she brought peace to his soul. "Bed," he murmured. He stood, chuckling when she yelped.

"I can walk, you know."

"I know." He wanted her in his arms for as long as he could have her. When he reached the bedroom, he lowered her to the mattress. He had a sound machine on the night table that sometimes helped him sleep, and he reached over and turned it on. Because her coconut scent made him think of the beach, he selected the ocean.

"Are we at the beach?"

"Yes, and I'm admiring the pretty girl walking by in her tiny bikini." He unzipped her hoodie. "I'm trying to think of my best line because I have to meet her." He leaned down and kissed her. "I might die if I miss my chance."

"Oh, you better have a good line then."

"So much pressure. Sit up." He slipped the hoodie off, then slid his hands under her sweater. "No bra?" If he'd known that, his hands would have been sneaking under her sweater all through dinner.

"Didn't see the point. My girls are happier when they're free."

"I'm happier when they're free."

She laughed. "Like that's a surprise."

That right there was what she did for him...made him

laugh with her. When he was with her, his mind quieted. "What about panties. You commando down there, too?"

"Whether I answer that depends on how good your pickup line is. You don't even have one, do you?"

"I got one. You ready?" She nodded, and he said, "Do you have a map, beautiful girl? I just got lost in your eyes." Her lips twitched, and he knew she was trying not to laugh. "Hey, it's a good one."

"It's terrible. Got another one that might work better?"

"How about this one, beach girl? I can't tell if it's an earthquake, or if you just seriously rocked my world."

She rolled her eyes, then gave in to her laughter. "That's even worse. I'm afraid you struck out with beach girl."

"One more chance." He cupped a breast and rubbed his thumb over the nipple. "Okay, here goes. Would you mind giving me a pinch? You're so beautiful that I must be dreaming."

She pinched him.

"Ow. You weren't supposed to take that literally." He tickled her, and that resulted in a wrestling session, which somehow led to stripping each other's clothing off while laughing like children high on sugar.

"Oh, jeez, he's watching us," she said. "It's creepy."

He glanced over to see Duke sitting next to the bed, his body quivering with longing to join in the fun. He wasn't allowed on the bed, but any second now, he was going to decide he didn't care about that rule.

"Be right back." He got Duke out of the bedroom, then closed the door. During the minute it had taken him to do that, she'd rolled over on her stomach, and he stilled, taking a moment to admire that perfect ass. And for tonight, it was his.

Chapter Forty-Five

Harper's gaze was on the man crawling toward her across the bed, a predatory gleam in his eyes. She should have asked Skylar to come get her. It would have been the wise thing to do, but she wanted one more night with Kade more than she wanted to be wise.

The man was jacked, and she was afraid she might start drooling as her eyes took in a muscled body that was perfection. As much as she appreciated such a fine specimen of a man, especially when he was in a bed with her, she wished she hadn't fallen in love with him. But she had, and tonight was for making one last memory to take home with her.

When he was next to her, he lowered his face and nipped her bottom. "I couldn't resist having a little bite of your beautiful ass," he said when she squeaked.

"Never had my tush nibbled on before." The trick tonight was to keep things light, not let him see that her heart was shedding tears. He wouldn't want to know about the ache deep in her chest. She thought he'd reply with something funny, but his only response was a growl she wasn't sure how to interpret. Did it bother him to think of another man having his mouth on her bottom?

"Turn over, LT."

LT. He'd always made the two letters sound special, intimate. Tears burned her eyes, which was just silly. They were initials, nothing more. As she turned over, she willed the tears away, not wanting him to see them.

"So many places I want my mouth." He cupped a breast. "I think I'll start here and work my way down. You like that plan?"

"I approve."

His grin was pure wickedness. "While my mouth is here..." He swirled his tongue around a nipple. "My fingers are going to be here." He danced his fingers down her stomach to her sex. "Need to test for wetness. Hmm, wet, but not soaked yet. Need to work on that."

While his mouth made love to her breasts, alternating from one to the other, his fingers toyed with her with the skill of a maestro. She clutched the sheet in her fists as tension started low in her core and heat spread through her body.

"As much as I want to taste you, I'm not going to until you come on my fingers."

Everything he was doing—from the swirl of his tongue on her breasts and the little bites that were a kind of pleasure pain, to the feel of his fingers inside her, to the way he talked to her—made her feel like a volcano ready to erupt.

"Come now, Harper."

The volcano exploded. Her spine and the bottom of her feet tingled as euphoria crashed through her. He sealed his lips over hers, capturing her panting breaths with his mouth.

When her heart stopped feeling like it was going to pound itself to an early death, and he released her mouth, she snorted a giddy laugh. "You can't just order me to climax."

His smirk was full of male satisfaction. "I think I just did."

Okay, a point to him. She combed her fingers through his hair. "That was nice."

"Nice?" he sputtered.

She shrugged. It was amazing, but it was fun to tease him.

"I'll show you nice." He kissed his way down her body, and when his face was at her sex, he looked up at her. "You're going to eat those words and scream my name. That's a promise."

"If you say so." She swallowed a laugh when he glared at her, but she didn't miss the humor in his eyes. He lowered his head and buried his face between her legs. And, oh God, as he'd promised, she was soon screaming his name.

"Better than nice?" he said when he moved back up her body.

"Not too shabby. I might really be impressed if you can make me scream your name again."

"She throws down the gauntlet. Prepare to be impressed, my lady."

"We'll see." She was glad they were keeping things light. She didn't think she could hold back the tears if tonight turned heavy. "It's my turn to make you scream, though."

"Later." He moved up next to her, then grabbed one of the condoms from his night table. "We have all night, and believe me, I want your mouth on me, but right now, I need to be inside you."

There was something about a man rolling on a condom that was hot, and once it was on, she lifted her gaze to see he was watching her watch him. His eyes were hooded, his pupils dark and filled with desire, and when their gazes locked, one side of his mouth curved up. "You keep looking at me like that, H, and I'll be lucky if I last a minute."

"If you'd stop talking and do something, I wouldn't have…oomph." Well, never tell an operator to do something.

After tackling her and rolling them over until his body covered hers, he stared down at her. "You were saying?"

"I was saying something?"

He smirked. "That's what I thought." He brushed her hair away from her face, then his gaze fell on her lips, and then his mouth was on hers.

There had been tenderness in his eyes as he'd looked down at her, and she tried not to hope that this was more than just a fling for him. Still kissing her, he reached down and took himself in hand. As he slid into her, filled her, made love to her, and talked to her, telling her all the ways he wanted her, that hope refused to be banished.

Afraid her longing for his love would show in her eyes, she squeezed them shut. His mouth was on her neck now, one of his hands was under her, his fingers pressing into her bottom as his hips rocked, and his other hand was on a breast, those fingers playing with the nipple, sending tingling pulses through her. As the pleasure grew, so did the heaviness in her heart. She would survive without him, but she didn't want to. She didn't want to have to live with a broken heart.

"Eyes on me, Harper."

She opened them to see that his face was above hers, his

gaze locked on hers in that intense way of his. As she had earlier, she saw tenderness, a softness in them. She didn't doubt that he cared for her, and she reminded herself that that was what she was seeing, not love.

When she shattered, he held her close, and when he did, she held him. Each time during the night that they made love, she mapped his body with her hands, memorizing the feel of him. After tonight, that was all she'd have of him, her memories.

"Are you sure you don't want to take Duke?" Kade asked.

Harper shook her head as she swallowed the eggs past the lump in her throat. "He's happy here with you, Everly, and the lake." They were at the Kitchen, having breakfast while she waited for her dad to arrive. The last thing she felt like doing was eating, and she was having to force the food down. At least she wasn't bawling, but she wanted to.

"You'll come back to see him sometimes?"

"Sure." Probably not. Seeing Kade for a few days, then leaving again...no. She just couldn't. And when there was another woman in his life? Because the day would come when there would be, and seeing him in love with someone was something she couldn't bear.

Now that Theo Watson and friends were in jail and the threat gone, it was time to get her life in order. The Peace Corps was out. Before her life was turned upside down, it had sounded like an adventure, but she was adventured out. Although the little side business she had as an author assistant to make some extra money had fallen apart thanks to being dead, she could revive that, make it a full-time job, but that wasn't really what she wanted to do with her life.

There was one thing dancing in the corners of her

mind, but she wasn't sure if there even was such a job. While Kade had been inside the cabin with the SBI people, Chase had come to the end of the dock where she was sitting to tell her he was headed back to Charlotte.

"You were very brave, Harper," he'd said.

"I don't know about that. At least it's over and those men are in jail. I'll probably have nightmares for months."

He squatted next to her. "You probably will. We've rescued women and children who don't have the support system you do to turn to. You're one of the lucky ones. Your friends care about you, and I hear you're close to your father. Don't hesitate to lean on them." He glanced toward the cabin. "You know Kade will be there for you anytime you need him."

"I know." But she wouldn't ask him to be. "What happens to those women and children who have no one?"

"We try to connect them to organizations who can help them find a job, a place to live, someone to talk to. Sometimes it works, and sometimes even the ones with families don't get the support they need because their loved ones aren't able to deal with what happened. And occasionally, some are too damaged by the time we find them."

"What does that mean?" Was he implying they took their own lives?

"Let's not worry about that right now." He pulled a business card from his pocket. "Keep this, and don't hesitate to call if you need anything, even if you just need to talk."

Their conversation refused to leave her mind, and so the seed had been planted. But what to do with it? She needed to go home, rest a little, and do some thinking. Chase's card was in her wallet, and she just might be calling him soon with some questions.

"Harper," Kade said, then, "LT." He stared down at the coffee cup as he turned it in a few circles before he lifted his gaze to hers.

His voice was so soft and tender, it sounded like there was love in it. Excruciating seconds passed as she waited for him to tell her he wanted her to stay with him.

"I'm going to miss you."

There it was, he was letting her go. "I'll miss you, too." She swallowed past that lump that refused to go away. They were best friends. Of course he was going to miss her. He was never going to say, *Harper, I love you.* The door to the diner opened, and she pushed away from the table with a real smile on her face. "My dad's here."

As soon as he saw her, he held out his arms, and she ran to him. The tears she'd managed to hold in until now fell down her cheeks. At least she'd have the excuse that it was the emotion of seeing her father.

"Baby girl," he said. "I missed you so much."

That made her cry harder. "I missed you too, Daddy." She hadn't called him Daddy since before she was a teenager, and it was proof of how vulnerable she was feeling.

"It's really over?"

She nodded against his chest. "Yeah, I'm risen from the dead." Her friends were going to be getting some surprise phone calls over the coming days. She took her dad's hand. "Come. I want you to meet Kade."

She introduced the two men, and Kade held out his hand. "It's a pleasure to meet you, Dr. Jansen."

"It's David to the man who saved my daughter's life."

"She did a pretty good job of saving her own life, sir. Would you like some breakfast?"

"Thanks, but I stopped for coffee and a breakfast sandwich. It's a long drive home, and I'd like to get on the road."

Kade glanced at her, and she was sure that was sadness in his eyes. "I'll walk you out." He took some bills from his wallet and left them on the table.

When they stepped outside, Duke barked a greeting. She kneeled and kissed the top of his head. "You be a good boy, okay? I'm going to miss you." Him and his daddy so much.

"He's the real hero of the day," Kade told her dad. He untied Duke's leash, then grinned at her father. "Watch. Duke, roll over."

Duke sat, then gave them a pleased-with-himself goofy smile.

"He wants you to think he's missing a brain. Have Harper tell you stories about him." Kade held out his hand again. "It was a pleasure to meet you, sir."

"And I'm glad I got to meet the man I've heard so much about. Come see us sometime." He touched Harper's arm. "I'll be in the car."

Her father was giving them privacy to say their goodbyes, and a part of her appreciated that, but the hurting part didn't know if she could leave Kade without crying. He'd kissed her long and hard before they left the cabin this morning, and as they stood, inches apart, she'd willed her tears away. She would not cry, damn it. Not yet anyway. Not until she left, and he couldn't witness her tears.

"Call me when you get home, okay?"

"Okay." That was another thing she wouldn't do. She'd text him that she was home.

He slid his hand around the back of her neck, then kissed her forehead. "No more walking into strange warehouses, yeah?"

Somehow, she managed to smile. "Yeah."

"I…" He shook his head. "Just call me. That's all."

That's all. The tiny spark of hope that had refused to die finally did with those two words.

"Goodbye, Kade."

Chapter Forty-Six

Kade returned to his cabin, planning to stay for the rest of his leave. There was no one here who would talk to him, who'd ask what was wrong. Just him and Duke crying in their beer. He snorted as he walked up the steps to the porch. "We're a sad country song," he told Duke.

They'd lost the girl…well, he had. Duke would have kept her, given a choice. The dog had a brain after all. Kade stopped before going inside and glanced at the dock. An image appeared of her sitting there while laughing at Duke as he played in the water, and it was so real that he almost walked over there. He squeezed his eyes shut, and when he opened them, there was nothing but the empty dock.

When they'd said goodbye, he'd almost told her that he might be falling in love with her. But the *might be* had tripped him up. What did he know about the love between a man and a woman? Zilch. If he'd told her, she would have wanted to stay, and then he'd ruin her life. He'd rather be miserable than do that to her.

Miserable turned out to be the operative word when he walked inside his cabin. Everywhere he looked reminded him of her. He couldn't stay here, and when Duke let out a sorrowful whine, Kade walked back out the door. He wanted his brothers.

"Let's go home, bud."

The dog raced him to the truck.

Kade found his family in the backyard, where Parker and Everly were throwing a Frisbee to Fuzz and…another dog? Tristan and Skylar sat on the deck, watching them. Duke raced straight for Everly.

"Duke!" Everly screamed. He didn't stop when he reached her, and after knocking her over, he covered her face with kisses while she hysterically giggled. "I missed you so much, Duke!"

Fuzz ambled over to Kade and looked up at him as if to say, *Did you really have to bring him back?* The unidentified dog sat next to Parker and leaned against his leg.

Everly pushed Duke away and ran to him. "Uncle Kade! Did you see our new dog? Her name's Ember, and she smells fires."

He glanced at Tristan. "Smells fires?"

"Ember's an accelerant detection dog. Basically, an arson investigator."

"That's cool. Who does she belong to?"

"The Marsville Fire Department now," Tristan said. "Apparently, Parker put the department on a waiting list but thought it would take longer to get one. Her trainer delivered her to the firehouse yesterday."

"Red Lab?" Her red coat was rich and shiny.

"Yup. She's kind of prissy."

Skylar punched Tristan's arm. "She's just shy."

"Uh-oh," Kade said. Duke had noticed the new dog. "Duke, come!" Ignoring Kade, he gave a bark of excitement as he ran to her. Ember's ears perked up, and when Duke reached her, she rolled over on her back.

"He still minds well, I see," Tristan quipped, then frowned. "What's up with that? She gives Fuzz the cold shoulder but offers the goofball her belly?"

"I think she likes bad boys," Skylar said.

"Speaking of bad boys…" Tristan eyed him. "What are you doing home? Thought you were staying at the cabin tonight. Where's Harper?"

"Gone." He almost choked on the word, and there was that ache in his chest again. His brother and future sister-in-law were looking at him with pity in their eyes, and he couldn't deal with that. He should have stayed at the cabin, gotten drunk, and if he'd cried in his beer, there wouldn't have been anyone to see.

"What?" he said when they exchanged glances.

"Nothing," Tristan said.

Right. Nothing, other than they thought he'd screwed up. He hadn't, he'd done the right thing. They didn't understand that he'd done her a favor. He had to believe that. He glanced down at the red hair tie he'd slipped on his wrist after she left. "She's better off without me."

Skylar frowned. "Why would you think that?"

Tristan put his hand on her arm and shook his head. He stood and slung his arm over Kade's shoulder. "Let's take a walk, brother."

Kade almost refused, didn't want to hear whatever Tristan had to say, but hadn't he come home because he needed his brothers? For years, he'd used the military to distance himself from home, from the memories of a mother who didn't want them and an aunt who hated them. All he'd really done was shut his brothers out of his life.

Sure, he came home on leave throughout the years, but

he hadn't been there for them, nor had he let them be there for him. He'd helped with Everly when he was home for a few days here and there, even changing diapers, and he'd take foot rot from walking through the rainforest with wet socks for days over diaper duty. The point being, he'd left each time without a backward glance. It was Tristan and Parker who'd raised her to be the delightful child she was. They should resent him. Miraculously, they didn't.

As they walked past Parker, who was watching them curiously, Kade stopped. A part of him wanted to do one of his disappearing acts. He didn't do feelings sharing. But he wanted things to change, and one of those changes needed to start with his brothers. He waved Parker over. "Apparently, Tristan wants some brother time."

The sweetest smile crossed his baby brother's face, and when Parker reached them, he also slung an arm around Kade so that he was sandwiched between them. Why had he kept a wall between him and these two men for all these years? For the first time since being dumped at this house, he felt like he was home. His damn eyes burned.

They walked down to the pond, stopping near the willow tree. "Skye and Everly had a picnic under that tree right before Skye left me," Tristan said.

Kade remembered how miserable Tristan had been until he and Skylar worked things out. "But she came back."

"She did." He picked up a small stone and skipped it over the pond. "Now tell me why you think Harper's better off without you."

"I'd like to hear the answer to that, too," Parker said.

The urge to walk away from this conversation was strong, but if he did that now, he'd keep running. It was time to man up. "What do I know about relationships?

She'd end up hating me, and that would kill me. Besides, she didn't even try to stay."

"So she abandoned you, too?" Tristan said.

"What the hell are you talking about?"

"A long line of people who abandoned you...us."

"You're starting to piss me off, Dr. Phil."

His brother shrugged. "You've been pissed most of your life. Our father took off when Parker was born, and our mother left us on Aunt Francine's doorstep, never to be seen again. Aunt Francine sure didn't want us, so that counts as abandonment. Then you thought your best friend died, and although if she really had, it wouldn't have been her fault, once again it seemed like someone you cared about had abandoned you. Then, after you find out she's alive, she still leaves you."

"Where are you coming up with this crap?" But as much as he wanted to tell his brother to eff off, he couldn't deny that all of that was true, and like everyone else, Harper had left him. *Because you gave her no choice.*

"After our mother dumped us, Parker crawled into his shell and barely came out. You went in the other direction by acting out. I was sure that prison was in your future."

He couldn't argue that. "Is there a point to all this?" He didn't ask Tristan where he fit in the abandonment issues. His big brother had stepped up for him and Parker, something he still hadn't thanked Tristan for. He would as soon as he didn't want to punch him in the face.

"And I'll add my two cents," Parker said. "You've always seen everything as a joke, it's your defense mechanism. You pretend to have fun, but inside, you're dormant. You're afraid to feel anything."

He wanted to deny that, too, but hearing Parker say it, he realized it was true. "Not feeling anything is safer."

Could he change? He wanted to, wanted to be the kind of man who could make a woman like Harper happy. Even if he could change, there was still a big issue, and as long as he was sharing, he might as well share that. "She wants kids."

"So?" Tristan said.

"He thinks he'll make a shitty father," Parker said.

"I know I will."

Parker rolled his eyes. "Do you mean how you are with Everly? You love that girl, and you're her favorite uncle—"

"Hey now, I'm her favorite uncle," Tristan said.

"You both are, but I'm making a point here, so for the sake of conversation, Kade's her favorite." Parker poked Kade in the chest. "You're good with her. You think you'd love your own child less than your niece? That you'd be an ogre with your own kid when you treat Ev like a princess?"

Was that true? "Were you afraid of what kind of father you'd be when you found out you were going to have a baby?"

"Terrified out of my fucking mind. Same as you, what did I know about raising a child considering our role models? She wasn't planned, but the second I held my baby in my arms, I promised her I'd be the best father she could ever have. And you know what? It's been the easiest promise to keep."

"We don't have to be like our parents," Tristan said. "It's a choice. But you do you, brother." He squeezed Kade's shoulder, then Parker did the same, and they both left.

A choice. The idea of that was an explosion in his mind. He picked up some stones and skipped them across the pond. It wasn't that having choices was a novel concept.

Looking back, he now understood that he'd chosen to be a punk-ass kid when he could have been more like his brothers.

Once he'd gotten his head straight, he'd made the choice to be the best soldier he could be. Had it been easy? Hell no. He'd done it through grit, determination, and thousands of hours of training.

By believing that he'd be a lousy husband and father, he was choosing to let his parents steal away any chance of happiness with the woman he was in love with. It didn't have to be that way. He might have to work at it harder than some men, but Harper was worth the hard work, and he could be everything Harper needed. And with her, he'd always been able to be himself and she still liked him, maybe even loved him.

He could give her those children she wanted and be a good father as long as that was what he chose to be.

It was a choice, and he chose Harper.

He tossed the last stone across the pond, then went looking for his brothers. They were still in the backyard, standing together as they watched Duke play with Ember. He walked straight to his brothers and wrapped his arms around both. "Love you assholes."

Parker laughed. "You just couldn't leave out the *assholes*, could you?"

"Give him a break," Tristan said as he hugged Kade back. "He just had a come-to-Jesus moment."

"Yeah, I did. This probably won't surprise you, but I'm heading to Florida in the morning." He hoped he wasn't too late. "And don't get mushy on me, big brother, but thank you for putting up with all my shit over the years."

"It wasn't easy," Tristan said, laughter in his voice. "You tried my patience more times than I can count."

They returned to the house that now felt like a home, Kade laughing as his brothers reminisced about the trouble he'd gotten into as a teen. That was the thing about his brothers: they still loved him in spite of all the reasons he'd given them not to.

They'd reached the patio when the radio clipped to Parker's belt went off with an alert. "Have to go." He whistled, and Ember raced to his side. "Good luck with your girl, Kade." He squeezed Kade's shoulder. "Just be honest with her. Women like that."

"What do you know about what women like, baby brother?" As far as he knew, Parker hadn't gone on a date since returning home from France five years ago.

Parker laughed. "Absolutely nothing."

Tristan's phone chimed with a text, and after reading it, he said, "It's a wreck out on Running Creek Road. A tractor and a car, and the car caught fire. Skye and I need to go. Can you stay with Ev?"

"Of course, but I'm leaving in the morning, so be back before then." He had a woman to see and confessions to make.

Nothing would have stopped him from going to her the next morning except for the alert on his phone that showed his cabin on fire when he brought up the feed from his security cameras. Sheriff Lamorne turned out to be as useless as Tristan and Skylar had said he would be. The good news in the middle of all this was that Sorenson had been arrested trying to get on a plane for Thailand.

Kade called Chase after sending him a video of the bikers wearing the Road Killers colors who'd burned down his cabin in the middle of the night. "As much as I want to go after them, a trip to Florida is my priority," he'd told Chase.

"Go get your girl. Nick and I got this. By the time you

get back, they'll be turning against each other. The prosecutor's going to have a field day."

"Think Nick can get me an address for a Dr. David Jansen in Apalachicola, Florida?"

"Piece of cake. I'll text it to you as soon as he has it."

"Thanks, man."

"Just report in next week. That's all the thanks we need."

It took two days to deal with the local fire department, the sheriff, and the insurance company before he was able to get on the road. He'd intended to leave Duke at home, but the dog wasn't having any part of that. Kade had the weird feeling that Duke knew exactly where he was going and wasn't about to miss out on going to get their girl.

"You think she'll be glad to see us?" he asked the dog once they were on the road.

Duke looked over at him from the passenger seat and gave him a goofy grin, as if saying that was a ridiculous question.

"Hope you're right, dog."

Chapter Forty-Seven

The only way to keep from crying because your heart was broken was to keep busy. Harper had a life to plan, one that wouldn't have Kade in it, and as much as that hurt, there was nothing she could do to change it.

She spent her first day home closed up in her bedroom, and her father, seeming to understand she needed time to grieve, left her alone. She'd told him everything on the way back to Apalachicola, including that she was in love with Kade. She'd thought he would tell her that she'd been foolish to fall in love with a man like Kade.

Instead, he'd smiled and said, "Love always wins in the end."

She had no idea what that meant or how he could smile when her heart was irreparably broken. After giving herself one day to be sad, she wiped her tears away. Day two was spent on her computer, and on the third morning, with her research notes and a list of the things she wanted to cover, she got out the card Chase had given her and called him.

"This is Harper," she said when he answered.

"Well, this is a nice surprise. Is Kade there?"

"No. Why would you think he'd be here?" She'd fallen down a rabbit hole in her research and had managed not to think of him. Mostly, until she tried to sleep. And when she did manage to fall asleep, she apparently cried, because she'd wake up with tears on her face. She didn't appreciate that.

"Sorry, I forgot you said you were going home. What can I do for you, Harper?"

"Um, I was hoping you had a few minutes to talk and would be willing to give me some advice."

"About?"

There was wariness in his voice, making her think she was imposing on him. "Some career advice, but if you're busy, no problem."

"Career advice? I'll be happy to if I can."

Now he sounded relieved, and she wondered what he thought she might need advice on. "After what I went through, you said I was lucky to have a support system of family and friends. That there were people you rescued who didn't have that. That got me thinking. There's something that I think I'd love to do and would get a lot of satisfaction from if I can figure out how to go about it."

"Sounds intriguing. I have an idea where you're going with this but let me hear it from you."

"My job in the military was helping soldiers and their families find housing. I was good at it, and more often than not, I helped them with things outside of housing. I like helping people, and I want to help the kind of people you rescue. I want to help them find a place to live, find a job, be a person they can talk to…well, for those who need it and don't have anyone to turn to. I researched some of the organizations you mentioned, and that's something else I could do, learning which ones would be right for someone. I'm not sure I'm explaining this well, but—"

"You're explaining it perfectly, and I'd need to talk to

Nick, but listening to you makes me realize that we should have someone on board who does exactly those kinds of things. Would you be interested?"

"Oh, I wasn't suggesting you hire me, and I don't really think it would be a good idea."

"Can I ask why?"

Because she couldn't bear having a job where she'd see Kade on a regular basis. "I just don't think it would work for me." Her broken heart wasn't Chase's problem, so she didn't explain.

"I see. I'm still going to talk to Nick, and why don't you take a few days to think about it? If we can't work something out, I'll do a little research of my own and see if I can find another group like us who would be interested."

The way he'd said "I see" almost sounded like he really did. "Thank you, Chase. I'm kind of excited about this, but I wasn't sure it was something I should pursue."

"It definitely is. Give yourself some time to think about working for us. Call me in a few days."

"Yes!" she said after she disconnected. She wanted to talk to Kade, tell him about her idea and her conversation with Chase. She knew without a doubt that he'd support her, but she was still too raw to talk to him.

Elated after the phone call, she wanted to celebrate, but she didn't have anyone to celebrate with. Her father was at work, her closest friend was in Alaska somewhere, and Kade…no, she wouldn't think about him.

"To hell with it," she said to the empty room. She'd celebrate with herself. Because she and her dad occasionally liked to enjoy a glass of prosecco and talk about their day before dinner, he kept the wine cooler stocked with a few bottles. So what if it was midmorning? This was a special occasion.

After pouring a glass, she got out her dad's laptop. He'd left it for her to use until she could get a new one because she wasn't touching hers. She could take it to someone and get it debugged, but she still wouldn't trust it. Lunch was a late one because she'd fallen down the research rabbit hole again.

By the time five o'clock rolled around, she had pages and pages of notes and had finished one bottle of wine. She fixed a snack plate of cheese, crackers, and grapes, opened another bottle, and while she waited for her father to come home, she drank another glass. She couldn't wait to tell him all her news.

A little later, he called to tell her that he was held up at the hospital. Oh, well, guess the snacks and wine were all hers. A pity that. She giggled, then poured herself another glass.

"Cheers," she said, holding the glass up as she toasted herself. Maybe the trick to forgetting Kade was to just stay buzzed, because she hadn't thought of him once in the past five minutes. *Kade.* Tears welled in her eyes as soon as she thought his name. "Oh, no, don'tcha cry over that man, Petunia." Why was the memory of that smirk on his face when he'd called her that in Fanny's shop in her mind as clear as day?

The doorbell chimed. "I'm hearing bells," she said. "No more wine for you, LT." *Stop it! Stop with the Kade pet names for you.* The doorbell chimed again. She finished off the last bit of wine in the glass, then headed in the general direction of the door.

Why were there two of them? She tried the one on the left first and found nothing but wall, and it reminded her of the night she and Kade had tricked his roommate with the fake door. That made her laugh. She sidled over to the other door, and like magic, it was real.

She still had enough presence of mind to put her eye to the peephole before opening it. "Now I know I'm drunk."

"I hear you on the other side, LT. Open the door."

"You're a fidge…figment of my magine…gah! Imagination and too much prosecco. Go away."

"Are you drunk, Harper? You sound drunk. Please open the door."

"Don't trust my eyes." Wait, was that a bark? One she knew well? She opened the door, stumbled over her own two feet, and landed against rocks. Rocks with arms that caught her. The rocks were muscles. She giggled, she who never giggled…except apparently when her brain was prosecco pickled. Something wet touched her leg, and she giggled again. "Duuuke! I missed you soooo much."

"You are drunk," he said as he lifted her back on her feet.

"And you're Kade."

"In the flesh. Want me to pinch you so you know you're not dreaming?"

She snorted. "Nah. Dreaming. I'll wake up any minute and hate you for making me cry."

"It kills me that I made you cry, sweetheart."

Sweetheart? Didn't the man have enough pet names for her already? He really was here and not just a figment of her imagination, but why? "Why?"

He scooped her up in his arms and carried her inside. "There's only one answer to that question, snookums. Want to hear it?"

She wanted to be mad at him, but as hard as she tried to be, she couldn't find the anger. Another reason to never drink wine again. This man had crushed her heart, made her fall in love with him, and then stomped on that organ that kept her alive.

"Want to hear it, cuddle bear?"

"You think you're very clever with all the pet names." She gave him a grin that felt rather loopy. "You kind of are." Huh? What was she saying? That he was forgiven? Oh, hell no.

He carried her into the living room, plopped himself down on the sofa with her on his lap. "Well, Petunia, I am clever. You want to know why?"

She yawned. She just wanted to curl up in his arms where she'd always be safe and go to sleep, but then she'd have to wake up eventually, and she didn't want to let go of this dream she was having. "Don't go away," she said before closing her eyes.

Chapter Forty-Eight

"I'm not going anywhere," Kade said to the woman in his arms. She'd fallen asleep before he could tell her he loved her. It was for the best, though. They needed to talk, but not until she was sober and wasn't thinking she was dreaming. He met Duke's interested gaze. "She's asleep." It was probably a good thing she was drunk. If she'd been sober, she likely would have slammed the door in his face.

Duke padded over and looked at Harper, then he shifted his gaze to Kade with worry in his eyes.

"Don't worry, bud. She's ours."

The dog sighed as if that was all he needed to know, then he settled down at Kade's feet.

"You're mine and I'm yours," he told his sleeping girl, and that was how her father found them.

Kade expected the man to get one of his guns and shoot him, or at the very least, show him the door, but David only smiled and said, "I knew you'd come through."

That reception was a surprise, and after Kade carried Harper to her bedroom, the two of them tucking her into bed, they popped open a couple of beers and had a long talk.

Kade came away from that conversation with two re-alizations: that he wished he'd had a father like David, and that all her father wanted was for his daughter to be happy—and apparently he thought Kade was the man to make that happen. He'd added that if Kade broke her heart again, he'd learn that a father's wrath knew no bounds.

It was a sentiment that Kade could only respect, and he made her father a promise he meant to keep. He would never hurt her again. As for Harper, Kade would have to wait until morning to learn if she too thought he was the man who could make her happy. He'd never hoped for anything to be truer in his life.

The next morning, Kade was in the kitchen with David when Harper stumbled in with Duke—who'd chosen to sleep next to her bed—following her.

"Morning, sunshine," he said, smiling when she slapped her hands to her head.

"Don't talk so loud." She squinted at Kade. "Huh. I didn't dream you. Figured I didn't unless Duke ran away from home and managed to find me here."

He shared an amused glance with her father as he handed her the two ibuprofens and glass of water he had waiting for her. While she downed the pills, he poured a cup of coffee, added the right amount of cream and two sugars, then set it next to her on the counter. "Drink up, sugarplum. We got some talking to do, and you need a working brain."

David chuckled. "I think that's my cue to leave." He stopped next to Harper. "Don't leave without telling me. In person, not from a phone call saying you're gone." He squeezed Kade's shoulder. "Welcome to the family, son."

"What did he mean by that?" Harper said. "I'm not going anywhere."

"Bring your coffee and let's talk."

She followed him to the living room and sat on the opposite side of the sofa from him with her legs tucked under her. "Why are you here?"

"For you."

"I don't understand."

"Okay, how about this? I'm in love with you." Those were words he'd never thought he'd say to a woman, and it surprised him that he didn't stumble over them. "Before you say anything, there are things I need to tell you. I hurt you when my misguided brain thought I was doing what was best for you."

She blinked, and then blinked again. "Did you just say you loved me?"

"I did, and I'll say it again and again, but first I need you to listen before you say anything." The only way for her to understand and believe that he'd finally come to his senses was to bare his soul. So, he did. He told her things about his childhood that he'd never shared with her before, how he'd used the Army to put a wall between him and his brothers. How he'd used jokes and humor to hide his insecurities. He told her how he, Tristan, and Parker had been abandoned by everyone who should have cared for them. How that had messed with his mind, even to the extent that he'd believed he'd make a rotten husband and father.

"I always thought I'd never let anyone in, but you're the reason I was wrong." He moved next to her and trailed the back of his hand down her cheek. "I don't want to live my life alone. I need you in it. I just had to figure something out."

"What's that?"

"That what kind of husband and father I can be is a

choice. I choose to be a good one, the best that I can be, as long as you're by my side. I love you, Harper, so deep in my bones that I won't be whole without you."

"Kade," she whispered as tears rolled down her cheeks.

"I'm here, H. I'll always be here for you." He picked her up in his arms and carried her to her bedroom. Her father said he wouldn't be back until dinnertime, so he had all day to show her how much he loved her.

And later, when he held her in his arms, their bodies joined together, she said the words he longed to hear.

"I love you, Kade."

All was right in his world.

Epilogue

One month! An eternity. Harper was arriving today, and Kade walked through his living quarters on the third floor, making sure everything was perfect. He'd stocked his mini-kitchen with her favorite snacks and drinks. The sheets were clean, he'd bought another dresser that was all hers, and he'd made room for her in his closet.

They'd FaceTimed every day, but he needed to touch her, to hold her in his arms. The hardest thing he'd ever done, and that included any mission he'd been on, was to leave her behind when he returned home from Florida. She'd wanted to spend a few days with her dad before starting her new job.

He feared that she'd wise up and realize she could do better than him. Then he wanted to punch himself in the face for thinking that. He deserved to have a woman love him as much as the next guy.

He'd already participated in one rescue mission of five missionaries and their children who'd been captured in South America. Instead of the ransom the rebels were demanding, they got a surprise visit from an elite team of former special ops soldiers and sailors. The missionary families were now safely back home, and Kade had never been on a mission as satisfying as that one. He was going to love his new job. That Harper was now working for Talon Security was the icing on the cake.

As soon as she'd accepted Chase's offer, the Talon brothers had arranged for her to spend a month with an organization that worked with women and children who'd been rescued from sex traffickers. There were times during their FaceTime talk when she'd cried as she'd told him about her day and what the women and children had endured. It had taken all his willpower not to get on a plane and go to her so he could hold her in his arms and wipe away her tears.

"Are you sure this is something you want to do?" he'd asked during one of their calls. It was killing him to see her hurting.

"Yes, a thousand times, yes," she'd said through her tears. "I've found my purpose in life."

He understood, because so had he.

Passengers rode down the escalator on their way to the Charlotte airport baggage carousels. Kade searched the faces for the only one he wanted to see…and there she was. His girl. His heart bounced wildly in his chest. The moment Harper saw him, a wide smile crossed her face. That smile and the way her eyes lit up at seeing him almost brought him to his knees. He'd never dared to hope a woman would look at him like that, as if he was her world.

"Excuse me," she said to the person riding down in front of her. Then she said the same to the next one as she passed, and the next one as if she couldn't wait another second to reach him. When she made it around the last person in her way, he opened his arms, and she ran into them.

He closed his eyes and inhaled her coconut scent. "God, I've missed you, H. Let's go home."

After a stop at Talon Security that he'd hoped wouldn't take long but ended up being two hours, they were finally headed home. During the hour ride to Marsville, she held his hand while telling him about her time with the organization and what she'd learned. He smiled at her enthusiasm.

When he parked the truck at the house, he brought her hand to his mouth and pressed a kiss to her palm. "What I want right now and what I'm getting are two different things. Our entire family, including Andrew, three dogs, and a cat, are inside waiting for us. They're throwing you a welcome home dinner. That's what I'm getting. What I want is to pick you up in my arms, march right past them, and lock us up in my rooms where I'll spend the night showing you how much I missed you."

She smiled. "I kind of need my sugar lips fix. Maybe we could sneak away before they realize we're here."

The side door opened, and Duke raced out, followed by Everly, both heading straight for them. "I think we missed our window of opportunity to make an escape." He leaned over the console and kissed her. "I love you, Harper. Eat fast."

"I love you, too. So much, Kade. You're going to be amazed at how fast I can eat."

The next morning, after a pickle-and-eggs breakfast with Everly, Harper bundled up per Kade's instructions, and was now on the back of his bike with her arms wrapped around his waist. One of her favorite places to be.

It was a beautiful day, brisk but not too cold for a bike ride, especially with the heat warming her from the big male body she was pressed against. There were only a few stubborn leaves clinging to the trees, so the beautiful colors she'd marveled over on her first ride through Marsville were missing, but since the town was now her permanent home, she had every year to look forward to seeing them.

She smiled to herself, remembering her wish to find a town like Marsville to live in once she wasn't dead anymore. "Sometimes wishes do come true."

"What's that?" Kade asked, tilting his ear toward her and resting his hand on her knee.

"I said I love you."

"Love you back, buttercup," he said, raising his voice over the wind.

She laughed as he leaned the bike around a corner, the sound of the bike's foot peg scraping the asphalt giving her a thrill. Chase had told them to take three days off, and as they rode under a brilliant blue late-fall sky, she counted her blessings. The man she loved deeply loved her back, his family had welcomed her with open arms, and she'd somehow found her place in the world.

It didn't take long for her to realize he was taking her to the cabin, her favorite place to be. At the first sight of the lake, she lifted her face to the sun, and breathed in the crisp mountain air. Kade hadn't told her to pack a bag, so that meant they weren't spending their time off at the cabin. Bummer, that.

When he turned onto the driveway, he stopped and shut down the bike. He put his hands over hers, holding them against his stomach, and looked over his shoulder at her. "I haven't said anything before now because I didn't want you to be sad while you were away. You were sad enough as it was. And I didn't say anything this morning because I wanted you to enjoy the ride."

"You're scaring me. Did someone die?" Her mind immediately went to his former teammates.

"No, nothing like that." He squeezed her hands. "That motorcycle club burned down the cabin in retaliation for their three members getting arrested."

"What? The cabin's gone?"

"Yeah. I thought it was better to warn you before we rode up to it. But don't be sad, okay?"

"How can I not be? I loved that cabin."

"Me, too, but the ones involved are now sitting in jail, so there's that." He let go of her hands and started the bike.

As they rode down the lane, she braced herself for what she'd see. When where the cabin once stood came into view, she gasped. Even though he'd warned her, it was a shock to see nothing but burned ground. He stopped, and they got off the bike.

"Oh, Kade." He'd loved that cabin. It had been his sanctuary. His place to regroup after missions, during some of which he might have come close to dying. He'd never tell her of his close calls, but she didn't doubt there'd been more than she wanted to know about.

For her, his cabin had been where she'd fallen in love with him, where they'd made memories, and it hurt to see it gone. One of the things that she couldn't wait to do when she moved to Marsville for good was to spend time here on the lake with him and Duke. That wasn't going to happen now, and she blinked her tears away. She needed to be strong for him.

He shrugged as he wrapped an arm around her and tucked her against him. "We're going to need a bigger cabin anyway."

"Why? I thought it was perfect." It sounded like losing his peace place didn't bother him. It bothered the hell out of her.

"For all the kids we're going to have."

She blinked up at him. "Ah, was that a proposal?" If so, the answer was yes, yes, yes!

"Not yet. You'll know when I do." He winked.

This man! "Maybe I'll propose to you."

"You do that, snookums. I might even say yes."

* * * * *

Acknowledgments

This is the twenty-third time I've written an acknowledgment, and let me tell you, it's been an incredible journey since I wrote my very first one for *The Letter*, a Regency romance. I remember dancing through the house when my publisher sent me the cover art, singing, "I have a cover. I have a cover." Seeing a book cover with my name on it was a thrill like no other.

That was in 2013, and from the beginning when I didn't know anyone in the book world to now, I've met so many people and I've made many wonderful friends around the world, which means there are so many people to thank.

Always the first to thank are the people who read and love my books, especially Sandra's Rowdies (my Facebook reader group). Thank you for your friendships, for your emails, and for your reviews. Thank you for the fun times and the laughter. Keep on being awesome.

I need to send a special thank-you to Brandy, Clarissa, Christine, and Heather. Thank you, ladies, for the special things you do for me. You've helped make my life easier!

Book bloggers, thank you for the support and love you give to authors. You're our rock stars.

To my writer pals, Jenny Holiday, Miranda Liasson, and AE Jones, the three of us started this journey around the same time, and I will always be grateful that you are in my life. Love y'all.

Kerri Buckley, my Carina editor, thank you for being awesome! Deb Nemeth, my books are better because of you, so super thank you.

To my agent, Courtney Miller-Callihan, we've been together from almost the beginning, and thank you for so many things. Here's to many more years together.

And then, there's my family… Jim, Jeff, and DeAnna, you're my world. Love you to the moon and back.

About the Author

Bestselling, award-winning author Sandra Owens lives in the beautiful Blue Ridge Mountains of North Carolina. Her family and friends often question her sanity but have ceased being surprised by what she might get up to next. She's jumped out of a plane, flown in an aerobatic plane while the pilot performed death-defying stunts, gotten into laser gun fights in air combat, and ridden a Harley motorcycle for years. She regrets nothing.

Sandra is a Romance Writers of America Honor Roll member and a 2013 Golden Heart finalist for her contemporary romance *Crazy for Her*. In addition to her contemporary romance and romantic suspense novels, she writes Regency stories. Her books have won many awards including The Readers' Choice and The Golden Quill.

To find out about other books by Sandra Owens or to be alerted to cover reveals, new releases, and other fun stuff, sign up for her newsletter at bit.ly/2FVUPKS.

Join Sandra's Facebook Reader Group... Sandra's Rowdies: www.Facebook.com/groups/1827166257533001/

Website: www.Sandra-Owens.com

Connect with Sandra

Facebook: www.Facebook.com/SandraOwensAuthor/
Twitter: www.Twitter.com/SandyOwens1
Instagram: www.Instagram.com/SandraOwensBooks/

He's a father, a firefighter, and an artist. There is no room in his life for his sexy new neighbor. But when an arsonist threatens the woman his little girl thinks is perfect for her daddy, the game changes.

Keep reading for an excerpt from
To Hold and Protect *by Sandra Owens,*
the third book in her K-9 Defenders series.

just that that brittle doesn't mean our

Chapter One

"Arson," Parker told his brother, Marsville's police chief, as they walked through the house once the fire was out. It had been up for sale and was thankfully empty.

Tristan frowned. "That's three now."

"Yep." Parker kneeled next to Ember, his fire-accelerant detection dog, who'd alerted on several spots in the house. "Good girl." He held out his hand, and the red Labrador delicately took the treats from his palm. She was food motivated, the treats a reward for a job well done.

He'd collect samples to send to the lab, but he didn't need the results to know the accelerant was gasoline that had been poured on the floor. Gasoline burned downward and was the reason for the hole in the wood. It also formed a volatile air and vapor mixture above the origin of the fire that would then ignite. He looked up and noted the expected severe ceiling damage over this hot spot.

"So we got us a firebug," Tristan said. "What's the profile on an arsonist?"

Parker stood and stretched. "Young white male. Craves attention and power. Might get sexual gratification from the fire."

"Seriously?"

"Yeah, some do. But that profile doesn't mean our

firebug is a young white male. Could be older, could be a woman—although that's rare—or it could be kids. Statistically there are arrests in only about ten percent of arson fires nationally."

"That's not encouraging."

"Nope. I'm going to collect samples, then head home. You and Skylar still on for dinner tomorrow night?"

"Yeah, we'll be there."

"Great. See you then."

Although the fires could be unrelated, Parker doubted it. He hadn't pinpointed why yet, but these fires felt personal, like someone was…teasing him? No, *taunting* him. That was the word he was looking for.

He'd felt watched while his crew had been fighting the fire. As the fire chief, his responsibility was to direct the activities of his firefighters on the scene, and while he'd been doing that, the hairs on the back of his neck had stood up. He knew most everyone in Marsville at least by sight if not by name, and although he'd searched, he hadn't seen any strangers in the crowd who'd gathered to watch.

"Let's go home, Ember," he said after collecting his samples. They'd go to the lab tomorrow.

He made a stop at the station to drop off the samples. He was the chief of a small-town station located in the foothills of the Blue Ridge Mountains in North Carolina. The idea that they might have an arsonist working in Marsville was worrisome since the station operated with only a small crew, barely enough for the twenty-four hours on and forty-eight off shifts. Normally that wasn't a problem, but it could become one if the arsonist kept starting fires at the rate he or she was going.

The two Marsville fire engines and their one ambulance were back in their bays, and his crew were in the kitchen, throwing something together for dinner. He poked his head in. "Good job out there today, people."

"Wanna join us, Chief?" Ericson said. "Drummond's got plenty of pork chops on the grill."

"Sounds good but can't today. Next time." If he didn't get busy painting, he wouldn't have enough pieces ready for his upcoming New York show. Leaving his official fire chief's SUV in its bay, he and Ember got in his black-on-black Dodge Challenger Hellcat and headed home.

As he passed the house next door to his—which had been an empty eyesore even before Bob Landry had died—he noted a bright yellow VW Bug convertible in the driveway. Parker loved cool cars, but bright yellow was not a cool car color. His eyes were drawn to the woman on the porch and…his daughter? He slammed on the brakes.

"Sorry," he said when Ember gave him a dirty look from the passenger seat. He pulled in behind the VW. "Stay." He exited the car. "Everly Isabella Church, who gave you permission to leave the yard?"

"Uh-oh." Everly scooted next the woman. "Daddy called me three names. That means he's mad at me." She sighed. "I probably won't get any pickles."

She had that right. The most effective punishment he could give his pickle-loving daughter was to take her pickles away. "Does Andrew know where you are?" Andrew, their everything—housekeeper, cook, and Everly's manny—would blame himself for letting a willful little girl escape his watchful eye. He shouldn't because Parker himself had lost track of his sneaky daughter a time or two.

"No." She hung her head, then lifted the same brown eyes he saw every time he looked in a mirror. "I'm sorry, Daddy. I just wanted to meet Miss Willow."

His baby girl had him wrapped around her little finger, and although he wanted nothing more than to scoop her up and pepper kisses all over her face until she giggled, he didn't. She couldn't just go off on her own to her heart's content. The world wasn't safe, and nothing meant more than making sure his reason for living stayed safe. "Go home, Ev."

She peeked up at him through honey-colored bangs that needed trimming. He needed to take her to get a haircut, should have a week or two ago. "But, Daddy—"

"Now, Everly."

"Don't you think you're being a little harsh, Everly's dad?" said the woman, Miss Willow he supposed, after Everly ran from her yard to his.

"She's five years old. It's not safe for her to traipse around the neighborhood by herself."

"I wasn't going to let anything happen to her." She stood and held out her hand. "I'm Willow Landry."

Landry? A relative of Bob's then. Although he was irritated with her because she was a stranger and how could he know whether she'd let something happen to his daughter, he couldn't bring himself to be rude and ignore her outstretched hand.

Free spirit was his impression as he took in the straw hat, flowery dress, and cowboy boots. Long, curly strawberry blond hair, green eyes, a splash of freckles across her nose, and…well, she was striking. Not that she was his type. He inwardly snorted. Like he even had a type anymore. He hadn't since bringing his baby girl home from France.

He put his hand around Willow's. His first thought was how small and soft hers was, his second was *here she is*, and a weird charge raced up his arm. What the hell? He snatched his hand away.

"Parker Church," he managed to say. "Gotta go."

"Nice meeting you," she called after him.

He waved his hand over his shoulder, refusing to look at her again, and reminded himself that she drove a bright yellow VW Bug. He could not be interested in a woman who drove a bright yellow anything, no matter how cute those freckles dotting her nose were.

Later that night, Parker closed himself inside his studio, the first thing he'd spent money on when he'd sold enough paintings. His studio was behind the house of horrors he'd grown up in. Now it was a house filled with love that he and his brothers had made their own.

Only his family and a few Marsville citizens knew he was the artist known as Park C. His dream as a boy had been to make enough money from his art to take care of his two older brothers. Well, he'd accomplished that beyond his wildest dreams. Not that Tristan and Kade didn't contribute their fair share, but yeah…his wildest dreams meant his bank account had surpassed anything he could have ever imagined.

The surprise was that he'd also ended up a fire chief, making him the firefighter who painted. That amused him. After returning home from Paris, he'd signed on as a volunteer firefighter. The volunteer position became a paid one, and when the previous fire chief had retired last year, no one else had wanted the job.

At the time, one of his brothers was the police chief and the other was a Delta Force operator, so he'd decided he too should do his part to make the world a safer place. There might have also been a competitive impulse involved in that decision.

It was an odd combination of jobs, but that suited him.

He knew himself, and if he did nothing but paint all day and into the night, he'd lose himself in what he thought of as his painting fog. He'd forget to eat, bathe, forget he had a daughter, brothers, forget that a world existed outside his studio. Having to go to the firehouse each day saved him from that. Strangely enough, his firefighter job turned out to be good for his art, too. Time away from his studio gave his creative mind time to rest and reenergize.

But the last thing he needed was an arsonist on the loose. He had a show in New York in three months, and he still had five more pieces to paint. Although he was a fast painter, able to finish a canvas in a week between his time at the fire station and his daddy duties, he couldn't finish the final painting at the last minute since he needed to give it at least a week to dry and time to ship the canvases to New York.

Before he lost himself in a new piece, he went to Everly's space in the studio to see what she was painting. Even at five, his daughter was proving to be quite the little artist. She had more talent than he'd had at her age. Her favorite subjects were animals, and they had plenty of those for her inspiration. Her cat, Jellybean, was her favorite, and his brother Kade's dog came in second, probably because Duke was a clown. But Ember and Tristan's police dog, Fuzz, had their fair share of canvases.

She had an eye for the absurd, and her paintings always brought a smile to his face. In her current work, Jellybean was in attack mode, his rear in the air, his ears pinned back, and his eyes slitted as he prepared to attack Duke. She'd painted Duke with hearts hovering above his head and cartoon hearts in his eyes as he stared back at his favorite cat. She'd perfectly captured the relationship between the dog and cat. Duke loved Jellybean, and Jellybean lived to torture Duke.

As he did with each of her paintings, he added a tiny ladybug that she'd have to find. Once that was done, he returned to his easel. He'd already stretched the canvas and primed it so it would be ready for him to paint tonight.

He never knew what he was going to paint before he started. Sometimes it might be something he'd recently seen, and other times he had no idea where a piece came from. He never painted from a photo. He'd tried to once, a sunset he'd taken a picture of, and when he finished, he likened his effort to paint by numbers. For whatever reason, his art had to come straight from his imagination, and he often didn't realize exactly what he'd painted until he stepped back and looked at it.

After connecting his phone to the speakers, he selected one of his playlists, and with music blaring, he painted. Hours later, he came out of his painting fog and stepped back.

Standing in a field of cheerful sunflowers and wearing a flowery dress, cowboy boots, and a straw hat, a woman with strawberry blond hair, green eyes, and a splash of freckles across her nose smiled back at him.

"Well, hell."

Don't miss To Hold and Protect, *book three in the K-9 Defenders series by Sandra Owens, coming soon from Carina Press.*

www.CarinaPress.com

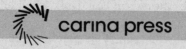
A woman on the run. A wounded SEAL who wants to become invisible.

Two strangers, one mountain cabin.

The sole witness to a murder, stuntwoman Rachel Denning thought she'd found the perfect hideout in a remote cabin just outside Asheville, North Carolina...until a strange man appears in her bedroom. After a few terrifying moments, she realizes it's a mix-up—he's not there to kill her—and Rachel finds herself with an unexpected protector in the form of a navy SEAL.

Read on for an excerpt from Mountain Rescue, *by Sandra Owens.*

Something wasn't right. The man wasn't acting like a killer. The men who worked for Robert were as cruel as he was. They didn't tease, and if they called her anything besides her name, it would be bitch. They especially didn't smile as if they really were having fun. If he was one of Robert's men, he would just kill her and be done with it.

Now that she could study this man, he...well, he was gorgeous in a rough bad-boy kind of way. A trimmed beard, more like a few days of scruff really, covered his face. A fresh scar ran from the corner of his right eye and down his cheek before disappearing into his beard. She almost cringed at seeing how close he'd come to losing an eye.

No, she wasn't giving him her sympathy, not when he was here to hurt her. Yet his eyes weren't mean or cold. The only thing she could see in them was curiosity as he stared back at her. They were pretty eyes. Hazel, the kind that would change with the color of shirt he wore or his emotions. Dark brown hair in need of a haircut scraped across the neck of his T-shirt. Then there was a body worth drooling over.

Stop it, Rachel. Stop noticing how hot he is. She was totally stupid for letting her mind wander when there was danger in the room. Because, while he was a feast for the eyes, she had no doubt the man could be dangerous when he wanted. Still, he wasn't emitting dangerous vibes, and that confused her because if Robert had sent him, she should be dead by now.

"What do you want from me?"

His gaze slid over her body, those hazel eyes heating. "I have some ideas if you're interested in hearing them."

Don't miss
Mountain Rescue *by Sandra Owens,*
available wherever books are sold.

CarinaPress.com

CAREXP1222